**Praise for Linda
Jane Bunk**

"Greenlaw's experience as a Maine-based lobster-boat captain brings verisimilitude to her descriptions of the people, the landscape, and most of all the wild offshore weather, all neatly rolled into a mystery with plenty of suspects." —*Kirkus Reviews*

"This debut mystery series is to be savored on all counts . . . Greenlaw [writes] with great joie de vivre and incredible skill." —*Library Journal* on *Slipknot*

"A sleepy Maine town, the local drunk found dead, a detective asking too many questions . . . No, not *Murder, She Wrote*—it's [Greenlaw's] first foray into mystery, and it's riveting." —*People* on *Slipknot*

"Greenlaw proves that she's as skillful a mystery writer as she is a fishing-boat captain—and that's saying a lot." —Sebastian Junger, author of *The Perfect Storm*

"Greenlaw has no trouble finding her sea legs in . . . this swiftly paced yarn." —*Entertainment Weekly* on *Slipknot*

"Bestseller Greenlaw introduces an indomitable heroine, Jane Bunker, in her strong mystery debut. A cast of memorable New Englanders . . . enhances a fast-moving plot, while the nautical details will appeal to fans of Greenlaw's nonfiction books." —*Publishers Weekly* on *Slipknot*

"The author's experience as a lobster-boat captain is apparent in her vivid descriptions of nor'easters and in her portrayals of the quirky residents of Maine's rural areas. An entertaining series, strong on setting."
—*Booklist* on *Shiver Hitch*

"One of the summer's best mystery novels . . . worth tossing in your pack!" —*Outside* on *Shiver Hitch*

"Greenlaw's third atmospheric mystery (following *Fisherman's Bend*) combines the author's knowledge of the sea with humorous accounts of small-town life."
—*Library Journal* on *Shiver Hitch*

Titles by Linda Greenlaw

SLIPKNOT

FISHERMAN'S BEND

SHIVER HITCH

BIMINI TWIST

SLIPKNOT

Linda Greenlaw

St. Martin's Paperbacks

SLIPKNOT

For information address St. Martin's Press, 175 Fifth Avenue, New York, NY 10010.

ISBN: 978-1-250-13576-6

Our books may be purchased in bulk for promotional, educational, or business use. Please contact your local bookseller or the Macmillan Corporate and Premium Sales Department at 1-800-221-7945, ext. 5442, or by e-mail at MacmillanSpecialMarkets@macmillan.com.

Printed in the United States of America

St. Martin's Press edition / April 2017
St. Martin's Paperbacks edition / November 2018

St. Martin's Paperbacks are published by St. Martin's Press, 175 Fifth Avenue, New York, NY 10010.

10 9 8 7 6 5 4 3 2 1

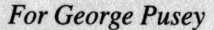

For George Pusey

ONE

"Why did you move the body?"

"The tide was coming in."

I was relieved that my now seemingly stupid question was not flagged as such by either tone or content of reply. The man I was soon to know as Cal Dunham spoke in an oddly pleasant, nicotine-stained voice. His reply revealed no inflections of "dumb broad," nor did he voice any of the questions that I assumed he might have liked to ask me. Why and how had I appeared, notebook and pen in hand and camera slung on shoulder, at the crack of dawn in the seaweed-strewn and barnacled ledges below the west side of the pier at Turners' Fish Plant in Green Haven, Maine, just as the body of Nick Dow was discovered washed up on the beach? Cal hadn't asked. So I assumed there was no need to tell him that I was a rookie marine consultant on my first assignment. I also needn't tell him that I was a freakishly early riser and had wanted to flounder through this initial survey of Turners' Fish Plant and property without witnesses to my newly embraced learn-as-you-go style.

"Jane Bunker," I said, leaning forward and offering a hand.

Although his hand was rough and calloused, his grip was as light as that of any man who's uncomfortable shaking hands with a woman. "Cal Dunham," he said hesitantly, as if unsettled by the normalcy of introductions in this extraordinary scene starring the dead body. Then— out of politeness, I supposed—Cal motioned at the body with an open palm and said, "Nick Dow."

Nick Dow—wasn't that the name of the man who had caused such a scene at last night's town meeting? It was impossible to make a positive ID while seeing only the back of a head, and a badly smashed one at that. Someone had hit him with something heavy to crush the back of his skull so thoroughly. The dark hooded sweatshirt was similar to what half of this town's population wore, so that was not a defining detail. The rope used as a belt was probably a staple in the Maine fashion scene, I thought as I snapped some pictures. Was this the same guy? I would have to check with my favorite chatterbox waitress at the coffee shop. Lucky for me that the first and only friend I'd made since moving here three days ago was the girl serving coffee. Audrey knew all and told all.

Once I'd established for Cal that I was not a reporter for the *Morning Sentinel,* and that I was a marine investigator employed by Eastern Marine Safety Consultants, and that I was indeed not "like the fireman who played with matches," my acquaintance of only five minutes was somewhat more forthcoming with information. He politely addressed me as Ms. Bunker, even after I insisted he call me Jane. He relaxed a bit and straightened from his crouch over the body, but for the large mass above his shoulder blades. Cool, an authentic hunchback, I thought. They've got one of everything in this tiny town.

Although my first instinct was to bombard Cal with questions to satisfy my growing curiosity about the dead man, and to note any theories he might have as to the whys, whos, and hows, I remained quiet, with my eyes riveted on the badly fractured skull. I didn't ask Cal a thing; I vainly believed I had somehow subliminally compelled him to share all he knew with me. But as disillusioned with my own extrasensory powers as I was, I must admit that Cal Dunham was simply presenting me with his alibi. The covering of one's own butt is powerful incentive while standing over a dead body.

This June twelfth had begun just like every other day in the past six years since Cal Dunham's retirement from offshore fishing, or so he told me as we conversed over the waterlogged corpse. He had risen with the sun, sipped a cup of Red Rose tea, and enjoyed a Chesterfield cigarette before slipping out the door without waking Betty, his wife of nearly fifty years. He had driven his Ford pickup the potholed three miles to Turners' Fish Plant—his place of employment, along with nearly everyone else in Green Haven who didn't go to sea. He had arrived one hour before the plant was officially open, sometime after the owner and bookkeeper, Ginny Turner. "The owner of the plant is your boss, and she's at work before you?" I asked, thinking about my experience with bosses and not recalling any who were on the job prior to me. Suspicious, I thought.

"She's part fish," Cal said in defense of his boss. "Certain types of fish surface at night. She spends the wee hours accounting bait, fish, lobsters, and clams bought and sold the previous day, settling up with the fishermen and diggers, and taking phone orders from customers down the coast to be packed and delivered each day. Everyone else in Green Haven is tucked into bed when Ginny is most productive. Everything was as usual until

I got out of my truck and saw Ginny at the end of the wharf. She's always up there"—Cal pointed to a second-story window overlooking the harbor—"hovering over the company checkbook like a gull on a mussel."

"What was she doing on the dock?" I asked impatiently. "And what were you doing here?"

I didn't bother explaining to Cal that I was not here to investigate a murder, as old habits are hard to break. I listened intently as he continued to fill in some blanks. "I guess I'm what you'd call the foreman around here. I take orders from the queen and give them to the worker bees. I always come to work early, just habit," Cal explained. "Anyway, when I looked to see what she was gawking at, there was ol' Nick, facedown."

Cal said that he and Ginny quickly agreed she should call someone while he pulled the cold and partially rigor-mortised body out of the incoming tide. "I figured she'd dial up the sheriff or the county coroner. Never thought the insurance company would get here first. Ain't that just like people, though? Worried about their pocket-books, with poor Nick here as dead as he can be."

Oh, how I was enjoying the flow of information I was not really privy to. And the unsolicited editorializing absent any intimidation from me was a gift. If I had stumbled upon a similar scene back in Miami, there wouldn't have been a drop of information that didn't first come through the filter of an attorney.

Cal appeared ill at ease in the presence of a female he assumed was here to question him regarding the body. From what he said, it seemed that his boss feared a wrongful-death suit, since the body had washed up below her dock. Again, Cal hadn't asked. So I would not confess that I was actually here to do a routine safety examination and survey of the fish plant and surrounding properties for insurance purposes. Coincidentally, this body had washed ashore. I've always been lucky that way.

I shrugged at Cal's disgust that I had arrived on-scene before the law enforcement officials. Accustomed to even less enthusiastic greetings, I began pacing off the piece of jagged shoreline between two rickety, slime-covered ladders secured to the west face of Turners' dock. "Well, if you ask me, which you have not," Cal continued, "you might want to do some moonlighting here at the plant. I think you'll find there ain't a lot to investigate in Green Haven—not like Florida. Dead bodies on the beach don't occur too much here."

Ah, there it was. A bit of my past had arrived in Green Haven. I snapped a few photos and jotted something in my notebook, but my mind was now occupied with questions unrelated to the scene. I wondered how much this stranger knew about my circumstances other than that I had come to Maine from Florida. Did he know that I had willfully given up a position as chief detective in Dade County to take this entry-level job? Did he know why I had chosen Down East Maine and the Outer Islands as my coverage territory? I checked my paranoia. Of course Cal couldn't know any of this. It was all very complicated. Hell, these were things I didn't fully understand myself. Without realizing it, I was staring at Cal as if trying to see into his head. He stood over the body, his well-toned, muscular arms across his chest. His full head of perfectly white hair was cocked to one side as he inspected my every move while guarding his fallen comrade. His countenance was grave but for a playful spark in his blue eyes. He had a calm about him that I found comforting. I liked Cal. He looked exactly the way I had imagined a seventy-year-old New Englander. Except for the hump, he looked like Robert Frost. Perhaps apprehensive with what may have been misunderstood as an admiring gaze from a much younger woman, Cal asked, "Why did you decide to come back to Maine after all this time?"

So, Cal knew more of my past than I had hoped. I gave him the short, rehearsed, and totally believable response: "Just tired of drug runners with fast boats and Haitians on inner tubes." I had no desire to confide in Cal the more personal reasons for my move. The fact that a relationship gone bad had resulted in my mentor's imprisonment was something I might never reveal. I grinned as I measured the gap between the lowest two rungs above my head. I released the bitter end of the metal tape, letting it recoil freely into the plastic housing with a sharp snap that punctuated the end of this topic of conversation. The gene responsible for the gift of gab had skipped a generation in my case, which was an obstacle I overcame on a daily basis. In the absence of anything worthy to say, I always bailed out of meaningful conversation or uncomfortable topics with sarcasm. In the most extreme situations, my responses were suitable for print on bumper stickers. Nervousness clipped my half of a dialogue to what I was once told could be read on any of the triangular wisdoms espoused by a Magic 8-Ball. Cal did not make me nervous, but his question had.

"Why not change careers?" Cal asked. "Seems easier than uprooting and moving all the way to Green Haven, Maine. Did you ever consider going back to school for something . . . well, something more appropriate, like nursing or hairdressing?"

Twenty years ago I would have jumped on Cal for his male chauvinism. At the age of forty-two, I didn't jump much anymore. Besides, I knew he meant no offense. I would have to get to know him a lot better before filling him in on the real reasons for my move north.

Apparently keen to my consternation, Cal politely

took his cue to change the subject. "I don't suppose the ladder was the problem. Nick was a good enough guy, even though he did irritate folks. He has a knack for pissing people off, but not to the point of homicide. Has a long history of getting liquored up at night when he's not offshore." The level of intoxication might account for the number of belt loops he missed while threading the old piece of rope around his waist, I thought. Perhaps threading a belt should be part of roadside sobriety tests. Cal went on, "He must have come here with a skinful and walked right off the dock. He doesn't have any family that I know of, so I wonder why Ginny would worry about getting sued. It's not that I don't like your company, but you are wasting your time here." So, I thought, human nature held its ground even this far north of the Mason-Dixon Line. My best friend and mentor had taught me this lesson long ago. Disinterest was the best lure for information. The less attention I paid to the corpse, the more I learned about Nick Dow. My mentor's wisdom hadn't been enough to keep him out of prison, but that's another story.

I repositioned myself to photograph the entire wharf, stepping over the body as comfortably as if I were straddling a length of driftwood left by the last ebbing tide. Cal spoke softly and fondly of Nick, clearly having trouble referring to him in the past tense. As I jotted a few notes and numbers on the first page of a fresh legal pad, I heard hurried footsteps *thunk*ing along the weathered planks of the dock above: at first faint, then close until stopping.

"Is everything all right down there?" The voice was as nervous as the approaching treads had been. I held the legal pad in a salute, shading the rising sun, and took a long look at Ginny Turner while waiting for Cal to answer the query I supposed was meant for him. Clearly not the most complimentary angle for a woman of such girth, I thought as I silently counted the rolls of lard like the rungs of the ladder. Ginny Turner was immense—even her forehead was fat. It was impossible to discern where the chins stopped and the chest began. My mental tally was interrupted at seven when Ginny announced in exasperation, "Oh, Gawd! Here comes Clydie! Of all people . . . Where is the fire department? I called 911 twenty minutes ago. Glad my house isn't on fire. Did you have to leave him right there, Cal? Can't you tuck his arm in? It looks like he died reaching for the ladder. Why did he have to die here?" Off she went, quicker and more gracefully than her aerodynamics suggested, presumably to make another call for help.

"Who's Clydie?" I asked Cal before the man now clambering over the ledges toward us could hear.

"Clyde Leeman, otherwise known as the harbormaster, is the town busybody. He ain't quite right in the head—a simpleton. He's harmless. Loves to complain and gossip, like a woman. No offense intended."

"None taken. In my experience, *all* harbormasters are simple." I was delighted to think this absence of intellect was a prerequisite for the position I had tangled with in every major port south of Charleston, South Carolina.

"He ain't really the harbormaster, although he acts like it. Clydie lives on top of the hill overlooking the whole harbor and a good part of the town. He likes to talk and loves to put the stick in the hornets' nest."

I could think of several people fitting that same description, and knowing it was best to avoid one whose life's ambition was to cause trouble, I made my way under the pier, over a ledge, and up a ladder on the opposite side before Clyde reached the beach now below me.

"Well, well, well, what have we here? I came down as soon as I heared the report on my police scanner. Oh, no. Oh, dear. Poor Nick Dow. I knowed it was him by that purple sweatshirt. Did you find him, Cal?" Clyde asked from under a chocolate-brown cowboy hat that looked more out of place than the body in the kelp.

"No. Ginny did. Speaking of Ginny, you know she don't want you on her property," Cal said as nicely as he could, considering the message was "no trespassing."

Clyde pushed black-rimmed glasses up the bridge of his nose and took a deep breath. Bouncing slightly on the balls of his feet, agitated, he exhaled. "I come all the way around the fence! I'm below the high-water mark! This ain't her property. The old bitch! She had no reason to fire me. I got a lawyer. He says I got a case. The money don't mean nothing to me. I don't care, but, but, but . . ." Clyde was sputtering like an outboard motor with water in the gas. I thought I saw him wipe a tear from under his glasses. Clyde continued a bit louder and faster. "I wouldn't work here again if they begged me. They said my eyesight was bad. Didn't trust me with the forklift no more. Well, I had my eyes checked and got a certificate says I'm fine. My lawyer says I got a good case to sue her ass. I don't want no money. It don't mean nothing to me. It's just the principle of the thing, Cal."

Before Clyde could draw another breath and resume the verbal pounding of his former employer, a siren could be heard coming from the direction of the center of the village. The siren served as fodder for Clyde's next thought, which he was quick to share. "Here come the Cellar Savers! Green Haven's finest! I ran for fire chief last election, and would have won, too, if that bitch hadn't turned the whole plant against me. If I was chief, I would have been down here today before *me!*"

Clenching my teeth to contain a chuckle, I inspected the plank decking on the top of the wharf. Clyde turned up the volume another notch to be heard over the nearing siren. "Who's that girl?" he asked. Cal explained that I was a marine investigator doing some work for an insurance company, to which Clyde gleefully exclaimed, "Oh, yes indeedy! She's going to sue Turners', too! Wrongful death due to negligence and lack of maintenance around this dump. Hey, girlie, look at them spikes, heads all stuck up proud like that. Anybody could trip on one and fall down here and smash his foolish head wide open. No railings! Did you get pictures of this ladder? How do you expect a man to climb out of the water with his head all stove in when he can't even reach the bottom rung?"

I did my best to ignore Clyde. Cal didn't bother explaining to Clyde that the "girlie" was ultimately on the side of Turners', whose insurance company would be on the defense in any lawsuit, should there ever be one, which, if Cal was right about the possible scenario, would never be filed. I was only doing my job, just in case.

Forgetting or ignoring the fact that he was no longer welcome on the premises, Clyde diligently made his way to the top of the dock, where he became busy shouting directions at the man behind the wheel of the ambulance. With the way his shouted instructions and hand signals diametrically opposed each other, it was purely coincidental that the converted bakery delivery van negotiated the tight three-point turn without meeting the demise suffered by Nick Dow. The makeshift ambulance came to a stop, followed closely by a police car sporting bold lettering—HANCOCK COUNTY SHERIFF. Two teenagers, one in fisherman's boots and the other in stylish athletic shoes, stepped out of either side of the ersatz ambulance. Cal said hello to them, calling them by the names Eddie and Alex. Eddie, in the boots, had frizzy blond hair and eyes that had that puffy pot smoker's look; Alex was clean and alert, with black hair and eyes that flashed with what I discerned as sheer irritation. I was certain Alex was the young man who had been humiliated in front of the entire town last night.

Visibly uncomfortable with the task at hand, Eddie and Alex stood waiting for someone, anyone, to tell them what to do next. A uniformed officer emerged from the police vehicle. He stood erect and ceremoniously placed a wide-brimmed hat identical to the one worn by Clydie upon his flat-topped head, prompting the first greeting. "Howdy, partner." Clyde swaggered closer. "I'll bet you wish you'd deputized me when you had the chance. Could have saved you a trip today."

The sheriff dismissed the overzealous Clyde with what could have been interpreted as a nod but could as easily have been a nervous twitch with no intended significance. Clyde shadowed the sheriff as he conducted a thoughtful and methodical surveillance of the area, looking everywhere but at the body by Cal's feet. The two ambulance attendants, still awkwardly awaiting instruction, stood dumbfounded, with their hands shoved deep into their dungaree pockets. Eddie's jeans were well worn and ragged at the cuffs, which dragged on the ground. Alex's Levi's appeared to be new and had crisp creases that ran the length of his lanky legs. Amused and intrigued, I found their unfamiliarity with this scene of death strangely refreshing.

My presence was so conspicuous that the newcomers on the dock must have assumed I had a very good reason for being there—although all three waited for a clue to my identity rather than risk a question they figured even Clydie knew the answer to. I began double-checking all measurements and digital images I had captured thus far. The sheriff donned mirrored trooper glasses so that he could more discreetly watch my actions. Clydie patted his own breast pockets for sunglasses and disappointedly came up empty. "Will you gentlemen please help me with Nick before the tide reclaims him?" Cal sternly yet politely interjected into the confused silence.

"Sorry it took us so long to get here, Cal," said Eddie, who, on closer inspection, indeed appeared to be stoned. He opened the back door of the van. "We were about to leave the dock at the sound of the cannon when Ginny called on the VHF and asked if we could help out by driving the bakery truck—um, ambulance. I was hoping we could get an EMT to come over, but I guess they're both racing to get offshore for the new season, too." Alex remained silent as he shot Eddie a look of disgust that I assumed was prompted by impatience with his partner's apologies and explanations to the group of adults with whom Alex clearly had zero interest. The young men worked mostly against each other but finally managed to wrestle the stretcher from the back of the ambulance while Cal explained that it was too late for an EMT and that they needed only to deliver Nick to Boyce's funeral parlor.

"Twenty minutes till the shot of the cannon!" Clydie enthusiastically announced, holding his wristwatch a mere inch from his face. "Eleven boats all fighting for next year's quota. The newspaper says it will be like *Survivor, The Amazing Race,* and *Deadliest Catch* all rolled into one. The government's really gone and done it this time. A lot of folks will be pretty upset about Nick's pool, too. Hell, I put a ten-spot on the *Sea Hunter* myself. Guess I can kiss that farewell, to judge by the status of my bookie." On and on Clydie rattled. The men, accustomed to his prattle, paid little attention while I discreetly took a few more notes. "Hey, his back pocket looks empty! Cal, did you take his black book? I sure would like to have my ten bucks back. Maybe the book and all of that money is drifting around the harbor!"

The parking lot adjacent to Turners' Fish Plant was quickly filling with cars and pickup trucks and a steady stream of employees. Women in hairnets, and men in the rubber boots that I had just now overheard referred to as Green Haven wing tips, trickled down the wharf and formed human puddles around the van they had come to know as the ambulance. Shallow gasps of scared surprise and sighs of sadness escaped the growing crowd of townspeople and plant workers as they realized the source of this highly unusual activity involving the county sheriff. The sheriff, clearly appreciating an audience, had scrambled down the ledge to join Cal, who had remained stoically by the body. With Clyde Leeman by his side, the sheriff tried in vain to appear at ease this close to a dead body in a town where, I couldn't help but notice, the law was unwelcome. Except for Clyde, the Green Haveners moved away from the sheriff as he passed. Some shot dirty looks in his direction. In an attempt to justify his badge, the sheriff began directing the young men carrying the stretcher. "Lug that thing down here. Give them some room, folks. That's it."

Amazed and intrigued with the notion that perhaps nobody at the location—with the exception of me—had ever seen a corpse outside a silk-lined casket, I tucked my notebook into my messenger bag and closed my jacket over my camera. With hair that was neither long nor short, not really dark or light, and a build that could best be described as average, I had always been good at disappearing in a crowd. I wondered as I glanced offshore at the island that loomed in the distance, interrupting an otherwise pristine horizon, how my life would have been different had my mother not plucked me away from my island birthplace and planted me in South Florida. Yes, I thought, that must be the Acadia Island I had wondered and fantasized about. If I had been raised there, I wondered, would I be here now as a real member of this assembly? I must still have family there.

Florida had been the most exotic and faraway place my mother could imagine when she decided to escape Maine with her two children; my brother, Wally, was just an infant. I thought the three of us were moving to another country by the time the Ford LTD station wagon rattled over the border of Georgia and into the state that would become our new home. Nearly thirty-eight years later, I could still hear the whoop my mother let out when she read the sign welcoming us to Jacksonville, as clearly as I had from my cozy nest of blankets in the backseat of that old car. As if we had been chased the length of the eastern seaboard by something that couldn't penetrate the northern border of the Sunshine State, my mother declared us free. So at the age of four, I decided that my mother was different from other mothers.

My familiar stroll down this well-worn path of imaginative memory was cut short by a high-pitched screech and a flood of tears from a woman right beside me. Too well dressed to belong in the scene, I thought, the screamer stood out in the sea of long white lab coats—the plant's traditional uniform. This woman's reaction to the sight of Nick Dow's lifeless body was telling. Perhaps they had been lovers. Except for this one outburst of emotion and a few gasps that had slipped from behind hands trying to contain them, this body had been viewed nearly as casually as an abandoned shell that once housed a hermit crab. I was struck by how different this scene was from the many I had witnessed in Dade County. Maybe this coolness was the Yankee way. Or maybe no one had liked Dow much. Ginny Turner's reaction was significantly different. Ginny was quite dismayed at her own misfortune of a delayed start to this morning's schedule. If this had occurred on one of Florida's beaches, a southern Ginny would have closed up shop for the week and been home baking for the funeral festivities. There would be a lot of crying and carrying on. Someone would have thrown him- or herself on top of the body by now. These northerners were quite different. My mother had never meshed with Floridians. I was beginning to understand that the difference was ingrained. Although I had never known exactly what my mother had fled, I understood that my retreat north was every bit as calculated as hers had been.

As I brushed by the sobbing, overdressed woman whose face was buried in the neck of a consoling bystander, I heard single chopped syllables staggering through all her gulps and sniffles. From what I could piece together of the almost unintelligible hysteria, I knew that, at least in the mind of one woman, this death was not a simple drunken misstep off a dock. Something had "gone . . . too . . . far."

Alex and Eddie, I learned from Cal, were high school students fulfilling their civic requirements for graduation; they were also sons of two of Green Haven's most prominent cod fishermen. The sobbing woman was Alex's mother. The boys were working as a team to maneuver a backboard type of stretcher alongside the corpse. Cal joined the two in rolling Nick Dow onto the clean white sheet covering the thin mattress on the board while the sheriff and Clyde held the opposite side of the stretcher, keeping it from sliding away on the slippery rocks. The body slowly shifted from stomach to side and flopped bluntly onto its back in the middle of the mattress, giving me my first formal introduction to the face belonging to the man I was struggling to remain disinterested in. The air was still—even the gulls went mute. The five men surrounding the stretcher stiffened and immediately backed away. Spooked, Clyde Leeman stumbled and fell on his rear end, then crawled quickly away like a crab, his eyes fixed on what looked like a blood-filled hole in the middle of the deceased's otherwise stark white forehead. "He—he—he's been sh—sh—shot!" Clyde stuttered.

As naturally as the men had scrambled to distance themselves from the horror of murder, I moved in close with my camera clicking. The sheriff was on his radio, calling for assistance from the state police, as Ginny Turner tried unsuccessfully to pry her employees away from the scene and to their various jobs in and around the plant. A mixture of relief and disappointment was shared as I flicked the limpet from the deceased's forehead. "Relax, folks. It's just a seashell," I said, impressed with my authoritative tone. The entire crowd let out a sigh. I zoomed in on the green campaign-style button pinned to the victim's chest. I pulled out my notebook and sketched the pin with the same block letters: YES!; the "Y" was artfully drawn windmill blades. Just as I added a dot to complete a question mark, a shot rang out that momentarily stifled the chaotic motion and buzz surrounding the onlookers, now speculators and surmisers. I instinctively hit the deck by diving onto the beach. I rolled for cover behind a large rock and reached for the gun that I no longer carried. All jaws dropped, and eyes were on this strange woman lying in the seaweed.

Stunned and confused, I remained behind the shelter of the boulder, gathering my wits. Cal approached slowly with both palms up, as if to say, "I'm unarmed." He offered me his large hand, which I gratefully accepted. He helped me to my feet and said, "That was the cannon shot signaling the start of the codfish season." I tugged my jacket back into place and pulled a tendril of hair from my eyes, tucking it neatly behind an ear. After making certain that the only damage I had sustained was to my ego, Cal added, "You ain't in Florida anymore, girlie."

TWO

By the time Nick Dow's corpse had finally and officially been pronounced dead by the county coroner, who had driven all the way from Bangor, it had been in and out of the bakery truck four times that I had counted. I couldn't avoid a silent comparison of Dow, all tucked in and shrouded by the traditional white sheet, to a loaf of bread being shoved in and out of an oven. When the bakery ambulance refused to start, it was towed off the dock behind a pickup truck fully loaded with a tower of lobster traps that until now I had assumed were nothing more than very popular lawn ornaments. This small town just kept getting smaller, I thought. The stack of traps pulling the bread van was followed away by the sheriff, a state police car, and a handful of kids on bicycles. From what I could gather, this was the only funeral procession Nick Dow would have.

The morning air was so clear that it hadn't taken long for the sun, now well above the horizon, to penetrate and soften patches of sand between the ledges steeping in the tepid yellow light. This late-June sunshine infused the mud, barnacles, and seaweed with warmth enough to send wafts of musty air in the opposite direction. The incoming tide licked rings of salt from rocks along the shore and quenched its thirst in pools that had been left by the last ebb. Herring gulls left perches and worked feverishly over a school of bait fish that simmered in a malformed oval of the harbor's surface off the end of the pier.

As the last bicyclist pumped, crested, and vanished over the hill, the scene changed dramatically from chaos to all business. Cal Dunham was able to resume his duties as plant foreman and chased all employees off to their various jobs. As much as I wanted to pay Audrey a visit at the coffee shop and hear all of the scuttlebutt surrounding Dow's death, I diligently stuck to the task at hand. I had been sent to the plant to perform the primary steps of a total value assessment and safety survey. Eastern Marine Safety Consultants hired itself out to insurance companies needing surveys, research, and other information pertinent to insure, reinsure, or settle claims. I was low man on the totem pole, performing the legwork and making no decisions. Wishing to retain my new job and paycheck, albeit meager, I pulled the checklist from my bag and got busy. Although it was difficult for me to generate any excitement about my new career, I did have a spotless work ethic and a tendency to be a perfectionist. In doing appropriate homework, I had basically memorized the entire Occupational Safety and Health Administration website and every link to and from, so I felt relatively comfortable in spite of my lack of experience. OSHA set all federal guidelines for safety in the workplace, and I had been told I should consider their standards the Bible.

A hydraulic winch (no visible emergency shutoff) hummed as it pulled blue plastic crates from the ocean and placed them one at a time on a digital scale (power cord exposed to elements) where two men (not wearing hard hats) worked together stacking the crates onto pallets (loaded beyond capacity) lifted and carried away gently by the tines of a fork truck (no clearly marked, designated traffic area). Each pallet of crates was delivered to the back of a waiting eighteen-wheeler where a husky man (inadequately clothed) in the refrigerated box worked expertly with a pallet jack (ergonomic nightmare) maneuvering dripping pallets (dangerously slippery—no nonskid) to fully utilize the tight (not properly lighted) space and fully load the truck. Okay, I thought, too much information. I might never get beyond this one workstation! Perhaps just a walk-through inspection with general comments would suffice for now. So I proceeded without the notebook and checklist and tried to get an overall feel for the safety of the work environment. I fought the urge to make a note of the absence of fire extinguishers and first aid equipment and, before I knew it, was making my way around much quicker.

Tons of fresh herring were sucked through a giant straw-like duct from the belly of a boat at the side of the wharf as diesel fuel was pumped back aboard through a smaller rubber hose. The simultaneous pumping on and off came in surges of differing cadence, creating a syncopated beat to which the rhythm of the plant kept pace. From the other end of the duct, shimmering silver and blue cigar-sized fish leaped like spawning salmon onto a belt that conveyed them through a stainless steel tunnel where they exited caked with salt. At the end of the belt, freshly salted herring fell into drums marked BAIT. After a drum had filled, it was whisked away by a young man wielding a hand truck. An empty drum replaced the one in motion at the end of the belt before even a single fish dove to the concrete floor. Impressed with the smooth operation, I winced at the thought of how much electricity the place used. No wonder seafood is so expensive, I thought.

With the back of my hand, I parted the heavy strips of plastic hanging from the top of an extra-wide door frame and entered the plant. Still-steaming crabs were plunged from stainless steel vats into ice water and dumped onto a drain board lined on either side by women armed with miniature steel mallets and delicate picks resembling dental tools. The women brandished the picking tools with amazing speed and dexterity. Although I saw no headphones, each woman along the table appeared to be working to an individual and personal beat. Half-pint containers that filled quickly with tidbits and shreds from crab bodies were topped with whole clumps from sections of arms and claws placed artistically before covers were snapped and sealed. Clams were shucked and fish were filleted. Packers, sealers, and stackers all performed their parts with the grace of dancers. Hand trucks, pallet jacks, and forklifts transported product to and fro with the comfortable, calculated near-collisions of a synchronized trapeze act.

Amid the bustle of the plant activity, I became the answer to the question "What's wrong with this picture?" My mauve-on-plum mosaic blouse tucked into low-waisted khaki bell-bottoms looked quite flashy among the white over black topped with hairnets. Like a marble thrown into the gears of a machine, I zigged and zagged abruptly to stay out of the way while snapping a few pictures. Through an unmarked exit, I stepped from the cool fluorescence of the inner plant into the warm sunlight of the wharf. Extending from the back of the plant was a very large plastic duct about two feet in diameter. This was the gurry chute, from which spilled gallons upon gallons of bloody and gut-filled liquid with its unique stench into the harbor. Good thing I'm not working for the EPA, I thought as I backed away from the gory mess. "Watch yourself, dear," the man controlling the hydraulic winch warned as a crate of lobster brushed the top of my head, parting my hair. I apologized for being in the way and moved into the path of an oncoming forklift laden with boxes marked FROZEN MACKEREL. The forklift driver hit the brakes, sending his cargo to the pavement, where box tops flew and hundreds of mackerel stiff with frost skidded, attempting one last splash.

"Oh, I am so sorry," I again apologized. I stooped to collect the mackerel that had come to rest around my feet. The driver cheerfully began repacking his load, forbidding my help. I gladly stepped aside, and within minutes the frozen mackerel were again boxed and en route. I marveled at the pace and productivity of all that went on around me. It was a sweatshop environment—I wondered why the employees appeared so happy. These people may have been at a loss when confronted with a dead body, I thought, but they were certainly handy with dead fish.

Having completed the tour with minimal necessary measurements, notes, and photographs of Turners' Fish Plant, I had more than I needed to file a report. I wondered if I would be asked to investigate the scene of Dow's death. Probably wishful thinking on my part. Although I agreed with Cal Dunham's opinion that no suit would be filed with regard to a wrongful death, as there were no known beneficiaries, I couldn't shake the feeling that something was being swept under the rug. The state police officer, also a member of the Dunham family, had assured me that there would be no autopsy, since they suspected no foul play, and only a routine toxicology report would be done, as required by state law. That report, everyone concurred, would show only what they already knew: Nick Dow was a lush. But the degree to which his skull had been smashed indicated, to me at least, a very long fall before hitting bottom. I could not buy it. Something was wrong here.

Ducking around a corner to the edge of a parking area, I placed a call to my boss, Mr. Dubois, who was quick to remind me that I was no longer a criminal investigator. I disliked having to report to a boss after so many years of being trusted with much more responsibility, and I understood that the boss was uncomfortable with me as well. It seemed that upper management had drawn straws, and Mr. Dubois had chosen the short one. He was stuck with me. Since Ginny Turner had requested the presence of an insurance representative, he had said that this was an opportunity to update the file as well as to inspect the plant operation for OSHA requirements. That a body had been discovered just as I had arrived to perform a survey was not a calling or a sign, he said. In fact, he was adamant that the death was none of my concern. He went on to explain that Ginny, whose original intention in calling the insurance agency had been to increase the value of the plant's policy, had called again early this morning, when the body was discovered, to cover her ass and avoid any financial outlay. I heeded his warning that Ginny would not be pleased with the resulting list of required upgrades to bring her business into compliance with new, stringent regulations. These changes, costly to the plant owners, would protect the insurance company in potential future claims. And "we" had been hired and paid by the insurance company, he scolded. According to protocol, Turners' would be given one month to make all necessary changes or risk being dropped from insurance coverage. This development was not news I was eager to deliver to the Ginny

Turner I had come to know thus far, but I had my marching orders. After claiming a low cell phone battery, I almost hung up on Mr. Dubois as he continued to lecture me.

The boss was probably right, I reasoned. I was no longer a criminal investigator. That part of my life had been left down south. Perhaps the right thing to do was to notify the state police with my doubts. They would likely send a detective to investigate, and I could be a Good Samaritan. I had all the photographs of the scene, and I was sure that Cal would cooperate by answering any questions. I quickly dialed Information and was connected to the state police. Following three automatic voice prompts, I was greeted by a human being who claimed to be the detective whose territory included Green Haven. I launched into what I considered a professional courtesy call, but the chief detective cut me off rudely. "Yeah. Right. I heard all about it at six A.M. Some drunk fell off a dock and drowned. What do you want from me?"

"I believe an autopsy will show the cause of death was not drowning. The victim's skull was fractured to a degree that indicates something more than a fall," I said. Following a pause I felt was required to add some credibility, I went on, "I just moved here from Miami, where I was employed as a criminal investigator for over twenty years."

"How long have you been in Maine?"

"Three days."

"Green Haven ain't Cabot Cove, and you're not Angela Lansbury. Are we done?"

"I can supply pictures of the corpse. Won't you at least send someone here to do some preliminaries?"

"Lady, the last time I sent a unit to Green Haven, the car ended up in the clam flats. Your new neighbors don't take kindly to law enforcement, so unless I get a call from someone more established, a drunk fell in the water . . ." The line went dead, leaving me to believe he had hung up on me. Well, at least I had tried. I could now resume my menial tasks with a clear conscience, even as the mystery nagged.

I looked up and into the window of the office that I imagined enjoyed a panoramic view of the wharf and thoroughfare. There sat Ginny Turner, phone pressed to her ear, just as Cal had described. I decided it might be prudent to give her a heads-up before presenting her with a long, expensive list of to-dos that would soon be on its way to her insurance provider. So, up the external stairs I went. At the top of the stairs, I let myself through a heavy wooden door into what appeared to be a waiting area. Two chairs upholstered in the "harvest gold" that was fashionable in the 1970s straddled a low table littered with issues of *National Fisherman* magazine and many thin copies of *The Working Waterfront.*

Although the entrance to the inner sanctum was closed, Ginny's voice flowed with the stream of daylight through the gaps between door and jamb. As I raised a fist to rap on the door, a headline glared and caught my eye from the glossy June *National Fisherman*: GREEN HAVEN, MAINE, WEIGHS IN ON NEW COD REGULATIONS— PAGE 37. Curious, I dropped my clenched hand and sat to read and wait, thereby not interrupting Ginny, who sounded very busy. As I took a seat, my buttocks forced air from the vinyl-covered chair, resulting in a faint flapping between the top of the cushion and the backs of my thighs. I held my breath, anticipating a blast of immediate verbal wrath from the other side of the door. But the haggling over the price of salt persisted, so I relaxed and flipped through the magazine to page 37.

I skimmed the editor's note at the top of the page,

which explained the venue for what appeared to be a series of letters written by Green Haven fishermen in response to an article in the previous issue entitled "The Expense of Saving Fish." Reading through the letters, I quickly learned of the common thread.

I could see both sides of the debate. I sympathized with the fishermen, who were so heavily regulated and trying to make a living. And I understood the environmentalists' concern for dwindling fish stocks. I detested groups like Greenpeace, which always seemed to target the wrong enemy. On the other hand, I winced at the sense of entitlement expressed by many fishermen. Didn't everyone have to cope with government interference? Blah, blah, blah, I thought as I read more of the usual rhetoric. As I didn't yet have anyone to kibitz with, I knew I would keep all opinions to myself as I read the final letter, airing the only opposing view.

It was written by one claiming to be a longtime deckhand who had served aboard much of Green Haven's cod-fishing fleet. He had, according to his letter, witnessed the near-annihilation of the species and had been privy to blatant disregard of laws and outright cheating among the various captains and boat owners driven by greed. He had seen the senseless killing of tens of thousands of immature fish for the harvesting of those few marketable. The letter was passionate and well written, making it weighty and credible. I froze at the signature: It had been composed by none other than Nick Dow. Dow hadn't made many friends with this letter, I thought. Not along the waterfront, anyway.

As I sat and waited for Ginny to give the phone a break, I surmised that if there were to be a murder investigation, this letter would be considered a piece of evidence. It must have pissed off a lot of Green Haven residents who depended on the commercial harvesting

of fish for their income. But could a letter drive someone to murder? Perhaps it had been forged to frame Dow
and put him in harm's way. Well, none of this was my
concern. I was a marine safety consultant and insurance
investigator, not a criminal investigator. Murder was no
longer in my repertoire. I could now sleep at night. But
I closed the magazine and slipped it into my messenger
bag. Old habits die hard.

From the other side of the door came the slamming
down of the phone's receiver. Before I could collect myself and approach to knock, I heard a rapid and, I sensed,
frantic and agitated dialing. Only five digits—a local
call. I sat back once again and waited for Ginny to complete this call before I delivered my preliminary findings
of the plant's safety features. "Hello. This is Diane from
Scudder Investments. Is Blaine Hamilton there, please?"
Fascinated with Ginny's disguising her voice as well as
her identity to the party on the other end, I nearly fell
out of the chair, straining to get my ear closer to the door.
Wasn't Blaine Hamilton a primary player at last night's
now infamous town meeting? If I remembered correctly,
he was the primary proponent of the construction of the
offshore wind farm.

My landlords, Alice and Henry Vickerson, had en-
couraged me to attend the meeting, which they'd said
could lead to a defining decision for my new hometown.
They had warned me that the wind farm proposal was a
bitterly fought battle currently dividing Green Haven's
community. Even with their warnings, I was surprised
at the amount of anger demonstrated in the small town's
public forum. I had never imagined the meeting would
turn into a near-brawl instigated by the town drunk, who
was now dead. The corpse, I was certain, had sported a
button with a slogan that appeared to be in *support* of the
offshore power generation, in spite of what I'd witnessed

as his boisterous *opposition* at the meeting. Had the
button been pinned to his sweatshirt after his death?
Ginny Turner was the one who had found the body. And
now she was carrying on a secret conversation with
Hamilton, who I gathered had the most to gain by pushing through the project.

The tiny town keeps on shrinking, I thought. Ginny's physical appearance denied the most logical
conclusion—an illicit affair. I held my breath through
an endless pause indicating that Ginny had been placed
on hold. As she continued with a greeting in her own
voice, just above a whisper, the door at the foot of the
stairs burst open, letting in Cal Dunham and all of the
noise of a busy working dock.

Cal stood in the doorway, calling orders to a man in
a diesel truck whose engine rumbled, annoyingly drowning out any information I might have overheard. The
door banged closed behind Cal, who climbed the stairs
purposefully while leafing through a handful of loose
pink pages that I assumed were orders or receipts or
something of that nature. Cal nearly tripped over my feet
in the small alcove, then greeted me with the familiarity
and warmth of an old friend and ally. "Any leads yet?" he
asked playfully.

"Not looking for any. Accidental death, right?"

"Right. Someone accidentally bashed Nick's head in,"
Cal said as he twisted the knob of Ginny's office door.

"I'm on it," I confided.

"I know." Cal opened the door wide and dropped the
pink sheets in the middle of a cluttered desk, behind
which sat his boss, who was no longer on the phone. "Almost one thousand pounds short," he reported to Ginny.
"How could we lose ten crates of lobster?"

"Arrrrr! We didn't lose them! We've been ripped off,"
yelled the fat lady as she slammed a fleshy fist into the

middle of her desk, upsetting a box of gaily colored paper clips that pattered like sleet on frozen grass as they fell. "Maybe I'll hire a security guard. Who do you know?"

Cal thought for a few seconds before responding with a slight smile, "Clydie's looking to sign back on."

"That halfwit! I wouldn't hire him to guard seagull crap!" Ginny sounded disgusted with Cal's attempt at humor.

"You'll have trouble hiring anyone in their right mind, with dead bodies washing ashore here and all. The insurance gal's here to see you." Cal left the door open and smiled and nodded to me as he left. I was even less eager to speak with the seething mound of irate female than I had been before. Cal descended the stairs carefully and vanished into the bustle and bright sunlight.

"Come right in, dear," Ginny said, her voice softer than I had experienced thus far. I entered the small office, which was positively bulging with desk and woman. A straight-backed wooden chair beside the desk reminded me of one I had occupied in the principal's office on more than one occasion during my elementary education. Ginny offered the chair with the sweep of a very large arm whose flabby mass, beneath a tight short sleeve, continued to move long after the arm itself had stopped. I collected a few of the multicolored paper clips from the small seat where they had landed during Ginny's fit, returned them to their cardboard home, and perched myself precariously on the chair's edge.

"Poor Nick Dow. But who called you?" she asked suspiciously.

"Actually, no one called. I'm here to survey your property. You requested an increase in value, so a new survey needs to be submitted along with your application," I explained.

"Oh! Well, that's fine! Can I get you a cup of coffee?" Ginny offered with forced sincerity.

Following a brief and contentious discussion of what I had found regarding the plant's substandard safety features and changes necessary to meet OSHA requirements, Ginny Turner was ready to explode. Each item on the preliminary list worked to turn up the pressure within the core of this bloated lady. Each time Ginny slammed the desktop, the fleshy heel of her hand picked up another paper clip that clung to her sweaty skin. Pink and purple paper clips went unnoticed by Ginny and were joined by blue and yellow in consecutive desk poundings. Though I have never been the type to be intimidated, I was somewhat entertained by the theatrics. "Mrs. Turner, I am just doing my job. Don't you want to provide a safe working environment for your employees?"

"My employees are lucky to have jobs! OSHA shut down the sardine factory and displaced over fifty of this town's hardworking folks who never realized they were earning paychecks in a death trap until some city slicker like you came along and put them out of work." The fist went down again.

"You don't provide your employees with minimal safety equipment, basic first aid, or even protective working apparel."

"Apparel," Ginny sputtered. "Some of these people don't have indoor plumbing!"

"You could be put out of business by a single personal-injury victim with a good attorney," I reasoned.

"Attorney, schmirney!" Ginny was nearly breathing fire from her fully risen yeast-dough lips. "We don't operate like that in Green Haven. We take care of our problems without invoking the law."

I took a deep breath. "So I've noticed." I felt my eyebrows disappear beneath my bangs.

"What is *that* supposed to mean?"

I was pleased to realize that this insurance gig was, at least for the moment, more fun than I had anticipated. Feeling my exit cue had come, I rose to my feet and turned on a heel toward the door. "You'll be hearing from me," I promised over my shoulder with a tone that implied "I'll be watching you." As I closed the door behind me, something (I assumed a stapler) crashed into the other side with enough force to have been hurled by Roger Clemens. Certainly enough force, I noted, to have put a pretty good dent in my skull had that been the intention.

THREE

It was such a glorious sunny day that the strain in the back of my neck caused by confrontation—not to mention the mysterious death—could be soothed with a little massage from Mother Nature, I thought. Taking one last look around, I wandered to the far end of the longest pier jutting from the bustle of the plant's nucleus. A solitary loon paddled by as effortlessly as a decoy adrift in the slight breeze, seemingly oblivious to the many herring gulls swooping, darting, and squawking overhead.

Working docks that ringed the harbor like spokes on a wheel were alive with activity. A stern trawler—which I assumed was one of the dozen or so boats engaging in the codfish battle that I had been hearing about—threw lines from splintered pilings at the dock closest to where I stood. Backing down with a plume of black smoke that quickly dissipated to a colorless exhaust, distorting the landscape I viewed through it, the boat turned and headed to sea. New homes that otherwise gleamed in fresh white paint and pristine cedar decks appeared lackluster through the boat's heavy exhaust. I imagined they were similarly occluded when seen through the boat's sun-damaged Plexiglas windows. I thought the boat's captain must appreciate his weathered windows, since they softened the newfound quaintness that spread with every forced sale of a native's homestead. Scanning the shoreline, I noticed a sprinkling of holdouts who had perhaps refused to sell. These less manicured houses and a few dilapidated places of business were a tribute to the rusted yet proud vessel making its way seaward. Three men in carpentry aprons, perched along the ridge of the tallest roof in town, waved hammers high in salute to the fishermen who clung to their seagoing heritage. It certainly hadn't taken me long to choose sides in the debate over land use. I had been here three days and was already thinking like a lifer.

The controversy imposed by the new cod-fishing regulations that had gone into effect at the shot of the cannon were quite similar to problems caused by the implementation of quotas on commercial fishermen, in my experience. I had spent many a summer vacation fishing with the man who was my mentor and had become my best friend, and his outspokenness on regulations had perhaps tainted my opinion. But from what I had gathered, a system that tallied pounds caught this season in order to properly allot individual quotas for next year created unnecessary competition between individual fishermen. Fishermen who traditionally worked together would be desperate to outcatch one another for their own financial survival. The stakes were so high that I knew it could become heated enough to result in sabotage or worse.

The departing boat cleared the obstacle course of skiffs hanging on moorings and faded into the narrow channel that ran the length of Green Haven's waterfront. The red navigational buoy off the end of the pier bobbed almost imperceptibly in the flooding tide, while the water rushing by it produced endless whirlpools that appeared magically from the base of the buoy, as from the perpetual dipping of an oar. The effect was mesmerizing. As I followed the boat's progress offshore, I admired the large island that loomed, almost intimidatingly, in the distance. Sparsely scattered houses on Acadia Island were mere dots in a low overcast of spruce green. I wondered how my life would have been different had my mother remained on that island. I had absolutely no memory prior to the day we left, and I couldn't help being curious. Would I someday muster the courage to venture out there and introduce myself to my family?

If the scarce bits of information I had extracted about them from my tight-lipped mother over the years had been accurate, this alleged family might not welcome their long-lost relative with open arms. The extended clan was apparently not too excited about my generation. They needed workers. They needed fishermen. They needed members who would be able to pass along the family name. The birth of a girl had been bad enough. But when my brother came along equipped with much less than what was required, my mother fell from grace with her in-laws. So, she maintained, she had stolen us away to save us. As I matured, I realized that what my mother had done amounted to kidnapping. She had stolen us away from our father and his family, but as no one ever came looking for us, I figured no one cared.

"Hi, Miss Bunker."

Startled, I nearly fell off the end of the pier. "Cal! You scared me! I'm just admiring this beautiful day," I said.

"Yeah, cocker, ain't it?" The screech of a table saw through plywood distracted Cal. "They're putting a new roof on the old sardine factory. Gonna be condos. Don't know what they'll do about the smell." This thought brought a mischievous smirk to his face.

"That larger island is Acadia, right?" I asked, pointing offshore.

"Yes. Look, you can see the houses. Only see them when it's wicked clear. The eastern shore is where all you Bunkers are from. That great span of open water to the right of Acadia is known as Penobscot Ridges."

"Isn't that the proposed site for the wind farm?" I asked, ignoring the comment about my family. I knew the answer but was looking for an opinion or at least another detail.

"Yes. That tiny puddle of the entire North Atlantic Ocean is causing quite a ruckus around here. It's been the most productive bottom for cod since before I was born. Green Haven's bread and butter for decades. It's been closed to fishing for the last five years or so, to allow the fish a breeding ground. Now the fishermen want to harvest what's there, and the wind farm people want it for their own."

"Where do you stand?" I asked.

Cal chuckled and gave me a look that I assumed meant I had crossed a line. I had noticed that these Mainers all suffered lockjaw when politics were questioned. I knew not to expect a real answer.

He said, "I can see both sides. Ginny asked me to come down and see if there was anything I could help you with."

"Does that mean 'get lost'?" I asked with a chuckle of my own.

"She didn't say that, but I imagine she'd relax a bit if you were to disappear," Cal said.

"Banished along with Clyde! I guess I didn't make a very good first impression." I began to walk, escorted by

Cal. Cal and I could become friends, I thought as I bade him goodbye at the gate.

Bound for the coffee shop on foot, I began to appreciate the proximity of things. In Miami, I never could have imagined walking to work from home, then from the job to have coffee. This was a wonderful change of pace. The price of gas was outrageously high, especially on this thin peninsula of an outpost. Happy to leave my old gas-guzzler parked, I could almost calculate the money saved with each step. Thrifty to a fault—my detractors might say cheap—I had always watched my pennies. And with the new job, I would have fewer to pinch. I had never been high on what I had come to think of as "frugal pride": that tendency of people to respond to a compliment on a particular item by quoting its exact price and percentage saved in the bargain. Whatever happened to a simple "thanks"? I preferred to keep my thrift closer to the vest.

Within five minutes of a brisk walk along the quaint and narrow Main Street, I found myself entering the coffee shop under a neatly painted wooden sign that read HARBOR CAFÉ. No neon in this town, I noted. The entire Main Street, lined with curiosities and antiques housed in small, neat emporiums, was, to my eye, quintessential New England. Private homes were a mix of newly renovated and in need of paint—those, I assumed, housed fishing families. The less manicured houses were fortressed with neat stacks of lobster traps and piles of buoys painted as nicely as the neighbors' fences. A badly cracked blacktop sidewalk that ran the north side of the road was hemmed by lengths of beautifully polished local granite; a melding of tradition and progress and another indication of slight contradiction inherent in transition of place.

The coffee shop's interior was exactly what one would

expect from its outward appearance. Square wooden tables and straight-backed chairs were spaced like pieces
on a checkerboard. Glass salt-and-pepper shakers with
shiny silver tops were yoked together alongside rectan-
gular paper napkin dispensers in the center of each table
and at three-stool intervals along the breakfast counter. A
white menu board announced daily specials in bright
inks. The inclusion of doughnuts and pie and the absence
of grilled Cuban sandwiches was something that would
take some getting used to, I thought as I calculated
what I could order and remain within my self-imposed
three-dollar breakfast budget. Virtually every seat in the
place was taken by someone who fit right into the scene.
The air smelled of delicious comfort food, and coffee
was served in heavy white mugs with thick, chunky han-
dles that would support only a two-finger grip. The only
anomaly was Audrey.

Heavily tattooed, pierced, spiked, and dyed, Audrey
was Green Haven's local color. She single-handedly
waited, served, and bused every station in the coffee
shop. When I first met her, she'd told me that she was
eighteen. I suspected she'd lied, adding a year, but didn't
particularly care. Somehow Audrey heard the door close
behind me over the din of townsfolk happily and noisily
lingering over coffee and plates of food, often shouting
over and across tables. Audrey waved at me and pointed
to the breakfast counter. By the time I wound my way
there, Audrey was slapping both palms on the Formica
as if she were playing bongo drums. Confused because
all of the stools were occupied, I stood behind the broad
shoulders and sunburned neck of a patron and waited for
Audrey to show me to a seat. The man with the sunburned neck turned and exposed a most handsome and
kind face. Smiling, he quickly stood and offered me his
stool. Strong, handsome, and polite! I hoped Audrey

would introduce this blond Adonis, but she thanked him and asked him to please say hello to his son, Alex, for her. I would soon learn from Audrey that this was Lincoln Aldridge, the man touted as Green Haven's most desirable and eligible bachelor and the ex-husband of Lucy Hamilton, the elegantly dressed woman from the dock. Audrey was clearly more concerned with her social life than mine, which was understandable, and Lincoln was gone before I could even say hi. I promised myself I wouldn't miss the next opportunity.

"Hey, girlfriend!" Audrey said enthusiastically. "How do you like my town so far? You've been here three days, and you've witnessed a brawl at our town meeting, and now dead men are drifting ashore!"

"It's not the sleepy hamlet I anticipated," I answered.

"The only hamlet around here is the one-egger we serve with cheese. Want one?"

"No, thanks, Audrey. Just coffee and a blueberry muffin, please." She flipped the mug at my place right side up and poured strong steaming coffee right up to the rim. Either she remembered that I drank it black, or she didn't care whether I slopped onto the Formica.

"Wow. Isn't this late for the breakfast rush?" I asked as I tried to lift the mug without spilling.

"Yes. But there's *a lot* to talk about. I can't believe my ears. Before his bloated body was left by the tide, Nick Dow was nothing but a drunken, no-good bum. Now that he's dead, everyone in town is claiming special rights to his last day on earth. Weird."

The stools were close enough to necessitate contact at elbows and knees with the folks on either side of me. Disturbed by the lack of personal space, I hoped that Audrey would at least introduce me to the woman on my right, who was nearly in my lap and clearly a player in the conversation that I had just entered. "I saw him stumbling along when I let the cats out last night. He was still alive at ten o'clock," the sixtyish woman with a long, thick gray braid confirmed. "I even offered him a sandwich. I've always done that with Nick when he's down hard. I wonder if I was the last one to speak to him. God bless his soul."

"Oh, Marilyn!" Audrey rolled her eyes rudely. "I've heard six versions of supposed last conversations already this morning. Like, who gives a shit who spoke with him last?" Introductions were clearly not part of coffee shop etiquette. Audrey continued as if speaking to two people who knew each other. But now that I'd heard her name, I was sure that Marilyn was one of the two owners of the hardware store and gas pump across the street whom everyone referred to as the Old Maids. I wondered where her partner was.

The man on my other side leaned in close and slightly over the counter before chiming in. "Marilyn, I believe you saw Nick closer to ten-thirty. Remember, I offered him a ride home. He declined, saying that he was headed to the boat. His arms were full of groceries, but he didn't want any help, poor fella." I realized that the man was actually a woman, and now I knew where Marilyn's partner was.

"I hate to burst your bubble, gals," Audrey said with a fully loaded tone of sarcasm. "But little Johnny Bray claims to have shared milk and cookies with Nick after a bedtime story. And I think that was well after ten-thirty. Nick was always so good with the young ones. He'll sure be missed." Dropping a wet sponge on the counter, she placed her hands on her hips to deliver with extreme sass. "Give me a break, Marlena! Until this morning I had never heard anything but disparaging remarks about Nick Dow. Now he's gone, and you were offering him food and transportation! Just last week the two of you accused the bastard of pissing on your geraniums. Before nightfall you'll be circulating a petition to nominate him for sainthood. Can you spell 'hypocrite'?"

"It's not right to speak ill of the dead," Marlena defended.

"Oh, relax," Audrey said. "I'm just pointing out that when someone dies tragically, everyone left behind wants to establish some meaningful relationship or connection to the deceased. Don't be so uptight."

"Uptight? I'm not uptight," Marlena said as though she'd been scolded. Turning to me as if looking for an ally, she repeated, "I'm not uptight."

Beating the countertop like bongos again, Audrey made sure she had our attention before speaking. "No, you're not uptight. You just lay awake at night wondering whether or not 'anal-retentive' is hyphenated. And I don't care how dead Nick Dow is, I'll never forgive him for what he did at the town meeting!" Off she went with a plastic tote to clear dirty dishes from tables, where she was adamant about sharing her low opinion of Nick Dow with anyone who might want service. From a table across the room, Audrey clanged a spoon against a water glass until the coffee shop went silent. "Announcement! Announcement! We've got an eleven-forty-five heart-to-heart with the fallen hero right here! Free coffee! Woo-hoo!" she teased as she danced around collecting dishes, and the buzz of gossip grew again.

"That girl is such a smart-ass. Why do we like her so much?" Marilyn asked no one in particular with a smile. Audrey charged through swinging doors to the kitchen, and I heard her barking orders from memory. The women on either side of me confessed that they had not attended the town meeting and wanted to hear what had transpired to get everyone in such a tizzy. Before I could begin to report what I'd witnessed, Audrey was hopping the length of the counter toward us, filling cups and juggling bagels as she came. She recounted the evening in great detail. I added an observation here and there, but Audrey was into the telling and editorializing. It was interesting for me to learn what Audrey understood as the truth of the situation, keeping in mind her huge crush on Alex Aldridge, which she had confided to me. "You gals don't get out much. Here's the straight skinny for you and the newcomer. Yes, I know you were there," she said before I could interrupt. "But having lived here for only three days, you couldn't possibly begin to understand the nuances of Green Haven. Well," she began, "just about the whole town was in the gymnasium to debate pros and cons of the construction of a wind farm off the coast of Green Haven. Even the hermitlike inhabitants of Acadia Island—an outpost of the township—had come ashore to gather information and weigh in on the hotly debated issue that was, prior to the public forum, only a rumor. In hindsight, it had been a terrible mistake for Alex Aldridge to sit right next to Nick Dow, the drunken fool. And now poor Alex must surely regret the entire evening." I suspected that most of this was for my benefit, as the Old Maids must have been in Green Haven long enough to be aware of the background information. I filed away Audrey's description of my people.

Audrey went on, "The vibes were bad from the very beginning. The fact that the community was divided on the wind farm was evident in the seating. The opponents of the issue—many of the wealthy summer folks, about half of the active fishermen and their families, and approximately fifty percent of the plant employees—were in the bleachers behind the home team's bench, the end of which Alex had squeezed next to Dow, just prior to the meeting being called to order, and directly in front of Jane and me." Oh, so she had noticed that I'd been seated right beside her. I felt honored to have a part in this dramatic retelling.

"On the opposite side of the issue and basketball court sat more wealthy summer folks and the rest of the fishermen and plant workers. Those in favor of wind-generated power were an unusual mix of affluent transplants and homegrown downtrodden. The clannish Acadian Islanders"—another not very complimentary term for my kinfolk—"sat among the proponents with Green Haven's tree huggers, clammers, and worm diggers, in the bleachers normally occupied by fans of the losing varsity basketball team. At the end of the court, under the south-end hoop, was a long folding table that was otherwise seen only at potluck dinners and the annual church bazaar. Perched in folding chairs at the table were the town's five selectmen and two 'energy experts' dressed in suits, one of whom the sight of must have turned Alex Aldridge's stomach: Blaine Hamilton." Wow, I thought. And to think Audrey had only a few hours to rehearse.

"The proper and distinguished Blaine Hamilton is the third and very recent husband of Alex's mother, Lucy. Alex feels that Hamilton is too old to be with his mother and too much of a jerk to be referred to as Dad, so he refuses his mother this request." None of us dared question this omniscient knowledge Audrey had mystically absorbed. "The Hamilton family has been summering in Green Haven since the town was established. Blaine inherited his family's arrogance and palatial compound and all of Granite Bluff, the very private and gated thousand acres, off-limits to anyone lacking the proper pedigree, unless hired to serve in some fashion. Most residents of Green Haven detest Blaine Hamilton for one trivial reason or another—some can't put a finger on why they dislike him, they just do." I had been at the meeting, and so far, this was all news to me. The Hamilton history piqued my interest. In my experience, greed was nearly always a factor in murder cases.

"There are no clear lines in this battle." Audrey refilled my mug and delivered my muffin, which had been split and grilled with butter. "The wind-power issue is splitting families and friends, and it cuts across economic and social status and political ideologies.

"Then who should sashay into the gym with all eyes on her but Alex's mother. Poor Alex must have been totally humiliated. Lucy Hamilton's skirt was shorter than those worn by Green Haven High's cheering squad, and the cut of her red cashmere sweater exposed more cleavage than anyone would be comfortable with." I, too, had noticed the scantily clothed woman and recognized her as the wailing mourner on the dock this morning, but I kept my mouth shut and listened to Audrey.

"The fact is"—Audrey insisted on saying "fact" a lot—"that Alex is embarrassed by his mother's poor reputation, a scandalous renown that she seems to enjoy enhancing. Lucy had strongly suggested, to the point of coercion, that her son attend this meeting in support of his new dad." I nearly choked on my coffee, wondering how Audrey knew this. She must have fantasized a conversation with Alex. "Alex's attendance was neither in support of Hamilton nor in opposition to the wind farm, contrary to what his chosen seat suggested, but rather, to appease his mother." I resisted the urge to blurt out, "How do you know?"

This could go on all day, I thought, and never get to the substance. When Audrey left for a moment to tend to the cash register, I was able to bring the story up to the actual meeting before Audrey took over again. "The first selectman tested the microphone by tapping it with the tips of his fingers, thereby calling the meeting to order."

Oh my God, I thought. Too much detail. "He welcomed the audience and informed them that this was an opportunity for all townspeople to gather facts and ask questions regarding the construction of a wind farm in Western Penobscot Bay. There would be, he said, a series of meetings prior to the annual town meeting in March, when a nonbinding advisory question will be added to the ballot.

"'What do you mean, *non*binding?' yelled a red-nosed Nick Dow from the bench. 'Are you wasting our time?' Poor Alex must have wanted to crawl under the bleachers as all eyes focused on what appeared to be his teammate, who stood slightly off balance, wringing his hands inside the pouch pocket of his hooded purple sweatshirt. The crowd silently waited for the selectman to answer the accusation." The Old Maids were enthralled, and their intense focus egged Audrey on.

"The selectman said that this process will be different than what we're used to, because it falls under section two-nineteen," Audrey said. "We don't control the permit. Section two-nineteen is a state statute that grants permits for utility projects such as the proposed wind farm.

"So now Nick Dow stood and screamed, 'Our input means nothing!' Pointing across the court with an unsteady gesture of his right hand, he continued belligerently, 'You incestuous bunch of mongrels can slink back to that rock you call paradise. You add nothing to this town. All you do is take, take, take . . .'" I didn't actually remember the third "take," but I let it slide for argument's sake. "Some folks were booing and motioning for Dow to sit down, but he kept hurling insults at broader and broader targets until he included every faction and family on both sides of the court. Others joined in the shouting until the gymnasium was roaring. The selectman banged the microphone on the table in an attempt to restore order, to no avail. A few people were trying to leave. There was pushing and shoving. Old Mrs. Holmes struck a bearded granola with her purse." I recalled the weapon being an umbrella, but that didn't matter.

Audrey the clairvoyant really began waxing philosophical. "Nick Dow succeeded in poisoning the sacred ground of the basketball court—historically the town's great uniter." Go, girl! "That court has always leveled the town's social hierarchy. The kid of the worm digger is as revered as the doctor's son. Both wear the same shoes. This is the only place everyone cheers, hopes, and prays for the same outcome. The Green Haven Herring Gulls are the pride of the town! In this arena, Green Haven has risen above the larger and more affluent of the entire state of Maine. They even beat Portland." The drama queen ramped it up for the finale. "On game nights, at the sound of the whistle on center court, Alex Aldridge is the most loved golden boy. Nick Dow, now standing on the bench and slurring loudly through cupped hands, had managed to disgrace this gymnasium where folks at a Friday-night game are more reverent and community-spirited than in church." I thought I heard one of the Old Maids sniffle.

"The shouting and shoving escalated. A man in a plaid shirt passed by us holding a bloodied nose. Someone had to do something. Someone had to get the instigator out of our beloved gym. Brave Alex grabbed the sleeve of Dow's salt-stiffened sweatshirt and jerked him down from the bench. Pulling him close to be heard, Alex spoke directly into Dow's ear. 'Come on, Nick, let's get out of here. We need to sober you up. Dad's expecting you aboard the *Sea Hunter* first thing in the morning.'" I had not personally heard what was said, so I could neither challenge nor confirm Audrey's younger ears. "Nick placed both hands in the middle of Alex's broad chest and pushed him away with uncanny whiskey-bolstered strength. Alex tripped over someone behind him, went down onto his rear end quite abruptly, and slid on the seat of his jeans across the polished hardwood, skidding to a stop at mid-court." A pause for effect left us breathless. "This motion in the middle of the chaotic sidelines hushed much of the noise. Nick Dow staggered close and stood over Alex as if to help him up. Speaking loudly and clearly enough for everyone to hear, Nick said, 'Why are you here? You're not old enough to vote. Besides, no matter what the state decides, you'll be supported by one of your daddies.' Poor Alex looked horrified. He sat, unable to get up, soulful black eyes blinking wildly. Dow did a very crude bump and grind. Thrusting his pelvis, he bellowed, 'Who's your daddy?'" Audrey actually did a great Dow impersonation, I thought.

"Most of the crowd was disgusted by the obscene display, though a few degenerates were amused. Alex sprang to his feet and ran from the gymnasium, totally humiliated.

"And that, gals, is the gospel." Audrey made another quick sweep through the dining area and into the kitchen, returning before the doors stopped swinging. The more I learned about Nick Dow suggested that he had many possible enemies, regardless of the "syndrome" Audrey had pinpointed so accurately. Dow had certainly upset everyone who'd attended the meeting. Any fisherman in the area must have been aware of the letter he had written denigrating their livelihood. Between his outburst at the meeting and the campaign button he'd worn, he would have generated enemies on either side of the wind farm issue. The list of nonsuspects was shorter than the suspect list at this point. Handy, I thought, that everyone assumed Dow's death had been a drunken misstep.

Otherwise, all of this relevant background information would have to be pulled through clenched teeth.

Most of the customers had left by now, and the Old Maids were making preparations to get across the street to work, mumbling about being lucky to have missed the meeting, and verbalizing sympathy for Alex Aldridge. "Alex will be fine," Audrey said protectively. "He's getting a basketball scholarship from Boston University. Ticket out of town! He can tell his new friends that his mother died during childbirth." This last was kind of rough, I thought. But not knowing Lucy Hamilton, I delayed judgment. I thought about all that Audrey had revealed of Green Haven's community and wondered if her beloved Alex was capable of murder. Or what about his mother?

I knew better than to ask Audrey her opinion of what Alex or Lucy may or may not have been capable of. Given all she had said, she would certainly be dismissed from the jury. As Audrey scraped scraps from plates into a garbage can, I winced. Half a doughnut plopped into the trash along with an untouched slice of toast. What a waste, I thought. I wrapped the uneaten half of my muffin in a napkin and placed it carefully in my bag. I figured it would suffice as lunch.

FOUR

In light of the flood of information that had gushed from young Audrey with each tipping of the coffeepot, I decided to shuffle the order of business that I had planned to conduct this morning. Working strictly between the lines of survey and insurance documents was going to drive me insane. I needed a hobby. Solving the mystery surrounding Nick Dow's death was going to satisfy my lust for something more challenging. Clandestine investigation of murder was so much more interesting than checking off boxes on official forms! My first priority had now become meeting the Hamiltons. Blaine and Lucy were, conveniently, the owners of *Fairways,* a forty-two-foot Hinckley—one of the more coveted crafts of knowledgeable sailors—but out of the price range for most. Like a hefty percentage of watercraft in the area, commercial and recreational alike, *Fairways* was insured by Top Notch Securities, a division of the largest marine insurance company in the East. Blaine Hamilton had requested a routine insurance survey of his vessel months ago, and now that Eastern Marine Safety Consultants had representation in the area—namely, me—they had been hired by Top Notch to perform the survey. The boat's inspection was, of course, the means for me to survey its owners and to hopefully get a more mature, less emotional take on the pulse of Green Haven and the series of events that had led to the death of Nick Dow. As long as the death remained accidental, everyone would be generous with opinions. I knew well that when murder is suspected, people suddenly get very quiet.

Slipping behind the wheel of my 1987 Plymouth Duster, I tossed my messenger bag onto the seat beside me and buckled up. The model of my ride was, in reality, a Turismo, but I referred to it as the model preceding my car, since Duster seemed a much better fit for the driver. I stomped the gas pedal to the floor three times and turned the key. The engine started with a roar and quickly idled down to a purr. Staring at the fuel gauge, I willed it to move above the big "E." It did, but just a hair.

I had been driving around on fumes, refusing to pay the nearly three dollars per gallon charged at every pump south of the causeway that separated Green Haven from the civilized world of moral, nongouging purveyors of petroleum. I was waiting for another legitimate reason to travel north of the twisting strip of connecting road to justify the forty-mile round trip. I had done the math and knew that the extra miles driven would inhale the dime saved per gallon. But it was the principle of price-comparative shopping that kept me coasting by the single pump in front of Island Hardware and Variety, known to the locals as the Old Maids, after the two sixty-somethingish gals with whom I had shared coffee earlier.

I understood that small-town proprietors demanded loyal patronage from locals. For business to survive, they absolutely needed a solid customer base among the year-round residents. I had been warned by Cal that the Old Maids took this demand for loyalty to the extreme. I would eventually frequent this staple of the community, but not today. With my right hand, I blindly searched my bag for the directions to Granite Bluff while steering with the left. Keeping my eyes deliberately on the road ahead, I was unable to discern whether the two figures in the passing peripheral storefront had actually waved a friendly hello or beckoned me to come in.

"Hi, gals. Bye, gals. Three bucks a gallon? Not today, gals." I spoke loudly, with the confidence of anyone enclosed in a speeding car with the windows rolled up tight. My fingers found the envelope on the back of which Cal had drawn a primitive map of the area, with arrows leading to a boldly printed G.B. I held the map in the center of the Duster's steering wheel while navigating the route through a maze of tiny shops lining the narrow Main Street, and headed out of town the "western way."

The road twisted and turned up and down small rolling hills strewn with granite boulders, sun-dappled blueberry fields, and patches of spruce trees grown so thick that as I cruised through their shade cast over the road and back into splotches of bright sunshine, I was intermittently cooled and warmed. Entry into each black shadow was saluted by sunglasses pushed from nose to forehead and back to nose at exit. Up and down the glasses went until I was convinced that I had missed the Hamiltons' driveway. I wondered why people of their stature would choose to live so far from civilization. Then I recalled something I had read in researching Maine prior to my move. New money desired addresses such as Bar Harbor or Kennebunkport. Old money stayed where it was born. If Audrey had her history straight, the Hamilton fortune had been born in Green Haven. I had already noticed that Green Haveners referred to the more touristy Maine towns with the same derogatory adjectives used in Miami about South Beach.

Slowing the Duster to a crawl and looking for a place to turn around, I calculated how much time and gasoline I had wasted in getting lost. I completed a seemingly endless series of steep turns that bent sharply one way, then the other. A straightaway and large clearing on the left, divided by a private drive marked on either side by granite pillars of intimidating size, elicited a sigh of relief. It was precisely as Cal had described. A sizable brass plate framed by intricate masonry on the right-side pillar read, GRANITE BLUFF—1879. Quite formal, I thought, and stopped between the pillars. Perhaps I would announce my arrival with a quick, courteous phone call. The Hamiltons were not expecting me for another two hours.

Pulling a cell phone from one of the many caverns of my bag, I was surprised to see a strong signal but not so surprised to read "low battery" on the phone's display. Yet another reason to travel to Ellsworth, I surmised. My landlords had warned me of the cost of electricity and cautioned me to use it sparingly. Given my tendency toward frugality, I'd heeded this advice. I simply must invest in a twelve-volt charger to be used in the Duster, I thought. But this would require running the car's engine at three dollars per gallon. Electricity was thirty-two cents per kilowatt-hour. Outrageous! Perhaps the Old Maids carried car chargers. There was a Wal-Mart in Ellsworth. Forty miles round-trip . . . The path of my daily existence was scattered with what I had come to call my "Scottish dilemmas." I tossed the phone back in the bag. I would arrive unannounced and ridiculously early. Oh well, I thought, it might serve my ulterior motive to catch the clients off guard.

One quarter of the way into the mile-long drive to the Hamilton estate, I was taken with the swells and gentle grades of earth and shallow grassy troughs connecting perfectly sculpted mounds on either side of me. I felt as though I had been magically transported to the Old Course at St. Andrews. This was exactly how I had imagined it on my many total submersions into every written work on the subject. A raised plateau overgrown with a distinctly different hue of green and distinguishing texture easily could have been a tee box anywhere in Scotland. Not that I'd ever been there; I just knew. Rolling down a window, I took a deep breath, confirming that the ocean was near.

Cresting a long, slow climb to the highest peak in the vicinity, I eased the Duster to a stop and reveled in the rare sensation of the moment—comfortable in loneliness and not totally understanding the happiness that I equated with the sensation of being home. I had come to know that home was a feeling, not a physical location. Down below the acres of lavender meadow, lush with lupine in full bloom, water and land melded in a most un-Mainelike fashion. It was an easy union of green and blue and not at all the usual contentious juxtaposing of jagged ledge and frigid sea that the estate's name conjured. Although my mother never admitted to missing anything about Maine, she had on occasion described its raw, natural beauty in terms quite dear. I now had a real picture to enhance her verbal illustrations.

I released the brake and rolled from wild, intrinsic beauty to the more manicured area surrounding the Hamilton complex. The main house was a large, stately shingle-style cottage. With neither window boxes nor balconies, the estate was handsome, with its masculine trappings of stone walls, a detached barn, and various outbuildings. As I parked and climbed out of the car, I visually followed a boardwalk to a granite pier from which hung an aluminum ramp connecting a square floating dock. Tethered to the float lolled an eggshell-type dinghy that was, I assumed, the means of transport to the sailboat moored peacefully in the center of this secluded cove.

Like all coastal communities with which I had become familiar, there was an obvious segregation of work boats from pleasure craft in the Green Haven area. There was the working harbor, where the lobster boats swung on moorings and bigger commercial vessels chafed against worn pilings of old piers. And there was the basin, with its fancy full-service marina, where most of the sail- and power-driven yachts were pampered. My mentor had always bristled at the distinction of boats between commercial and non as "pleasure" and "work." He maintained, and I had come to agree, that reality suggests more homogeneity: Boats are boats. *All* boats are work, and no vessel is strictly pleasurable. However, even without the distinction, boats live in different neighborhoods defined by income. *Fairways* was in a class all her own, I thought as I made my way around the front bumper of the Duster.

The path from the parking area to the front door was covered with seasoned mussel shells, the color of which recalled the lupine along the drive. The brittle shells crunched underfoot and warned those on the opposite side of the screen door of arrivals. Before I was able to knock, the woman of the house pushed open the door, invited me to come in, admonished me for being early, and introduced herself as Lucy Hamilton. I had previously seen her from across the high school gymnasium and on the plant's dock. Now my impression was that Lucy looked like Cher. "I'm sorry, Mrs. Hamilton. I wanted to call, but my cell phone is dead. Shall I leave and come back later?" I asked politely.

"No. He's not doing anything. I'll get him." Lucy

rolled her large dark eyes and pulled her long, silky hair from where it rested on breasts that rose like biscuits from her red dress. She whipped her dark locks behind her head and let them cascade onto well-tanned shoulder blades. She turned on a spiked heel of a strappy shoe, took two steps toward an arched doorway, cupped her hands around fully glossed lips, and shrieked, "Sweetheart! The insurance lady is here—earrrrrrrrr-ly!" She turned and retraced the two steps, flashed a "say cheese" smile, and said, "He'll be right down. Let me take your bag." Lucy grabbed my messenger bag with both hands, lifting its bulk from where it rested on my opposite hip.

"Oh. No, thank you. I'll need my bag," I said, and calmly removed it from Lucy's heavily jeweled fingers. With the quickness of a spoiled girl whose mother had taken away the last bonbon, Lucy snatched the bag again, this time pulling the strap hard into my neck.

"It's lovely. It's a Seabag, right? I have to get some of these for my boutique." Lucy's fingers were turning white as she tightened her grip. I leaned away from her in an attempt to rip the bag from her grasp again. Lucy was bracing herself so as not to slide along the hardwood. "I *need* some of these *bags,*" Lucy continued through clenched teeth. "They're made from recycled sails, right? Very chic now—recycling. And so nautical! Was this one sewn by ladies in prison?"

"No." I lurched with my full weight into the strap that I always wore across my chest, unwilling to lose a tug-of-war with the prim Madonna. I could, I assumed, twist Lucy's spindly arms off at the shoulders, but I found it more amusing to watch her struggle.

"It is an authentic Seabag, isn't it? Every bag is an original, right?" Lucy was almost groaning from the extent of physical output needed not to relinquish the bag to its owner. "I just *love* this one! How much did you pay for it?"

The strap was being tugged so hard into my throat that I could barely speak. "I made it myself," I whispered.

"Ewwwww!" Lucy recoiled from the bag, releasing it as if she had discovered that it contained snakes. I fell backward with the sudden release of counterweight and stumbled into a table, sending a very large and ornate vase to the floor, where it exploded into tiny fragments and dust. Before I could blink, Lucy had frantically pulled something that looked like a yellowed envelope from the mess and tucked it into a small drawer in the table. After she smoothed the front of her dress, her hands landed on her hips, where they remained as she joined me and stood speechless over the pile of rubble that I thought looked like kitty litter. Blaine Hamilton rushed into the room.

Blaine Hamilton had a presence that was friendly and familiar. Although his boat moccasins were well worn, his chinos sported a perfect crease, and his green flannel shirt appeared to have been starched. Except for his shoes, Blaine's clothing was crisp and fresh, like what was worn by the male models in the L. L. Bean catalogs I had been given by my landlords, perhaps as a subtle suggestion that I upgrade my wardrobe to something less Miami.

"Oh, my! Are you all right?" Blaine approached me with his right hand extended. I took his hand and, before I could fully execute an apology for the vase, was interrupted by the impatient woman in the red dress.

"She tripped on the Oriental rug. *She's* fine, but look at your poor parents!" Lucy turned and snapped at me, "It *was* an urn, not a vase."

"Touché" was all I could manage.

"Oh, dear," Blaine said. "Well, they always wanted their ashes scattered around the shore. Where's the broom?"

"In the broom closet," Lucy sniped sarcastically. It was clear that she was not budging from what I suspected was sentry duty at her self-appointed post between the drawer where she had tucked away the envelope and anyone who might want to peek inside, like me. Blaine hustled out of the room, leaving Lucy and me glaring silently at each other over the remains of his father and mother.

"That urn was worth more than your annual salary," Lucy hissed in a loud whisper.

"That's not giving much value to the urn." I smiled. "I'm sorry. We seem to have gotten off on the wrong foot. I'll go survey the boat with your husband and be out of your hair."

"*You!* Alone with *my* husband? Over my dead body! A lot of people want what I have. You can forget your scheme and go back to Florida with the rest of the reptiles that crawl around on their bellies."

And there it was. The only drawback of being a woman in a place regarded by most as a man's world is the insecure, jealous female who thinks you're after her husband. Blaine Hamilton wasn't my type. He wasn't at all like Lincoln Aldridge. Did everyone know I came here from Florida? I wondered. I quickly passed this off as the result of small-town gossip. I gracefully bowed out of the seething stare and attempted to portray disinterest in the drawer and in Lucy's husband. "Yeah. Whatever." I detested the dangling "whatever" response and hoped Lucy did, too. Letting my eyes wander around the room, I finally focused on a series of portraits lined up like a perp walk along the far wall. The portraits, all men, were handsome and dignified and not at all like the last of their bloodline—Blaine Hamilton. As Blaine scurried back with broom and dustpan and proceeded to sweep up his folks, chatting the entire time about nothing consequential, I grew fond of him. Blaine was soft and warm. His portrait would look like a caricature in the company of those it would join someday.

I began strategizing on how to get some time alone with Blaine to pump him for his account of what had gone down at the public meeting preceding the death that I was certain had not been an accident. How could I shake the suspicious wife? I would think of something. I just needed to be patient. I also would have loved a few seconds alone with that drawer, but I doubted that would happen. Lucy caught me staring at the drawer and moved to block my view of it. Fidgeting uneasily with her charm bracelet, she said, "The remains of the most affluent and superior people reduced to a dustpan . . . I never thought I'd see the day. What a disgrace. Does your employer carry liability insurance on *you,* Ms. Bunker?"

"Lucy, darling. Please try to be polite to our guest. Accidents happen," Blaine wheedled.

"She's not our guest, and most accidents are covered by insurance. Come on. Let's get this over with. I have to be at the boutique at eleven." Lucy swept her right arm toward the door, inviting and insisting that Blaine and I exit ahead of her. Blaine grabbed a ball cap from a hook in the entryway, pulled it on over his thinning curly hair, and held the screen door for the ladies with his foot while cradling the full dustpan to his chest. The three of us marched along the mussel shells with me in the lead and moving quickly. I wondered how Lucy was faring with her heels, but I never glanced back to check. Once we were on the boardwalk, the heels clicked closely behind. I nearly ran the length of the granite pier and stopped abruptly at the top of the ramp, where Lucy almost ran up my back.

"Ms. Bunker, we'll only be a few minutes sprinkling the ashes around the shore. Then I'd be delighted to show you *Fairways*. Come on, sweetheart," Blaine said to Lucy.

Lucy ran her eyes along the shore, where the tide had receded, exposing a narrow band of clam flats. Then she looked down at her shoes. "I'll just watch from here. But hurry. I'm meeting Victoria Cole at the shop. She's always good for a grand. How long will this survey take?" Lucy asked me.

"Well, I'm not sure." I hesitated, hoping to discourage Lucy from joining us aboard the boat. "Your vessel hasn't been surveyed since Mr. Hamilton, Sr., had it built, and you've made some changes, right?"

"Yes, yes, that's correct. There have been some changes—improvements, upgrades. That's why I need a new survey. I have no other plans for the morning. You can have all the time you need," Blaine chirped pleasantly. "Sweetheart, you can't be thinking of going with us. You've never been aboard *Fairways*. You'll surely have trouble climbing in and out of the dink wearing that dress." The use of the word "dink" for his dinghy reminded me that Blaine was indeed a member of the upper crust of society; watermen below the yachting class would have called the dinghy anything but.

"Don't you worry about me," Lucy warned. "I am no stranger to boats. I was born and raised in this town, on the water, *and* in a dress. My grandfather came here from Italy to fish," she added proudly.

"I thought your grandfather came from Poland to work as a stonecutter in the granite quarry," said Blaine.

"Yeah. That, too." Now Lucy sounded irritated. "Come on. Snap it up!"

"Yes, dear." As Blaine made his way to the edge of the water, Lucy followed me down the ramp and onto the float. I untied the dinghy's painter, jerked the tiny boat around by the bow so that it lay with its side against the float, and hopped down into the stern seat, leaving the bow for Lucy, as she appeared to be the lightest of the three of us. Not to be outdone, and taking her cue from me, Lucy pushed her hair from her face, took a deep breath, and moved to the edge of the float adjacent to the dinghy's bow. As she attempted a step onto the tiny triangular seat, her dress stopped her foot short of making contact. She quickly withdrew, hiked her dress up a notch, and tried again. I had allowed the slight breeze to blow the bow off just enough to keep the seat out of reach of the fully exposed leg. Again Lucy withdrew to a secure and square stance on the dock. "Need a hand?" I asked.

"No." Lucy shrank into a deep knee bend and reached for the painter, the bitter end of which was lying on the middle seat. Her long, perfectly manicured nails were one inch short of the line. She placed her knees on the float, gripped the starboard oarlock with her left hand, and stretched with her right. She easily grabbed the line, exhaled in relief, and gave me a "see, I can do it, too" smirk. She triumphantly pushed against the dinghy to right her full weight back on the float. The boat moved out, rather than her weight up, leaving Lucy neither here nor there. She arched between boat and float like a human bridge. She held fast, seemingly trying to decide whether to lunge for dinghy or dock. The gap between the two widened, flattening the arch in her back to nearly horizontal. There really was nothing I could do to help at this point, even if I had wanted to. All Lucy managed to utter before splashing was "My shoes."

Blaine came sprinting down the ramp in time to see his wife treading water. Her wet black hair was plastered to her tiny skull, which bobbed up and down like that of a seal looking for a mackerel. I switched myself into the middle seat, placed the oars in their brass locks, and maneuvered back to the edge of the float. I hopped onto the dock, secured the dinghy, and moved quickly to assist Blaine, who was pulling his wife out of the ocean by her fragile-looking arms. Although, of course, I did not laugh, I was amused; I knew I was seconds from a real visual of the expression "mad as a wet hornet." We worked together to haul Lucy first onto the float and then to her feet. The red dress clung to every curve, like a peach in heavy syrup to the side of a bowl.

I didn't know whether Lucy's trembling was from cold or rage, but I broke the silence with an explanation to answer the puzzled look on Blaine's face. "I think one of her spikes got jammed in these boards on the deck," I said, dragging the toe of my sensible shoe along the crack between two eight-inch planks. "Ouch! Look at those legs! There must be a barnacle factory down there," I said, drawing all attention to Lucy's shins. Rivulets of salt water trickled from the lower hem of the dress, over her knees, and onto her shins, where they mixed with blood from multiple scrapes. The shredded panty hose did little to contain the streams as they irrigated Lucy's very expensive-looking shoes. Lucy's fists were balled up tight. Her entire body stiffened with what I perceived as extreme ire and indignation.

"Sweetheart, are you all right?" Blaine winced with what I understood to be apprehension and anticipation of a lashing wrath I was certain Lucy was fit to deliver.

"I'm fine," Lucy answered calmly as she smoothed her dress and pulled her dripping tangles behind her head, then let them plop onto her back, which was stippled with goose bumps. "Ahhh. First swim of the season. Quite refreshing. I need to shower and change before meeting Mrs. Cole." As she sloshed past me, Lucy hesitated long enough to slit her eyes, clotted with damp makeup, and mouth something unreadable at me. She went up the ramp slowly and gracefully, with a seemingly forced nonchalance.

I stepped over the puddle left by Lucy and called out, "Nice to have met you, Mrs. Hamilton. Sorry about your vase."

Lucy never turned around, but she threw her head back, said "Urn" to the sky, quickened her pace, and disappeared up the boardwalk.

I climbed nimbly into the dinghy and took the rear seat, facing Blaine, who held the boat against the float while I got settled. Pushing off, Blaine placed the oars in their locks and pulled strongly and rhythmically toward the majestic dark-hulled sailboat. The size of the dinghy mandated a physical closeness that I found strangely warm and comfortable. With each dipping of the oars, the dinghy rose up slightly, forged ahead, and settled back into a short glide before the next powerful stroke.

I shook myself from the lazy state that so naturally lulls the one in the stern seat. Knowing that my time alone with Blaine would be brief, I initiated conversation with "Interesting hat," referring to his cap. Its embroidered endorsement for the wind farm very much reminded me of the button pinned to the deceased. Seemingly relieved to have the stillness interrupted, Blaine apologized profusely for his wife's lack of manners, excusing her actions with an explanation that led naturally to the questions I had come here hoping to ask. "Lucy is distraught over the death of Nick Dow. She hasn't been acting at all normal—beside herself with grief, I suppose."

"They were friends?" I hoped for more.

"Well, sort of." Blaine lifted the starboard oar into the

boat and tucked the glistening blade under the stern seat. One short backstroke with the other oar landed the dinghy gently against the side of *Fairways*. Blaine grabbed the edge of the three-runged ladder that hung over the rail and waited for me to climb aboard the large vessel. I did not budge. I sat waiting for more of an explanation. It eventually came. "Not friends, exactly," he continued. "Lucy had taken Nick on as a project, like a community service. She accompanied him to A.A. meetings, delivered meals to his place, took calls from him at all hours . . . I suppose she's feeling somewhat responsible for his death, since he was clearly fully intoxicated the evening of his accident." Blaine motioned toward the ladder with his free hand and said, "After you."

One of my few assets was something innate that compelled others to open up to me. Wanting to hear more but not wanting to appear overly interested, I climbed over the rail and onto the deck of *Fairways*. Blaine followed. As he secured the dinghy to a cleat, I said, "That town meeting was my first look at Green Haven. I didn't have a clue what was going on."

"You're fortunate to not know. It was appalling, wasn't it?" Blaine's soft voice was lower than what I assumed was normal for him as he recounted the same sequence of events that I had heard from Audrey in the café earlier this morning and had witnessed myself last night. Of course, Blaine's take on the episode was centered on Dow's misbehavior and how his actions had riled the town to the breaking point. He did not make any mention of the contentious wind-power proposal and how this had disturbed an otherwise complacent community. So I supposed his recounting was, in part, a way of dismissing any responsibility he might otherwise have to face for the meeting's outcome.

I went about the business of surveying the Hinckley

while Blaine supplied a few pertinent details of Dow's fated evening, including the fact that Lucy had stayed out all night following the mayhem at the gymnasium, supposedly looking for Dow and her son. "She was worried about Alex. He was verbally attacked and publicly humiliated by someone whom only she hadn't given up on. Not to mention that it was all because of my wind farm proposal. It's become my pet project. The money I've spent . . . That's pressing particularly hard on Lucy. She knows that wind power will be great for Green Haven, and she supports my efforts, but she's a native and has strong ties to tradition and the town's fishing heritage. Green Haven is under a lot of stress. Progressives and traditionalists are butting heads. Many folks are torn—they don't know which side they're on. Change, even when it's for the good, can be gut-wrenching."

By the time I had inspected every nook in the bilge, every corner of each crawl space, every inch of rigging, and every other system aboard, I had as much detailed knowledge of the vessel's owner as I did of his ship. The boat had been maintained to a T, and as my mentor would say, she was ship-shape, Bristol-fashion. Blaine Hamilton did not quite share the same harmony, in my opinion. This was not to say, I thought, that he was a wreck—just not at ease with his lot in life. He seemed unhappy. Blaine had amply apologized not only for his wife's rudeness but also for his money. It was clear to me by the time we rowed back ashore that Mr. Hamilton felt unworthy of his birthright. The constant denials endeared him to me, as I'd been born with nothing and still had nothing but *was* content. I was glad that Blaine was not the ogre that Audrey had made him out to be. My suspicions that he could have had a hand in Dow's death had been quelled, but his explanations, coupled with his wife's actions, had put Lucy in the running for prime suspect.

The cynic in me couldn't help but wonder if this had been his intention all along.

As we entered the house, I smelled the lingering sulfur from a freshly lit match. No need to ask for a drink of water, I thought. Lucy had already burned the mysterious envelope.

Blaine signed the application required by Top Notch Securities to increase the insurance on *Fairways,* and I bade him farewell and wished him luck with the wind farm project. Blaine walked me to the Duster and opened the door for me. "Wow, nonelectric windows. My first car had manual windows. Neat!" I sensed that Blaine was sincerely fascinated with my old wreck, so I was not embarrassed as I stomped the accelerator three times and turned the key. Blaine closed my door, waved goodbye, and backed away from the car. I stared at the gas gauge, willing it to move above the big "E." It did, but just a hair.

FIVE

I jammed the Duster's transmission into park. After I'd turned off the ignition, my hand lingered on the door latch as I inspected a new wooden sign through the windshield. The thoroughly weathered board—it must have appeared sometime after I'd left my apartment this morning—clearly marked the parking space as mine. JANE BUNKER had been scribed in penmanship identical to that which designated the three other spots for VICKERSON and CUSTOMERS ONLY. Apparently, my landlord, Henry Vickerson, had been busy with his burning tool again.

I grabbed my messenger bag and squeezed through the narrowly opened driver's side, being careful to not allow the Duster to make contact with the Vickersons' shiny new Cadillac. Maybe it was my imagination, but the twin plastic dachshunds perched on the ledge behind the Caddy's rear seat appeared to be bobbing their heads and wagging their tails as maniacally as they had been this morning. Although I had yet to witness the dogs' eyes light up, Alice and Henry had assured me that they were wired directly to the car's brake lights. The box of Kleenex sitting proudly on the car's dash in its hand-crocheted American-flag coat was another reminder to me that good taste is not universal. Alice had promised a similar cover for the tiny bathroom in the apartment I rented from them. So far it had not been produced, and I hoped that Betsy Ross might renege.

Strangely enough, I liked my landlords very much but was careful to keep them at arm's length, as they would, I thought, gladly take over my life if given the opportunity. The rental apartment over the Vickersons' business space and next door to their residence of fifty years was affordable and clean, the only two adjectives requisite in my short search for quarters in Green Haven. Henry and Alice were a bonus, in a way, since they were a wealth of information as well as a source of food and entertainment. Their business, the Lobster Trappe, was what could best be described as a self-contained flea market. Nautical fleas, that is.

Although it was just approaching five-thirty, I felt like a teenager sneaking in after curfew as I tiptoed through the maze of inventory for sale in the yard. I was looking forward to spreading out all the notes and reports I had gathered, and hoped to tie up some loose ends. After my official duties were out of the way, I planned to spend some time on my extracurricular project. Some time alone might help me connect the fragments. The death of Nick Dow, pending fishing regulations, the wind farm proposal, Ginny Turner and her plant, Lucy Hamilton's strange behavior, and the town meeting in such a small community must be linked.

Ducking under lobster buoy birdhouses and wind chimes and around tables displaying dory window boxes and codfish weathervanes, I weaved my way to the entrance. A large sign over the front door that read THE LOBSTER TRAPPE was another testimonial to Alice's taste and Henry's handiwork. It was shaped like a crusher claw, and the bold black lettering stood out sharply against the obligatory red background. The lobster is to Maine's tourism economy what the alligator is to Florida's, I thought. Somewhere in the middle of this country are households whose windowsills are full of pure junk memorabilia carted home from East Coast vacations. I thought it might be prudent for the boards of tourism in various states to regulate the crap sold that is supposed to represent something worthy of a midwestern family's annual one-week road trip. Does there exist a happy couple in Kansas actually wearing T-shirts stating that MAINE IS FOR LOVERS and I GOT CRABS IN MAINE? Or is there a man in Utah sporting a shirt that says I GOT SCROD IN BAR HARBOR? How could this possibly contribute in a positive way to the local economy?

Digging a key from the bottom of my bag, I chuckled and wondered why the landlords bothered with a lock. Was there any possibility that someone might trespass and steal something that had probably washed up on the beach? Closing the door behind me, I laughed again at the list of store hours, with the new addition of OR BY APPOINTMENT—367-2216. Did there exist a potential customer who might call for an exclusive showing of this assortment of junk? Driftwood and beach glass, knick-knacks, sand-dollar and starfish Christmas ornaments, used bait bags, miniature lobster-buoy key chains, and T-shirts silk-screened AYUH! lined the corridor to the back of the showroom, where I climbed the stairs to my place.

After gently closing the door behind me, I dropped my

bag on the wooden crate that served as a coffee table and hung my jacket on a peg beside the door. I removed the clips that had held my effort to grow out bangs tight to my scalp all day. I sighed as my body relaxed, with my hair free to dangle.

I hung on the refrigerator door and searched the cool space for anything that might resemble dinner. Emerging empty-handed, I promised myself a trip to the grocery store in the morning. I missed the daily three-dollar lunch specials of more rice and beans than I could eat at my favorite Cuban spot in the old neighborhood. I wasn't much of a cook. In fact, the rare occasions upon which I made the effort to produce anything more elaborate than a sandwich or bowl of cereal had been during my very few weeks of blissful live-in relationships so sporadically scattered over the last twenty years.

I was not one to recall certain dates in my personal history; rather, I marked the passage of eras with the evacuation or eviction of myself from some corresponding, once wonderful, albeit brief tryst. I hadn't made the grade of detective in 1989; I'd made the grade of detective after Vincent and prior to David. I hadn't taken all of my mother's advice, but what she had told me about men seemed to stick. In her opinion, men should be treated as library books. They should be borrowed and, when nothing more could be learned from them, returned. I had certainly avoided late fees. Now, in my usual "between men" status, I threw a handful of Orville Redenbacher into a pot and onto the stove.

"Hail to the popcorn," I muttered as I absentmindedly emptied the contents of my sailcloth bag onto the top of the round cable spool serving as the kitchen table. Fresh flowers stood erect in a vase that just fitted in the hole in the center of the table—the thoughtful yet disturbing touch of Alice Vickerson, who apparently wandered in and out at will. Setting my laptop computer on the table between the bouquet and me, I plugged the end of a cord into the side of my camera and began to download all of my photos to date. Once the download was complete, I organized groups of shots into separate files, the most interesting to me being the file I labeled "Dow," which consisted of a series of pictures of his corpse on the beach.

Clicking through the photos slide-show fashion, I paused on a full-length shot of the body. Something looked amiss. Zooming in, I blew up Dow's midsection and focused on the knot that secured his rope belt. Strange choice of knots, I thought. Having spent most of my summer vacations at sea, I was somewhat of a knot know-it-all. The slipped sheet bend appeared to have been tied backward. I wondered if Dow might have been left-handed. Dismissing this as inconsequential, I shut down the computer and tackled the mountain of paperwork required by my employer. As I shuffled a stack of insurance forms, the phone rang, causing me to drop the pages and lunge for the telephone. "Hello," I answered.

"Hi, Miss Bunker. This is Cal. Sorry to bother you, dear, but I have a cousin who works at the county lab in Ellsworth, where the autopsies and toxicology stuff are done. She just called, and of course, this is on the QT, but I thought you might like to know the results of the tests on Nick Dow."

I was both surprised and pleased that Cal had phoned. As I tried to pry the results of the tests from him, his end of the conversation became abrupt. Cal shed light only on the phrase "clammed up." The harder I pushed, the tighter his shell squeezed together. I imagined him nervously fingering a cigarette. As with clams, the water runs from the closed shell as through a sieve. But the meat remains concealed until the mussel hinging the shell relaxes.

I swore an oath of secrecy and listened patiently as Cal explained how his cousin could lose her job if word got out that she had shared confidential information. All water, no meat. As Cal told the cousin's life history and why this job was so important to her, I was distracted by Alice Vickerson, who was waving at me through two panes of glass. I waved back, wishing I could escape full exposure to my landlords while on the phone, but the curly cord kept me tethered to the wall and directly in front of windows facing the Vickersons'. Alice held up an index finger, indicating that I should wait for something, and disappeared.

I listened as Cal continued pissing the watery, irrelevant information on and on about his cousin and this bit of classified information that he would like to deliver in person. I assumed that Cal had learned from his cousin what I already suspected. Dow had not fallen onto a rock or drowned but in fact had been struck from behind with a large, heavy instrument. Cal's hesitancy to deliver this news over the phone was understandable. Accidental death was now murder, and murder was not commonplace here. Cal again went on to explain what kind of trouble this would be for his cousin if the leak were to be detected.

I was mentally forming a list of suspects in what had just been confirmed, to me at least, as the murder of Nick Dow. "Will you take me to Dow's house?" I asked. "We can discuss the lab results on the way."

"Oh, geez, I don't know, Miss Bunker. That might be dangerous." Cal sounded apologetic.

"I'll go alone, but I'll need directions." As I waited for Cal's reply, Alice reappeared in the window below and held up a large strip of cardboard on which was printed DINNER? I flashed a thumbs-up and immediately regretted doing so, but my regrets were fleeting, as my focus was on getting to Dow's for a snooping expedition.

Cal had resumed his nervous economy of word. "Going alone. Bad idea."

"Then take me! You can wait outside in your truck."

"No. No good."

"I'm a big girl. All I need are directions. Please, Cal?" I nearly inadvertently called him Clam.

"The wife goes to church tonight." Cal's tone had softened to contemplation.

"What time can you be here?"

"Oh, geez. Eight."

The distinct stench of burning popcorn spun me from the window, which wound the phone cord around my shoulders. The top of the stove was on fire, and black smoke billowed to the ceiling, where it quickly engulfed the fire alarm, sending a shrill beeping to anyone within quite a radius. "See you at eight!" I moved quickly toward the blazing stovetop, ripping the phone's base from the wall. I turned off the gas burner, but the flames had already climbed the wallpaper and were consuming an oil painting of the Gorton's fisherman and its driftwood frame. In the seconds it took for me to decide to leave the apartment rather than attempt to reconnect the phone and call 911, Henry Vickerson flew through the door with an extinguisher blazing, his tiny wife following close behind. Although the fire was doused immediately, Henry continued to spray the extinguisher until its contents were totally exhausted. A yellow chemical dust settled and coated all horizontal surfaces in the kitchenette while the smoke slowly found the open door.

I wondered what was appropriate in this situation. What should one say first? "I'm sorry" or "thank you"? I stood with the dead receiver still pressed to my ear and the cord wrapped tightly around my chest, the rest of the phone and a small piece of plaster resting against a thigh. "I was going to call the fire department," I said.

"Ha! Just as well you didn't," Henry said as he peered at me over the top of his wire-rimmed glasses. "The Green Haven Cellar Savers—that's what everyone calls them. This would have become a controlled burn of the entire neighborhood!" Draping an arm around the shoulders of his petite redheaded sidekick, he added, "You should have been here when they were training volunteers up in Boyce's blueberry fields."

"Oh, it was just awful!" said Alice gleefully. "If firefighters from all over Maine hadn't arrived, Green Haven would have looked like your popcorn!" The elderly couple shared a look and broke into laughter.

I extracted myself from the entwining cord and set the phone on the spool table. "I'm so sorry. How careless of me. Look at this mess! Of course, I'll be responsible for all repairs and cleaning. You won't evict me, will you?"

"Evict? Are you kidding?" Henry peered at me over the top of his glasses again. "You're the best thing that's happened to us since the storm of seventy-eight! What a nightmare. Remember that, dear?" he asked Alice.

"Like it was yesterday," Alice replied. "The kids were out of school for two weeks, helping clean up the shore. I've never made so many sandwiches in my life. Not to mention the loss of power. Try flushing toilets with buckets of ocean lugged up that hill! It was great!"

Somewhat amused with being compared to their local epic disaster, I smiled. "Am I still invited to dinner?"

"You bet! Come on, dear." Alice pulled Henry toward the door. "He'll get the shop vac and get the dust up while I get the food on. We'll worry about the rest tomorrow, while you're at work. You can set the table for us. We need to get you out of here by eight. And when you come home, we'll expect a full report. We want the straight skinny on the lab results. I'll bet that bum was high on drugs!"

How could the Vickersons know what Cal had told me in confidence? Could these innocent-looking elderly folks possibly have bugged the apartment?

Before I could either play dumb or confront the spies, Alice came clean. "We share a party phone line with you. When you or we get a call, the phone rings in both places. Didn't we tell you that? You jumped on the phone before we could tell whether it was your ring or our ring. Because we were expecting a call, Henry picked up." Now I realized why Cal had done the clam impersonation— party phone lines must be common in Green Haven.

"And listened?" I asked.

"Guilty. Both of us. Speakerphone."

Bewildered by the total lack of privacy in my home, I swallowed hard. I now clearly recalled the Vickersons' explanation of the party line, but I found it impossible not to pounce on a ringing phone. Was my ring two longs and a short? I decided it didn't really matter much that they'd overheard my conversation. Cal hadn't divulged anything to "us" other than his cousin's problems. I assumed that the news of a murder would travel quickly, so the Vickersons would be only a half-step ahead of the rest of Green Haven, and only if I chose to share Cal's secret information. The Vickersons assumed that the info would include evidence of drug abuse, which would support a theory of accidental death. I did not have to tell them that Dow's head had been brutally smashed from behind, as I knew Cal would confirm at eight. Obediently following Alice, I hustled to keep up with her short, rapid strides. In an attempt to leaven my thoughts and join my landlords in their amazingly lighthearted acceptance of the near-disaster, I said, "Whoa, Mrs. V. Where's the fire?"

SIX

This would be my third dinner in as many nights in Green Haven with the Vickersons, so as I set the table, I already knew where to find all that was needed and where each of us would sit. As I pulled yellow linen napkins through nautical-blue rings, I quickly scanned the dining and living rooms, noting any changes since my last meal taken with Alice and Henry. Ah, there it was. Henry had shifted the order of the miniature sailboats competing in the regatta on the mantel. The Lightning was now edging out the Laser, while the Bullseye had fallen back. I knew that before the evening was over, Alice would have rearranged the boats to a configuration she considered more aesthetically pleasing, in spite of her husband's insistence that the Laser would be the fastest of the three. As opposed to my scantily furnished studio, the Vickersons' home was busy—like a circus. This place was a virtual knickknack heaven. The array of colors and shapes filling every square inch of space was like the interior of a kaleidoscope.

Eight o'clock wouldn't come quickly enough, I thought,

so great was my anticipation of the news Cal would soon deliver. It was official. My life as a mere marine safety investigator and insurance surveyor had been short-lived. I was eager to get back onto the horse of criminal investigation from which I had been thrown. I had been foolish to think I could leave the past behind so easily. I knew my insurance gig would be a great cover, opening doors to much of Green Haven as well as supplying funds for life's necessities, my personal list of which was fairly simple.

I placed the lighthouse salt and pepper shakers on the middle of the life ring in the center of the tablecloth and wondered how thorough the pathology would be. Would Cal have a report that included possible murder weapons? Had telltale fragments of rust or wood splinters been found in Dow's crushed skull? Had there been signs of a struggle? And (my all-time personal favorite detail) what had been found under the victim's fingernails? Unless it was cocaine, rat poison, or someone else's skin, the fingernail scrapings never added much in the way of evidence, but they always intrigued me. In the past, I had been absolutely spellbound by not only the amount but also the wide variety of matter dug out from under even the most immaculately manicured of nails. I once overheard a pathologist in Miami refer to me as "that female cop with the fingernail fetish."

I deeply inhaled the garlic Alice was pressing into a heavily buttered skillet in the kitchen. "Oh, Mrs. V.! That smells great. What is it?" I asked as I positioned myself to peer over her shoulder.

"Garlic-and-lemon-sautéed mussels over pasta. I hope you're hungry. Henry picked enough mussels for an army!"

I bit my tongue before I could say, "Mussels again?" "I'm starving. Will this recipe go into your cookbook?"

"Perhaps. We're still experimenting and inventing. I wasn't crazy about last night's dish. Fresh mint, as it turns out, really overpowered the mussels. Sorry you had to suffer through it with us!" As Alice chopped and stirred the next possible addition to the Vickersons' *All-Mussel Cookbook,* I explained that all I had eaten today was the blueberry muffin from the café. "Oh, God! The café? And you're still standing? They change the grease annually. Henry and I made that mistake just once. Good thing we have two bathrooms," Alice said as she lit a burner under a pot of water. "There. Come sit and relax. Will you join me in a glass of wine?"

As alcohol was not in my budget, I gladly accepted and sank into an overstuffed chair facing the bay window that overlooked the working waterfront asleep below. I sipped the merlot and nibbled the cheese, crackers, and pickled mussels (again for the cookbook) that Alice, the consummate hostess, set beside me before disappearing into her bedroom. I watched through the window as the sun began to show signs of setting. Yellow faded, and growing orange was refracted by windshields of boats lying still on moorings in the flat, calm harbor. The plant was a large, dark fracture in the otherwise pristine shoreline ringed with white-painted clapboard houses, picket fences, and gardens maintained to perfection. It stuck out as an eyesore, interrupting the scenery I imagined was otherwise enjoyed by every household on the hill.

When Alice emerged from her bedroom cradling a bright pink weekly pill organizer, inhaler, and nasal spray, I knew it was time for the nightly medication exhibition with full running commentary. Although I found it humorous, I was mildly disturbed that Alice did not consider her medicating a private matter. Shouldn't this be taking place in the bathroom? I wondered. Alice set the full pharmacy—prescription and over-the-counter—in a neat display on the table between us. There was no sense in ignoring her, I had already learned, as she would insist on my rapt attention through every chemical swallowed, inhaled, or snorted, and would complement each with an explanation of its target ailment.

"Let's see," she began. "Today is Thursday, right?" She popped open the compartment labeled TH, which housed half a dozen pills and capsules. "My fibromyalgia has been just awful today!" Alice placed a pill in her mouth, gulped a slug of wine, put her head back, and swallowed. "Ahhh, that should do the trick." I wasn't sure whether she was referring to the pill or the wine. After downing drugs for arthritis, blood pressure, water retention, and allergies, while reciting possible side effects and complaining of exorbitant monthly costs for each, she shoved the nozzle of an inhaler into her pursed lips and pumped in a couple of healthy doses. The grand finale was the nasal spray. I'd almost thrown up the first time she snorted her sinus medicine in front of me, but now I was hardened to it.

Alice clearly loved putting on the demonstration, and I wondered who her audience had been before I moved in. Because I knew her routine, I was anticipating the discussion of her bowels. She would tell me precisely what time she had pooped or not today, and what she had eaten to precipitate whatever malady of her gastrointestinal tract she was currently experiencing. "I am able to keep my bowels on track with diet and exercise," she announced proudly. I silently hoped I would not be invited to dinner the day she decided an enema was in order.

The bowel movement's daily log was interrupted when Henry came through the door with the shop vac. "This little beauty would suck a golf ball through a garden hose," he exclaimed. Oh, good, no need to waste money on an enema. Henry stored the vacuum unit in a closet while Alice disappeared back to the bedroom, armed with all the accoutrements that had so enhanced the cocktail hour. "All cleaned up! The phone works, but I'll have to put it back on the wall tomorrow. Anyone ever call you Calamity Jane?" Henry laughed. "Do we have time for a little drinky-poo before dinner, dear?"

"There's always time for a quick one," Alice said cheerfully as she made her way to the liquor cabinet. "We believe in the quality of life, not the quantity. I won't burden you with my health issues, but I could die tomorrow. We have our cemetery plots all paid for, and our will is updated every six months." Alice acted as though she had not shared this personal information several times already in our short acquaintance. I found myself growing impatient and wanting to sneak a peek at my watch without seeming rude.

"Yes, it's important," agreed Henry. "All of our 'I's are dotted and 'T's are crossed. The business and property are in partnership—joint custody with right of survivorship, including the entire inventory. Winner take all!"

As they rambled on about death and proper preparation, I wondered about this joint custody with right of survivorship. Hadn't I just seen this term in a document and wondered what it meant? Now I knew. Sort of.

"Scotch, Jane?"

In the past two nights, the Vickersons had been quick to exploit my weakness for Scotch whiskey. Considering the pending shakedown of Dow's home, I thought better of getting too relaxed, and I refused anything more than a second glass of wine, which I nursed while the land-lords knocked back a couple of single malts as if they were Kool-Aid. Alice's face, fresh from a chemical peel, glowed a bit more with the warmth of imbibing. As she poured a generous second round for them, she applauded my strength of character and promised a nightcap when I returned from Dow's with information to share only with them. It tickled me that the old folks thought I could be bribed. I suspected they watched a lot of TV. "Do you think it might be dangerous to break and enter?" asked Henry. "What do you hope to find? Drugs? I think he was selling drugs. Maybe you'll uncover a drug ring right here in Green Haven! That bum was high as a kite all the time. If he hadn't drowned, he would have eventually overdosed or drunk himself to death. I hope Cal's cousin checked his liver—must have been the size of Texas!"

I made no mention of the pot calling the kettle black and happily obliged the couple this bit of drama. If they were part of Green Haven's rumor mill, it was best they believed Dow's death was accidental. I felt anxiety mounting as I tried not to visibly fidget. Eight o'clock couldn't come soon enough for me.

"Would you like Henry to go with you tonight? He's tougher than a boiled owl. And who knows what kind of riffraff might be shacking up in the abandoned crack house?" Alice offered as Henry tried to look mean.

"Oh, no, thank you. We'll likely just drive by. I have no intention of breaking in," I lied. "I'm just curious."

"Curiosity killed the cat," said Henry.

"Satisfaction brought him back," quipped Alice.

As we took our seats at the table, Alice served up nice portions of steaming pasta, topped with her sautéed mussel concoction, and passed around a crisp green salad. "Alice is right. It could be dangerous. If you're just being nosy, why not wait until daylight, when you might actually see something?" asked Henry. "Maybe you should think about this. Look before you leap." I took that as fatherly advice and was touched by his concern for my safety.

"Look before you leap?" Alice sounded disgusted. "He who hesitates is lost!"

"Patience is a virtue."

"A stitch in time saves nine?"

"I'm not sure that one works, dear," Henry said.

I had come to know these frequent exchanges as Ping-Pong proverbs, and I was sometimes amazed by how long Alice and Henry could volley. I inhaled the meal, hoping that Cal might pull into the drive early. I listened to the Vickersons' opinions, many of which pertained to Nick Dow, while restraining the urge to stare out the window for Cal's arrival.

"I'll bet that house hasn't been shoveled out since his mother died, and she wasn't known for her housekeeping skills," commented Alice. "She died, what, ten years ago?"

"Yes, dear, about ten years ago. His mother was weird, too. She practiced some type of witchcraft," said Henry.

"She was not a witch! She was a midwife." Alice loved correcting her husband. "She delivered every baby in Green Haven for over fifty years!"

"Witchcraft, midwife . . . same thing." Back and forth the two went; it wasn't bickering but more of a friendly discussion of differing views by two people who clearly respected each other's opinions. Henry and Alice simply agreed to disagree, which made a comfortable setting for me to be included.

Fortunately, Alice had not invented a dessert using mussels. I really enjoyed my slice of blueberry pie, though I had hoped not to have time for it. I could hardly pry my eyes off the clock. At precisely two minutes before eight, Cal's truck pulled into the parking area. I thanked Alice and Henry for dinner and again apologized for the mess I had made of the apartment as I placed my dishes in the sink. I bolted out the door while vowing to check back with them upon my return, secretly hoping they would have retired to bed by then.

Cal looked like a white crow perched behind the wheel of his truck. The hunch in his upper back was more pronounced now, and I wondered if this was an optical illusion or the reality of a hard day's work at his age. He held his cigarette outside the open window as he reached across the bench seat with his other hand and popped open the passenger door for me. I slid in, closed my door, and said, "Okay, Cal, what do you have for me?" I was nearly rubbing my hands together. Cal glanced up. My eyes followed his to the bay window above, where two red faces were pressed against the glass. Cal backed out of the parking spot using the mirrors and pulled out onto the street.

As he drove slowly up the hill and out of the town, I nearly went crazy with his silence. "Do you think they read lips?" I joked to break the ice. I got no reaction and regretted dragging Cal into this expedition. It was clear that he was a gentleman who would not think of letting a woman down; it hadn't been fair of me to insist that he take me to Dow's. "Cal, I appreciate your willingness to go with me, but that can wait. What did your cousin report to you?"

Cal took a deep breath before turning to me and dropping his bombshell. "There was not a drop of alcohol in the man's blood, nor any evidence that he had ever taken a single drink in his entire life."

cigarette, and drove along with the look of a man forced into doing something against his better judgment at the hands of a woman.

After less than a mile, Cal turned off the pavement into a narrow opening in some overgrown rhododendrons. The one-lane dirt road that I supposed was Dow's driveway was not well traveled. Deep wheel ruts of dried mud—divided by tall grass and weeds that tickled the underside of the truck—made slow, ambling turns left and then right. If we should meet an oncoming vehicle, one of the two drivers would need to back up some distance to find a spot to pull off and allow the other to pass, since trees and rocks lined the ruts closely on either side. As if reading my mind, Cal said, "Dow didn't drive and didn't receive many guests." That you know of, I thought.

"This road is creepy," I said excitedly. "It's like driving into an Alfred Hitchcock scene."

"Wait till you see the house. It would give Stephen King nightmares."

"Cal! You holdout! You've been here before?"

"Nope. My nephew drives the fuel oil truck for Dead River and has delivered here monthly for years. I've heard enough about it from him to be scared witless. Which is what I am for agreeing to this foolishness."

Expecting to see a dwelling around every corner, and sensing that we were moving slower and slower, I suspected that Cal's dread was growing at pace with my enthusiasm for a glimpse into Dow's life. I reminded my chauffeur that it would soon be dark and that darkness would surely enhance the creep factor. This threat resulted in a slight increase in the depression of the gas pedal and a corresponding bump in speed. It was finally faster than I could walk.

The evening had matured to dusk in full bloom when

SEVEN

"What?" I asked in disbelief. Cal repeated the shocking findings of the toxicology report his cousin had slipped to him, this time editorializing slightly. "So the town drunk wasn't a drunk," I said. I wondered how Dow had managed to fool virtually everyone in Green Haven and, more importantly, why.

"Drunk like a fox," Cal summarized, slowly and carefully turning his truck around in the middle of the road. "His grave should be decorated with an Oscar."

"What are you doing?" I asked as Cal completed his three-point turn and headed back into town.

"Taking you home. I thought you changed your mind about the field trip."

"Are you out of your mind? I need to get into his house right now! As soon as the news of his sobriety gets out, the place will be crawling with detectives. Come on, Cal. Give me fifteen minutes inside," I pleaded. Cal did not resist, nor did he have much to say other than some mumbling about never having seen a detective in Green Haven. He methodically reversed direction again, lit a fresh the narrow drive opened to untold acres of unmowed hay. An old farmhouse in midfield looked nothing more than abandoned in the distance. The road ended in a loop under a lone tree ripe with a flock of fat crows that complained loudly as they gave up their roost when we neared. The sun, just below the horizon, had drained the colors from the day, leaving the scene washed out in tones of gray and white. There was a certain stark and simplistic beauty about the place, I thought, and said, "Andrew Wyeth."

"All that's missing is the crippled woman," Cal responded just over a whisper. His awareness of *Christina's World* surprised and delighted me. My first friend in Maine, other than Audrey and the landlords, was slowly revealing himself as a fascinating enigma. Cal pushed pure white bangs that had fallen over one eye back onto the top of his head. "Going in?"

"The house is bigger than I imagined. I guess I was expecting something like a shack. I'll need more time."

"I have to pick Betty up from bingo in thirty minutes."

"I thought she was at church."

"They play bingo and cribbage in the basement on Tuesday nights."

"Gaming in the church. Must be a New England thing. The United Church of Reprobates . . . I like it. What time would you be back to get me if you were to take Betty home first?" I asked.

Cal looked at his wristwatch, did a quick mental calculation, and said, "Nine o'clock."

"See you then," I said, and hopped out of the truck. The vehicle was moving away as I slammed the door. So much for the age of chivalry, I thought as the tailgate was swallowed by the first bend in the drive. As I moved toward Dow's house, I was immediately engulfed in a cloud of mosquitoes. I walked faster and waved my hands over my head in an attempt to swat away the buzzing mass. I didn't know if the tickling around my exposed ankles was caused by the neglected grass or the bugs. But it nearly drove me insane in the short walk to the front steps.

A porch, probably elegant in its day, wrapped around the front of the house, the center of which was divided by a set of rickety steps. A shallow trough had been worn in the middle of each of the three steps, and the remains of a handrail teetered precariously. The house's clapboards retained only a trace of white paint, light flakes of which appeared to be so tenuously attached to wood, I thought they could be dusted away with the wave of a hand. The window left of the door was missing a couple of panes of glass, allowing shreds of a white curtain to ghost out and flutter in the slight breeze. A hollow whistling of the same breeze through the necks of twin propane bottles yoked by patinaed copper tubing inspired a tingle between my shoulder blades.

What had to be decades of garbage stuffed into green plastic bags formed mountainous heaps that consumed most of the porch. I pulled a penlight from my bag, and the beam confirmed the contents of the heaps as garbage. Raccoons had strewn their discarded dinner packaging, and flies were now enjoying what remained in pizza boxes, Twinkie wrappers, and tin cans alive with ants. Beyond the end of the porch and outside the window was the largest collection of empty soda cans I had ever seen. It looked as though Dow had simply thrown his empties through the broken window—the height of laziness, I thought. Now my impression of Nick Dow was as low as all I had heard around town. Slovenly white trash, I thought, realizing that Dow had lived in this dung pile up until three days ago.

I quickly ascended the steps and steeled myself for the

squalor I imagined I would find inside. The screen door, which had been patched several times with pieces of duct tape, opened easily. I was not surprised to find the inner door unlocked. As I pushed it open and stepped over the threshold, I held my breath, knowing that when I had to inhale, it would not be pleasant. Easing the door closed behind me, I strained to see my surroundings in relative blackness.

Frisking the wall adjacent to the entrance with my left hand, I found a light switch and flipped it on. To my astonishment, there were no scurrying vermin. In fact, the kitchen was, as my mother would say, as neat as a pin. The appliances were outdated, and the hardwood floors needed refinishing. But things were orderly and *clean*. There was absolutely nothing in the air that resembled the stench I had anticipated—only a faint musky smell that reminded me of tidal South Carolina. A lot can be learned about a person from the contents of his kitchen, I knew. So I began the search for clues to unlock the mysteries of Nick Dow.

By the time I had shuffled through all the contents of the cupboards and refrigerator, I understood that the disparity between the house's outward appearance and the reality of what was inside mirrored the dichotomy of its dead owner. Signs of neglect in the home's exterior would indicate to a reasoning intruder—which I was—even worse conditions inside. Were the ramshackle dwelling and surrounding pigsty an intentional facade used by Dow to enhance his reputation as a bum? Or did Dow simply suffer from some psychosis? The food in the refrigerator and freezer—including organic veggies, yogurt, and fancy cheeses—was a far cry from the mess scattered about the porch and yard. Dow's dump attested that he was a microwaver and junk-food addict, while within the kitchen were only delicacies of a healthy gourmet. And as the toxicology had indicated, not a single can of beer or jug of rum did I find.

Perplexed, I wandered into the next room and found a light switch. In all of my years of investigative work, I've found bedrooms and baths of murder victims always rubber-glove time. The gloves were for my protection. The characters I had investigated had been lowlife slime. Men and women who smuggled drugs and human beings and prostituted their own children for their next fix did not make beds or scrub toilets. Dow did. Murderers, druggies, and rapists did not read *Popular Mechanics* or *Scientific American*. Dow did. Criminals who had no regard for life except their own, who ended up dead at the hands of someone a bit more desperate than they, often slept on a filthy mattress on a floor riddled with drug paraphernalia and charred things that were not offerings to the multitude of religious symbols adorning bedroom walls.

I had moved to Maine in part to escape these things. And right now it looked as though I had. Dow's bedside table held no sex toys or X-rated videos. There was no giant flat-screen television, or even a television, for that matter. There were no personal photographs. There was not a single whimsical item to be found: no art, no games, not even a snow globe. When I looked in a closet, I found a set of golf clubs, much to my surprise. The woods had head covers monogrammed with ND, so there was little chance that they belonged to anyone other than Nick Dow. Rifling through the bag's pockets, I found scorecards from several courses in Florida and Arizona but none from any place in Maine. Pulling out a pitching wedge, I gripped and swung for no other reason than I could never resist doing so. A little stiff, I thought as I replaced the club. I hadn't played in weeks. Before moving through the next doorway, I noted the absence in the magazine rack of *National Fisherman* and wondered why Dow would write a letter to the editor of a publication to which he did not subscribe. It seemed I had a lot to learn.

A tidy and well-organized office did not surprise me at this point. But who would have believed that a fisherman and low-level bookie would keep such a neat desk and two three-drawer file cabinets? I thumbed through a stack of bills, all marked "paid," with dates and check numbers. Except for the absence of a phone bill, there was nothing unusual. No phone, no computer, nothing I could use to track down any contacts Dow might have had. Stacks of pads of white lined paper and an abundance of ballpoint pens indicated that all correspondence to and from this office was handwritten.

The leader of a gambling ring must keep a list or book of bets and debts, I thought. But where? I opened the desk drawers one at a time and scanned their contents, all of which contained typical office supplies. A plastic cup held paper clips, all standard silver save one. A multicolored clip similar to those used by Ginny Turner sat on top of the others. Coincidence? I doubted it.

As I moved around the side of the desk to the file cabinets, my heart raced like it had when I made my very first arrest so many years ago. Beside the far cabinet, on the floor, lay a large rusty tire iron. Dents and missing paint on the file drawers were evidence that they had been pried open and the locks broken. Could the tire iron also have been used as the murder weapon? There was no blood splattered anywhere and no blood or hair on the iron. Although it was not impossible, it was, in my opinion, unlikely that Dow had been killed here and thrown into the harbor afterward. In my experience, killers who used instruments as crude as a rusty tire iron were not meticulous about cleaning up after themselves.

The iron must have been used only to jimmy open the drawers. I hoped that who and why would be revealed by the contents of the drawers.

Slowly, as if expecting something to jump out, I opened the top drawer. It was stuffed tight with file folders. I opened the others and found the same to be true of all. The tabs on each folder were labeled with a name, last then first, in alphabetical order. The front file in the top drawer was labeled ABBOTT, ANDREW. I slid the folder from the drawer and opened it to find the official and notarized birth certificate of Andrew Abbott, signed by Martha Dow. Alice had said that Dow's mother was a midwife who had delivered many Green Haveners, so I assumed that her name was Martha and these files were her records.

Peeking into several of the folders, I found similar certificates and a few obituaries and other clippings in which the name on the birthing records also appeared. Midway into the top drawer were oodles of Bunkers; I had learned since moving here that it was quite a common family name. Walking my index and middle fingers through the tabs, I stopped at my name and pulled out the folder. I knew I must be running out of time, but I had to look. Although I was disappointed not to find the answers to any of the questions I had grown up and lived with, I was satisfied to see that I had indeed been born and that my mother was indeed my mother.

Tucking the folder back into its appropriate spot, I pulled BUNKER, WALLACE from the end of the Bunkers. A content and productive Down's syndrome child, Wally lived as an adult in an assisted living space in Florida; he would never have a need for his birth certificate. I knew his thirty-eighth was right around the corner, and I planned to send him some cool superhero stuff. Suddenly, a muted *thunk* jarred me from fond thoughts of Wally.

The sound came from behind the only closed door in the house. I strained to hear. *Thunk.* There it was again. Feeling naked without my gun, I picked up the tire iron from the floor and approached the closed door. I listened closely against the door. I detected a slight and constant whirring. A small electric fan, I thought. No, that wasn't it. Now I could hear a rapid, muffled *bloop, bloop.* I hesitated while deciding how best to enter the room. Should I throw open the door and stand back, or barge right in? *Thunk,* louder this time, sounding like a footstep. With the tire iron high over my head, I threw open the door and jumped into the middle of the room. It was dark except for an eerie square luminescence. The smell of southern salt marshes that I had detected in the kitchen was now overwhelming. Backing away from the strange, dim glowing box shape, I found the light switch on the wall.

An aquarium the size of a Volkswagen took up most of the space in the room. I was so exhilarated, I could barely breathe. The tank's aeration system bubbled and whirred. The glass sides appeared to be completely covered with green algae. The algae seemed to be in motion, and something was making its way out of the top of the tank. *Thunk:* It hit the floor. I moved in to see what had crawled out of the aquarium. A small green crab scuttled a few inches across the linoleum floor, like a cockroach. There were several other crabs on the floor, a few of which appeared to be dried out and dead. With my face nearly against the glass, I gasped in horror. The sides of the tank were not coated with growth; the tank was plumb full of crabs. There must have been thousands of them crawling around. Disgusting. I felt the sensation of something going up my pant leg. Crabs as pets? What kind of sicko was Dow?

Just when I had the urge to scream and run from the

house, lights flashed through the trees on the road and against the far wall of the crab room. Phew, I thought as my goose bumps melted like butter thrown onto a hot griddle. Thank God, Cal's back. I took a deep breath, turned out the light, closed the door, and went to the window of the kitchen to signal to Cal that I would be right out. As the truck pulled around the loop, the headlights flooded the kitchen, filling it with my shadow. Opening the door, I yelled, "I'll be out in a minute."

The icy realization that the vehicle was not Cal's hit me like gallons of Gatorade on a victorious football coach. The headlights flashed to high beams. Stunned, I stood, not knowing whether to retreat back inside or make a run for it. If I stepped back into the kitchen, I would be trapped in the house with nothing but a tire iron and golf clubs for protection. No phone meant no emergency call. If I bolted outside, I would be moving through open fields, where I could easily be run down by the truck. I froze in the doorway, unable to move in any direction. Blinded by the headlights, I knew the driver of the truck was getting a crystal-clear picture of me. If I ran I would be giving the vehicle's occupant reason to chase me, as if I had something worthy of taking the risk. I had nothing. So, scared stiff, I remained in the entryway in a stare-down that I knew could cost me my life.

EIGHT

The unmistakable high-pitched chattering and screeching of a belt out of adjustment grew fainter as the mysterious truck negotiated the turns returning it to the main road. I nearly collapsed in relief. When the noise had faded into the darkness, I let the screen door close me back inside Dow's house. I already knew I wouldn't tell Cal that I had been caught like the proverbial deer in the headlights by an unseen stranger. I returned the tire iron back to the floor where I had found it, and I wished that I had at least dropped it prior to exposing myself as a trespasser.

As I completed my final walk-through of the house, including the grotesque aquarium room, I picked up a dead crab from the linoleum and zipped it into the plastic sandwich bag that held my lunch on days that I packed one. As I tucked the Zip-locked crab into the pocket of my messenger bag alongside my cell phone, I was reminded of the need for a battery charger. As I retraced my steps through the house to ensure that everything was exactly the way I had found it, I did the usual mental gymnastics of figuring out which would be less expensive: shopping at the Old Maids' or driving to Ellsworth. Eventually, I would need to do one or the other.

Satisfied that I had not missed anything that might be an explanation of Dow's Dr. Jekyll/Mr. Hyde routine, I knew I would leave the house with more unanswered questions than I had entered with. I hoped that Alice and Henry would have overserved themselves with medicinal nightcaps and stumbled happily off to bed before my return so that I might avoid the inevitable grilling.

I left behind the garbage heaps on the porch, and I thought about how strange it was that in cities, where millions of dollars were spent on the high-speed and high-tech investigation and prosecution of heinous crime, secrecy to any degree was a myth of ancient lore. Full disclosure of every last detail of any search or research or interrogation or confession was given without question or thought of holding back even a single puzzle piece for future use. Years of bribes and leaks to the press had led to a policy and practice of leaving investigation open to the public. Law enforcement and the judicial system as a whole were cleaner that way—at least in theory. And yet here in Green Haven, Maine, something very odd was going on. Something that had culminated in murder. And it was unlikely that there would be any investigation other than mine, which at this point could be considered a mere dabbling, as I was absolutely unofficial. I was in the enviable position, I thought as I stood in the field at the end of the loop waiting for Cal in the dark, of not having to tell anyone anything. I needn't share the crab, the paper clip, the trespassing truck, the tire iron, or the contents of the file cabinets. My move north had been like stepping back in time to the era of Sherlock Holmes.

Cal's headlights appeared at nine on the dot. We shared neither greetings nor small talk. I didn't ask about his wife's bingo game. He didn't ask about the success of my mission. I didn't promise not to drag him into similar situations in the future. The night was warm. We rode with our windows down. My hair washed across my face and caused me to close my eyes. My exterior calm hid the turmoil within. Anyone could hide the truth, I thought. That was the easy part.

When my hair fell limp upon my shoulders, I realized that we had stopped in the visitor's parking spot at the Lobster Trappe. I was relieved when I opened my eyes to see the Vickersons' windows totally black. The only light in the vicinity was shining from my apartment at thirty-two cents per kilowatt-hour; I knew my goodbye would be hasty. Cal had already placed the gearshift in reverse when I opened the truck door and swung my right leg out. The small light on the roof of the cab was soft and kind to Cal's heavily weathered face. His eyes were on the rearview mirror, indicating to me that he did not intend to linger. Cal appeared to be more than ready to be done with his part in my caper. Stepping out of the truck and easing the door closed to avoid waking the landlords, I was uncomfortable leaving without a word. As usual, I had no idea what to say, though "good night" and "thank you" would have sufficed. "See you tomorrow" may have worked. Instead, I poked my head through the open window and whispered, "Talk is cheap."

The dashboard lights dimly lit Cal's easy smile and nod. His eyes never left the rearview mirror as he replied, "Yes, that's true. Supply and demand."

I hesitated before releasing the side of the truck. I took Cal's implication that the supply of conversation exceeded the demand as permission for me to remain silent. I left without even "good night" and was heartened to see Cal's headlights remain in my apartment windows until I stood inside and waved. They don't make men like that anymore, I thought. Perhaps I had been born a couple of decades too late.

The stench of burned popcorn permeated my living space. I wondered how I would ever fall asleep while breathing this air. I brushed my hair and teeth, slipped a cotton nightgown over my head, flipped off the light, and felt my way to the side of the bed. I fumbled and found the switch for the small lamp on my bedside table and turned it on. Beside the lamp stood a bottle of single-malt Scotch whiskey, a glass, and a handwritten note: "We trust that this will help you sleep. Your sheets are in the wash. Linens on your bed are on loan. Can't wait to hear about your night! Mr. and Mrs. V." Delighted with the twenty-five-year-old Highland Park yet dismayed with another affirmation of my total lack of privacy in a place where I paid rent, I was torn between appreciation and annoyance. Wasn't this the same contradiction of emotions explained time and again by friends with normal parents? Although I had never been abused in any way, I basically had raised myself with the help of my mentor, who had been my friend for over thirty years now. My mother called it making me strong and independent. The social workers found it bordering on neglect. I finally understood the frequent complaints of coworkers about meddling mothers and in-laws who let themselves into adult children's homes, doing laundry and leaving baked goods and notes about elves having visited. Through the years I had secretly wished for some parental elves. Fortunately, I thought as I poured a short drink of the caramel-colored liquor, my elves were lushes.

Tucking myself in, I buried my nose in the glass and was intoxicated by the peaty, almost seaweedy scent. The first sip tingled and left a smoky trail from the back of my tongue to the pit of my stomach. Why this sensation was enjoyable was beyond my comprehension. The indulgence was also beyond my budget, so I nursed the drink, savoring every dear drop while scribbling some notes on a pad. I had an appointment with Ginny Turner first thing in the morning to present the final and official list of upgrades and improvements that the plant needed to remain insured. I suspected this meeting would be most unpleasant. But it would get me back into Ginny's office, where I might gain some insight on her connection, if any, to Dow.

I didn't remember putting away my notes and turning off the lamp, but I supposed I must have as I squinted, barely awake, at six-thirty the next morning. Feeling a little guilty about sleeping an hour later than what was normal for me, I vowed to skip the nightcap in the future unless I had absolutely no schedule until later in the day. I quickly ran a cord connecting a printer to my laptop computer and printed out the plant's survey on the official form, all ten pages. A short, hot shower and instant coffee stayed me for the morning. After my seven A.M. meeting at the plant, I would visit the coffee shop for some real sustenance and perhaps a chat with the goddess of gab, Audrey. Maybe some of her loquaciousness would rub off on me. God knows I could use a little, I thought as I stared at the foamy brown sludge in the bottom of my coffee mug.

With the day forecast to be muggy, I decided on a short khaki skirt, a white tee, and sandals. I hopped into the clothes and put my still-wet hair into a tight bun and was ready to face the world—or at least Green Haven. Placing the Scotch in a cupboard, I wondered if the bottle had been full when the Vickersons left it. I hoped not. As I took one last look at its label, I wondered whether I would ever get to the Orkneys, or any other part of Scotland, for that matter. One dream at a time, I thought as I checked my figure in the reflection of the stainless steel refrigerator door. Not bad for forty-two, I thought vainly, and slung my homemade sailcloth messenger bag over my head, cross-chest fashion. With the strap pressing between my breasts, their size was accentuated, which was fine by me. Somehow, in the last twelve hours, I had transformed from the dowdy, conservative insurance lady to the new gal in town: the single, attractive, intriguing undercover murder investigator on a mission. I was full of anticipation for another showdown with Ginny Turner; the thought of ruining her day made mine.

The day, even at this early stage, was just what the weatherman had promised. Nothing like the heat of southern Florida but hot nonetheless, I thought as I walked through the parking area, past my Duster, and out to the edge of the road. The nice temperature coupled with the status of my car's gas tank compelled me to travel on foot. The plant was under half a mile away and all downhill. I hadn't worked out since leaving Miami, and my new job did not include a gym membership—one of the many bennies I had sacrificed along with a decent paycheck. Money isn't everything, I tried to convince myself as I wandered through the open gate in the chain-link fence in front of the plant. I could always walk for exercise.

Two steel fishing vessels were unloading their catches on either side of a finger pier jutting out from the plant's main building. The *Sea Hunter* and the *Fearless,* it appeared to me from the distance, were unloading codfish. My face flushed slightly with the thought that Lincoln Aldridge must be in the vicinity. "Good morning, Miss Bunker," called Cal cheerfully from his post as overseer of the unloading, weighing, recording, and transporting to the processing area. He stood more erect than he had appeared behind the wheel of his truck last night, as if he had somehow significantly deflated the hump in his upper back. Overall, Cal looked well rested.

"Good morning, Cal," I called back, and waved a hand. All work stopped as I passed. I was close enough to hear whispered questions of Cal and feel eyes staring and heads turning to follow my walk toward the stairs to Ginny's office. My new attitude had the desired effect. I was accustomed to admiring stares from men and at times longed for them. But it had been a while, a long while, since I had put any effort into my appearance and an intentional sway in my hips. I haven't lost a thing, I thought as I slowly climbed the stairs. I quickly checked my ego as I reminded myself that I had little female competition here at the plant among women clad in oversize lab coats, hairnets, and rubber boots. There was no way to make the required getup look cute.

"All right, boys, back to work! Haven't you ever seen a pretty woman before?" There was some low-level grumbling and a few chuckles as the workers obeyed Cal's order and resumed various duties aboard boats and on the pier.

Armed with the supreme confidence of a woman who can turn heads with a wiggle and a smile, I barged into Ginny Turner's office without knocking. Anticipating nastiness, I was nearly baring my teeth as I slapped the full ten-page report on the only corner of her desk not buried in something. The breeze created by the thrown report blew a cloud of powdered sugar from the abundance of whatever chocolate goodies Ginny was in the midst of consuming and onto the front of her navy blue shirt and moonlike face. Even the lenses of her glasses were dusted. At my usual loss for words, I stood awkwardly silent while the Pillsbury Dough Girl washed down a mouthful of chocolate with milk slurped from a one-gallon container. In the past when I had barged through closed doors unannounced, I had always done so leading with a loaded handgun. "Stick 'em up" or "Don't move" or "You're under arrest" was part of the protocol. Whatever came to mind now as an opening statement seemed toothless.

I wondered if perhaps my entrance had been a bit dramatic as Ginny calmly removed her fouled glasses and attempted cleaning them with her shirt. The shirt's hem was stretched to the max and resisted her pinching fingers. Following her third and final failed attempt to pull the shirt from her body, she simply rubbed the lenses across her mountainous bosom, back and forth, until a furrow was worn in the sugar that had settled there, exposing a stripe of navy blue. Now I knew why the fashion gurus advised no stripes on large folk.

Placing the glasses back in front of her eyes, Ginny gave me a long stare, up and down and back to where our eyes met. Her cowlike tongue did a full circumnavigation of her lips, leaving them glistening amid fields of white powder on her chin and cheeks. "Well, now, Ms. Bunker, I see you've changed your costume to contemporary trollop," she said with an evil smile. I was less bothered by the insult than I was by the realization that I did not possess her ability to come up with one so quickly.

I took a deep breath and wondered if she would have been so insulting with the barrel of a gun in her face. Realizing that it would not impress my boss if I pummeled a paying client within inches of her life, I smiled back and said, "Thanks for the fashion commentary, Mrs. Turner. My visit here is quite serious. This report of my survey of your property includes changes that must be made to bring the plant up to the minimum safety standards. The underwriters are giving you ninety days to comply. If you do not do so, your policy will be canceled."

Without another word, Ginny leaned across her desk and grabbed the papers I had delivered. She read silently. As she turned each page, her breathing got shorter and more labored. Her face got redder and redder, and sweat melted the dusting of powdered sugar into a thin paste. While she went through the report, I allowed my eyes to wander around her desktop and surroundings, and I wished I could have a few minutes alone to rifle through her things. I had sensed that Ginny Turner was guilty of something, or at least knew more than she had let on when I first met her. So far, she had done little to clear herself of my suspicion.

Both my contemplation of how to coerce Cal into letting me in after hours and Ginny's reading were interrupted by a sweet young voice over an intercom on the desk. "Mrs. Turner, Blaine Hamilton is on line one for you."

Mashing a button with a giant thumb, Ginny barked, "Tell him I'll call him back!" Scowling, she turned her focus back to the report. Interesting. Was she annoyed by the interruption or by the fact that I'd heard Blaine Hamilton had called? I knew Green Haven was a small town, but even so, I could not imagine what possible relationship could exist between Blaine Hamilton and Ginny Turner. I wondered if there was a way I could eavesdrop on the return call.

When the intercom chirped a second time, the sweet voice on the other end was even more timid, actually shaking. "Mrs. Turner, I'm sorry. Mr. Hamilton would like to confirm your seven o'clock meeting at—"

This time I thought Ginny's thumb would go through the desk. "I said I would call him back! What didn't you understand about that? Goddamm it!"

"I'm sorry, Mrs. Turner, but he—" Before another syllable could squeak through the tiny speaker, Ginny jerked the device's cord from the outlet, sending the small plastic box against the wall, where it fell to the floor in three pieces. It was very obvious that Ginny did not want me to know anything about her meeting with Blaine Hamilton. I decided I might just be in the mood for a walk this evening.

"You, Ms. Bunker, are dismissed," Ginny said to me.

"Dismissed? Do you have any questions? Do you understand that in ninety days, your coverage will be terminated if the requirements are not met?" I asked.

"I understand that these changes will amount to tens of thousands of dollars that I do not have. I understand that you could very well put me out of business. I understand that I am the largest employer in Green Haven and that many hardworking people trying to make an honest living will be cold and hungry without the income provided by the plant," Ginny said in a tone that was a little louder than necessary.

A very compelling position, I had to agree. If Ginny had not been totally unlikable, I might have started to feel bad about doing my job and coming down so hard on her. "Don't your employees deserve a safe working environment? Don't you care about their safety?" I shot back.

"My employees are first and foremost!"

"So I've noticed," I said quietly as I glanced at the pieces of broken intercom. This was my exit cue. Closing the door behind me, I hesitated long enough to hear the loud bang of something flung with great force against the other side and wondered if it was the stapler or a paperweight. As I descended the stairs, I considered Ginny Turner's violent temper and wondered whether, in the throes of a rage, she was capable of murder.

I found Cal standing with a group of three other men around the tailgate of a truck. The men were, I suspected by the lack of lab coats and hairnets, fishermen of the two boats whose decks were being scrubbed and hosed, all unloading apparently done. As I approached, I recognized the handsome Lincoln Aldridge, who had given me his stool at the coffee shop. Everything about this guy was attractive. Yes, very attractive indeed. I decided that this was my opportunity to be introduced. I hoped not to act as adolescent as I knew I could in the presence of someone I was so eager to meet.

I drew closer to the men and noticed that they were watching and discussing something on the beach below. Because of the height and length of the dock, I could not see the beach until I reached the truck parked at its edge. The shore, as far as I could see in either direction, was crawling with people. And this was not a sandy beach where people would come to sunbathe, swim, or sit and muse. I joined the spectators around the truck and thought it seemed as though the motions of the people along the beach were purposeful—as if they were looking for something. But they weren't organized like a search party; they looked more like an Easter-egg hunt— every man for himself. My interest was more in getting Lincoln's attention.

"Hey, Cal, what's going on?" I asked cheerfully. Cal responded politely, and what his brief explanation lacked in detail and enthusiasm was compensated for by the input from the fishermen to whom I was eventually introduced. Lincoln was even better-looking than I remembered from our brief encounter in the coffee shop. I grew nervous and focused on the other two men. Lincoln's son, Alex, I knew was the kid humiliated at the town meeting, Audrey's crush, and also one of the two boys who acted as ambulance attendants at Dow's beach scene. He couldn't have cared less about our introduction. The third man shook my hand and introduced himself as George, the captain's brother, the captain being Lincoln. Dying to strike up a conversation with Lincoln, I cursed my inability to do so. Unable to speak, I listened.

From what I could gather, half of Green Haven was searching for Nick Dow's little black book. A wad of cash also may have accompanied Dow into the drink, and some feigned a desire to find it, but from what the men told me, the real treasure for most of the searchers was the black book. Ultimately, I understood that the secret toxicology findings and autopsy report were not so secret after all. In fact, everyone seemed to know more than I did. I was surprised to hear that the consensus of the men was that Dow's black book held evidence that could convict many of the townspeople of a variety of things ranging from felony to indiscretion. Why, I wondered but dared not ask, were these men not included among those desperate to find money or conceal evidence that, if uncovered by the wrong people, could lead to imprisonment or divorce?

The disjointed conversation around the truck led me to believe that among the frantic searchers were people who would probably be counted among the suspects in a murder investigation if the black book were to surface. Why had nobody notified the authorities? Perhaps I should contact the state police again, I thought. Maybe, with this new development, the chief detective would be grateful for the lead rather than rude, as he'd been with my other attempt. Were my new acquaintances totally innocent and therefore unconcerned about the whereabouts of the book? Or did they already somehow know that the search would be fruitless?

The men soon ran out of talk. Cal excused himself to return to work. George and Alex returned to the *Sea*

Hunter at the request of their captain, leaving the two of us alone. "I have been secretly hoping to meet you," Lincoln confessed quietly when he knew that George and Alex were out of earshot.

Had I heard that correctly? "Really?" I smiled and blushed at my attempt to sound coy.

"Yes. I saw you at the coffee shop and wanted to say hello, but you were fully engaged by Audrey, who was no doubt professing her love for my son."

"Really?" This repetition fell well short of whatever feminine wiles I'd had in mind. I felt my face going beyond blush. Why could I not think of something interesting to say? Why was I incapable of flirting? I had to say something before he went back to his ship.

"Yes, really," he said softly, and looked down into the rusted bed of the truck. After a long, strained pause that I was unable to fill with even a comment on the weather, he said, "Well, I wanted to meet you. Now I have. It was a pleasure. If you'll excuse me, Jane Bunker, I have some errands."

"I'm scheduled to survey your boat this week," I blurted out as he climbed into the truck.

"Yes, I know," he said, seeming pleased that I had vocabulary beyond "really." He turned back to me, this time mesmerizing me with the sexiest blue eyes I had ever imagined. "I hope to get back out fishing in a couple of days. So let's make an appointment for either before I go or after I return. I'd like to clean her up a bit before you come aboard."

"Oh, don't go to any trouble on my account. I've been aboard some real wrecks!"

"We're not known for our housekeeping skills. Some advance warning would be greatly appreciated." Another long, awkward pause with the ball left in my court was saved by his suggestion of dinner.

"Dinner? Dinner would be great. I eat dinner every night. It's my favorite meal." Shut up, you babbling idiot! I thought. I must have sounded quite desperate.

"Tonight?"

"Tonight?" Oh, shoot, I thought. I already had an evening of eavesdropping scheduled. "Tonight is not good for me." Was I really turning down my first dinner invitation in Maine from anyone other than the Vickersons? I was blowing an opportunity to get to know the most intriguing bachelor in Green Haven. And I couldn't remember the last date I'd had or turned down.

"Tomorrow, then!" Lincoln said without missing a beat. "There's a meteor shower. I'll pack a picnic basket and take you to the most remote and gorgeous spot in the state of Maine to see the night sky. I'll meet you here at seven. What do you say?"

What *do* I say? Do I say you are the most romantic man I have ever met, and I am totally enchanted? Do I say let's skip the formalities and go to bed right now? Remembering my age, I pulled my wits together and said simply, "Great." No sense putting the cart before the horse, I reasoned. We said our goodbyes and our see you tomorrows, and I walked away consciously restraining my urge to jump up and down and shout "Hooray!" A date! I could not have fantasized this any better, I thought as Lincoln drove slowly by me to the gate. He stopped, looked both ways, and pulled out onto the main road. The unmistakable screeching and chattering of a belt out of adjustment grew fainter as he disappeared up the hill.

I had heard that same sound the night before, when I was out at Dow's.

NINE

I exited the plant property by the same gate through which I had entered, though I was far less poised on my way out. Confidence flagging, and wishing for something to hide behind, I had gone from sassy broad to total introvert at the speed of sound. I scolded myself to regain my air of superiority before anyone saw me squirm with self-doubt. What if Ginny Turner were looking out her window? How could I be so stupid? How could I fall for someone who was so obviously playing me? How could I gracefully back out of the date that I had so desired?

If Lincoln had been so eager to meet me, why hadn't he done so last night, when he had me trapped in his high beams? Maybe it had been the crowbar. I nearly laughed to myself as I imagined how I must have looked to the trespassing and unsuspecting Lincoln. Perhaps I would keep our date, I considered, if only to get to the bottom of what business he'd had at Dow's.

It may seem shallow, but I couldn't help thinking that

my fun clothes clashed with my mood. Not that Ginny's fashion commentary had had any effect, but if the remainder of my day was to be consumed aboard boats where I would be squeezing in and out and through cramped spaces never intended for human passage—spaces neglected since construction, except for insurance surveys—then I would be wise to run home and change into something better suited. And since changing my clothes might well be the only wise thing I had done since waking up that morning, I decided to do just that.

The Vickersons' gift shop was open, and both proprietors were putting the hard sell on a couple of tourists who were undecided about how a lobster-trap table would fit in at their home in the Hamptons. They listened to the logistics of strapping the table to the roof of their BMW, which was what Henry was recommending as I scurried through en route to my apartment. Alice stopped her sales pitch long enough to hand me a fax fresh off her machine. I thanked her and bolted up the stairs, relieved that she and Henry were too busy to talk with me.

The apartment was relatively dark, but rather than flipping on a switch and imagining the electric meter spinning like a whirling dervish, I opted for sunlight. I briefly admired the tugboat window-shade pull Alice had made in ceramics class, pulled it down and toward my waist, and slowly fed the recoiling roll above the large window. I stopped the chubby red tugboat at chest level, where it swung from a thin cord at the bottom of the shade like a pendulum, the cord bisecting my panoramic vista of Green Haven's working waterfront.

I removed and carefully folded the best my wardrobe had to offer, wishing I had saved the khaki skirt for another occasion (like a date). I wondered what I would wear to the stargazing picnic tomorrow evening. Was my interest in Lincoln still romantic? I wondered. Or was it a necessary part of my extracurricular investigation? The truth was, I realized as I stepped into an old pair of jeans and pulled a sweatshirt over my head, the fact that Lincoln had been at Dow's and known that I was there first only added to the anticipation and intrigue of a rendezvous.

Master of the quick change, I was sneakered, out the door, and back on Main Street before the Vickersons had swiped the credit card of the couple who I imagined were already experiencing buyers' remorse. As I walked, I contemplated many possible options for how to handle my pending date with Lincoln. Did I want to be alone with someone who might be capable of murder? Well, murder might be a stretch. After all, if Lincoln had a violent streak, he'd had the perfect opportunity to let it flare at Dow's and had chosen to leave instead. But he certainly had been involved with Dow at some level. My stride became stronger, and I threw my shoulders back and chest out as I passed a building in the midst of getting a new roof. I thought I heard a wolf whistle blown in my direction from the men banging shingles. Objectifying or simply appreciative, the buoy to my spirits was welcome indeed. Now all I needed was coffee.

The coffee shop was more quiet than usual. I surmised that most of the daily patrons were still scouring the shore for Dow's bankroll and book of dirty secrets. There was a middle-aged couple sharing a newspaper and a bagel at a corner table, an elderly gentleman in Top-Siders and plaid shorts waiting for a take-out order, and Clydie Leeman perched on a stool at the counter. I pulled the door closed behind me, which resulted in the ringing of the trio of cowbells hanging from the knob. Stifling the swinging bells by grabbing the ribbons from which they hung, I apologized for the intrusive racket to the couple glaring at me over the tops of their sports and style sections.

Audrey pushed through the swinging doors from the kitchen, carrying a paper bag with the grease of its contents noticeably wicking up its sides. "Good morning, Miss Bunker," Audrey called cheerfully. "Sit wherever you'd like. Be with you in a sec." I wondered how I had gone from "girlfriend" to "Miss Bunker." Audrey punched buttons on the cash register and collected money from the gentleman in plaid, who was indiscreetly checking out all of her tattoos and piercings. As soon as the man hit the sidewalk with his greasy bag, Audrey said, in true teenage fashion, "Take a picture. It'll last longer." There, I thought, was the old Audrey.

I was undecided about where to sit. I had mistakenly assumed the shop would be jammed full of townspeople gossiping and speculating about the now well-known scuttlebutt surrounding Nick Dow's secret life, and I'd hoped to be privy to all their theories, since I wanted to learn all I could while evidence and talk were fresh. My options were Clyde and Audrey. Then again, I could also use a solid meal. So perhaps all had not been lost in my walk to the coffee shop. Sliding a chair from under a small table between the kitchen and the restroom, I was nearly seated when Clydie invited me to join him at the counter. "No need to sit all by your lonesome. Come over here next to me. I don't bite!"

"Oh, sure. I'd love to join you," I lied as I watched Audrey roll her eyes. "I'll have the special. Scrambled with rye toast, please," I said to her as I took the stool from which Clydie had whisked his Stetson, making it clear where he intended me to sit.

"Coffee, Miss Bunker?" Audrey asked.

"Please."

"Clydie?" she asked.

"No, thank you, dear. I'll just stay and keep Miss Bunker company while she eats," Clyde said.

"I'm sure she's thrilled," Audrey said quietly as she poured coffee into my mug while digging into the front of her apron for a handful of tiny plastic creamers. After tossing half a dozen Mini-Moos onto my place mat, Audrey disappeared through the swinging doors, presumably to place my order with whatever hash slingers were employed in the smoky inner sanctum. Before the doors had come to a complete rest, she pushed back through them and hustled to a position across the counter from Clyde and me, resting both elbows on the orange Formica countertop and cradling her chin in her palms. Audrey's eyes flashed with youthful energy as she asked, "So, what's up, girlfriend?" Before I could answer, she specified what exactly she had in mind to discuss. "Have you seen all the idiots combing the waterfront for cash? Don't you think whoever killed Nick Dow robbed him first? And I mean, like, how many times has the tide come and gone since he washed up at the plant? Like there's thousands of dollars sitting under a clump of seaweed just waiting for someone to find it! I've got a better chance of finding a buck on the counter when Clydie leaves."

"I ain't leaving you no buck!"

"See?" As Clyde and Audrey discussed tipping etiquette, I realized that Audrey was right. There was little or no chance that any money would be recovered. So, I surmised, most of Green Haven was searching for Dow's black book.

"I'm not a gambling man," Clyde confessed. "But I'm ashamed to admit that I got sucked in by Dow. I put ten bucks on the *Sea Hunter* in the fish pool." He stared at his feet. "Lots of folks are in for a lot more. If I was them, I'd be down there poking around the mudflats, too."

A muffled voice penetrated from the kitchen, and Audrey vanished and returned with my breakfast. "You know, now Alex sleeps in Dow's bunk aboard his dad's boat. Isn't that sick?" Audrey continued as she slid salt and pepper shakers my way. "Sleeping in a dead man's bunk!" As Audrey and Clyde compared notes on Dow—both claimed to have known for years that he was not a drunk—I thought about Dow's bunk aboard the *Sea Hunter*. Hadn't I heard that Dow had worked for Lincoln sporadically for years? I had to get aboard that boat before Lincoln and his crew "cleaned her up." Having crawled around many a boat, I knew the hiding places were almost endless. I needed to do the survey on the *Sea Hunter* today, I decided. I ate my breakfast faster than usual.

As Audrey cleared my plate and silverware, I took the faxed schedule from my messenger bag. Let's see, I thought, what on my agenda could be put off until tomorrow so that I might get aboard the *Sea Hunter* today? The most urgent item on the schedule from my boss, Mr. Dubois at the agency, was to survey and report the damage by vandals to the electronics aboard the *Fearless*. Mr. Dubois had noted this as priority, since the cod boat could not safely go to sea without the equipment that had been sabotaged. I supposed this was true. Having gained an understanding of the importance of sea time for the boats in Green Haven's dwindling cod-fishing fleet, I knew it was critical for *Fearless* to get offshore as soon as possible to ensure their piece of next season's quota. I vowed to put the full-court press on whatever was needed aboard the *Fearless*. Once this was resolved, perhaps I would have time to sneak aboard the *Sea Hunter* before my eavesdropping expedition this evening.

Although it was painful, I left a dollar bill on the

counter, along with three others that covered my breakfast tab. Fifty cents would have been adequate, I thought. But I didn't have any change and was unwilling to wait for Audrey to make some, as she was nearing a breathless swoon in yet another lamentation of the object of her admiration's total ignorance of her existence. Clyde listened patiently, nodding in condolence and patting Audrey's fingers, which were fully bedecked in silver rings.

I slipped out of the coffee shop unnoticed and walked along Main Street in bright sunshine. As I neared the plant, I could see that the *Sea Hunter* and *Fearless* had moved from the unloading dock back to their usual berths around the corner of the main building. Two other stern trawlers were secured in the slots they had vacated, and the plant and surroundings were again in high gear, unloading, processing, packaging, and shipping. Cal's silhouette stood distinctly in the company of the other workers: The hump between his shoulder blades was prominent where others had a shallow recess. A slight bow and a tap of his forehead with two fingers, signifying a tipping of his hat if he had worn one, was Cal's way of letting me know that nothing went unnoticed on his turf. I found this comforting.

I walked the weathered planks of the wharf adjacent to the plant; the tide was as high as I had seen it since moving to Green Haven. The boats were bellied up proudly to the pier, the flares of their bows extending over the pilings to which they were tied. The *Sea Hunter* lay directly astern of *Fearless*. I understood why these two boats had not been named in the traditional female fashion. The *Sea Hunter* and *Fearless* were all about work. They were fairly brutish in their lines, with nothing pretty about either vessel. Far from pristine, the paint jobs were adequate to cover the rust. The boats looked— outwardly, at least—generally well maintained. I called hello to the captain and one-man crew working on *Fear-less*'s stern deck as I moved carefully around a telescope on a tripod in the middle of the narrow pier.

"Hi. I've been expecting you. I'm Alan Quinby. Everyone calls me Quin. This is my boy, Eddie. That's his foolish piece of junk in your way up there," the captain said, pointing to the telescope. Eddie looked humiliated as he nodded a silent greeting.

"It's not in my way," I said. "Hi, Eddie. I think we've met. Well, sort of. Weren't you one of the ambulance attendants on duty when Nick Dow was found?" Eddie had been the kid with the absent look on his face, staring at the sky. I recalled thinking that he had looked stoned. I was certain that he had been and was now.

"Yes," Eddie said, seemingly pleased that I had remembered him. "That's part of the civic duty required of seniors at Green Haven High."

I stepped aboard and extended a hand to the young man. "It's nice to see you again. I'm Jane Bunker."

"Hi, Jane." Eddie barely made eye contact.

"What's this Jane crap?" interrupted Quin. "That's Miss Bunker to you! Where are your manners?" In reply, Eddie squinted and flinched as if expecting to get back-handed.

After a cool "Nice to meet you" to his father, I immediately engaged in conversation with Eddie Quinby. My attention to the telescope, which he confirmed was one of three he owned, sparked real life into the otherwise inanimate Eddie.

"It's a great instrument for beginners. It's a Newtonian reflector. I keep it on the dock so that when I'm down here working, I won't miss anything. I saw Mercury at dawn and showed all the guys. Even my father looked!"

"I still don't know what the big deal is," grumbled

Quin. "Looked like a plain old star to me. Sometimes I think you make this stuff up. Point that goddamned thing in the air, and start telling stories about Venus or some garbage about a serious star that's part of a ship—"

"You've got it all confused, Dad. Sirius is the Dog Star. It's the brightest star and part of Canis Major. It's eight point five light-years away! Canopus is the star that's part of the constellation Carina. Carina is the keel of Argo Navis. That's the ship Jason and the Argonauts sailed in search of the Golden Fleece."

"Show me the astronauts!" Quin taunted his son.

"Argonauts. You can't see Canopus from here," Eddie continued, undaunted. "You need to be south of thirty-seven degrees north." I listened with interest as Eddie defended his passion to his father, who clearly regarded astronomy as a waste of time and energy.

In an attempt to have me join his side of the argument, Quin said, "Galileo, here, blew an entire paycheck on a tripod. Six hundred bucks! It ain't worth a damn." Pointing toward the tripod assembly on the dock and shaking his head in disgust, he scowled, then looked puzzled. "Hey! That's not your new tripod! Where's the six-hundred-dollar tripod?"

Eddie hesitated. Without looking at his father, he finally replied, "I didn't want it out in the salt air."

"That's a goddamn lie! You've never been a good liar. You had that tripod out in the salt air last week. I remember you showing George all of the fancy-ass adjustments one night when you should have been home in bed. It's no wonder I can't get any work out of you. You're up all night, dreaming about space. Now, *where* is that tripod?" demanded Quin.

It didn't seem to me that Eddie's stoned state was enough to numb him to his father's humiliation. "I think it was stolen."

"Goddamn right it was. How many times have I told you not to be so fucking trusting? You leave six hundred bucks laying around, you deserve to lose it, loser."

I was uneasy with the mounting tension between father and son, and with Quin's cruelty. But if looks could kill, Quin would be a goner, and Eddie would be heading to prison. Eddie stood flexing his hands in and out of tight fists and clenching his jaw so hard that his face turned red and beads of sweat formed at his temples. With any more goading from his father, Eddie might fly into a violent rage. He appeared to be at his breaking point. Before his father could prompt him to do something we'd all regret, I interjected, "I heard there will be meteor showers tomorrow night."

Eddie immediately snapped out of it and replied, "Yes. The Perseid meteors are generally the best showers of the year. There will be ninety to one hundred meteors per hour at the time of peak. Unfortunately, peak is at seven—still daylight. By the time the radiant is well placed, the waning gibbous moon will drown out a lot of the fainter falling stars." I began to realize that Eddie was accustomed to covering for his father's lack of decency. He was able to shift gears to avoid looking as embarrassed as he must have felt.

"Oh, really?" I tried to sound merely interested but was afraid my tone was sheer disappointment as I thought forward to my date.

"Don't worry. From the layman's standards, it'll be a great show."

Quin was visibly irritated. He zipped and unzipped the top four or five inches of his coveralls, up and down, up and down, while he examined what appeared to be a badly damaged fishing net on the deck at his feet. At a glance, I could see where a mistake had been made in the mending of the net that would make it impossible to have it absolutely correct, which I knew from experience was imperative to all fishermen. "You missed a pickup where the wing goes into the seam," I said, pointing out the error.

"You know twine?" asked Quin with more than a note of surprise.

"I fished my way through school. I had to mend to receive a full share."

"No shit. Thanks."

Thinking that I might like to impress Lincoln with my newfound knowledge of meteors, I engaged Eddie further while his father cut and fixed the mistake he probably had searched for and not been able to find. "I know nothing about the night sky. What would be the easiest star for me to identify?" I asked.

"That would be Sirius. It's found in Canis Major, or Big Dog. That's why we astronomers refer to it as the Dog Star." Quin snickered nastily at Eddie's inclusion of himself in the group "astronomers." "In ancient Greek times," Eddie continued resolutely, "the dawn rising of Sirius marked the hottest part of the summer. You've probably heard the expression 'dog days of summer.'"

"Yes, I have." This was perfect material for conversation with Lincoln. "How do I find this Dog Star?"

"Follow Orion's belt twenty degrees southeast to the brightest star in the sky. One fist held at arm's length is roughly ten degrees of sky. You can find Orion, can't you?"

Faster than I could confess my ignorance of astronomy, Quin displayed his astronomical impatience with his son's avocation. "Okay, Galileo. Back to work on this net. Miss Bunker has more important things to think about than the stars." Though I begged to differ, I thanked Eddie for the primer and promised to get a real lesson from him one clear night here on the dock with his telescope and inferior tripod. As I followed Quin up the ladder to the bridge, I couldn't help but think what an odd young man his son was. With the exception of his knowledge of astronomy, Eddie seemed quite unusual. Shouldn't he be obsessing about girls and cars at seventeen? Too much marijuana, I assumed. And the anger he had nearly lost control of was downright scary, I thought. I couldn't help but wonder about the six-hundred-dollar tripod. Eddie, I determined, was weird to the point of being frightening. Quin, on the other hand, was just rude.

Entering *Fearless*'s wheelhouse, I was taken aback by the extent of damage to every single piece of electronic equipment. Not only were the displays smashed, cords were severed and housings were crushed, exposing innards. "Wow. What a mess," I said as I pulled a pad and pen from my bag.

"Yup. All totaled. Can't even get parts for most of this stuff anymore. Guess I'll need new equipment," Quin said.

As I picked through the rubble, listing manufacturers and models of all the broken machines, what struck me most was Quin's nonchalance about the complete malicious destruction of his property. I had participated in many criminal investigations of property damage in my old line of work. In cases involving this degree of sabotage, recipients of such brutal treatment usually described feelings of nausea, disbelief, and personal violation. Many were moved to tears. Quin was unemotional. In fact, his biggest concern was not who had done this and why but, rather, how soon he would get a check to replace what had been destroyed. The first and only call he had made was to the insurance company.

As I did my work, Quin made the most annoying sounds with his tongue against the roof of his mouth. When he had managed to drive me almost insane, I said,

"The insurance company requires that you report this to the proper authorities."

"Why? I wouldn't press charges. Christ! I should thank whoever did this."

"The insurance company will not consider your claim without an accompanying police report."

"Yeah, yeah, yeah . . . I'll get someone down here pronto. I wonder if Clyde Leeman has any official forms." He snickered at his joke, which I found quite cruel. As I continued writing and snapping pictures, Quin chewed and spat fingernails and played with the zipper of his coveralls and picked a sore on his pockmarked cheek until it bled. By the time I'd finished and climbed back onto the dock, I was certain of two things: Alan Quinby was the most annoying man I had ever met, and he had destroyed his own electronics. But Quin's lack of integrity was not really my problem. My job was to survey and report the damage. I would not be asked to offer any opinions.

I said, "See you," to Eddie, who never looked up. As I walked by the telescope and tripod, I hesitated and backed up to a position from which I could look through it. I stood on my toes to line up my right eye. In the center of the circular view was a ceramic red tugboat dangling from the bottom of a window shade.

TEN

Fairly certain that nobody had seen me look through the telescope, I left it in the hands of the inferior tripod as I walked the pier at a consciously metered pace. If anyone were watching me now, they would see that I was neither nervous nor in a hurry to escape their view. I stopped before entering the shadow cast by the plant, faced the sun and stretched my arms wide, and threw my head back. Embracing the day and enjoying the warmth on my neck, I took a deep breath of the salt air, with all of its aromatics infused by the processing of fish and salting of bait. If the telescope had been employed even part-time to track my comings and goings, I now had the upper hand. Sure, I was creeped out that someone may have been spying on me. But I had nothing to gain by being apprehensive.

I couldn't dillydally long. I had a lot to accomplish today. Under the auspices of my "real" job, I had to survey two fishing vessels. The longtime owner of these sister ships had applied for hull insurance for the first time, a red flag to the insurance company.

Brokers and underwriters were loosening ties and rolling up sleeves in hot-flash-like response to new policies, inflated hull values, and increased claims by boats engaged in the cod fishery. The marine insurance industry had learned from hard-won experience the impact of poorly executed government regulations. Stringent legislation tended to become severe to the point of suffocating the participants whom the regulations were intended to protect. I had long ago observed that desperate people do desperate things. It's a simple matter of survival. Fishermen who had been diligent about paying soaring premiums and had never filed even the smallest claim were cashing out with unexplainable total losses of boats in waters too deep for recovery or investigation. This tendency to collect from the insurance company what had been paid in over decades had become, in some areas, a default retirement plan. The overwhelming sense of entitlement had trickled down to crew members. A back injury was the deck worker's 401(k). In many cases, I was becoming aware, it was not possible to distinguish legitimate claims from bogus ones. As a result, my workload was far heavier than what someone in my position would have experienced a few years ago.

Absolutely any proposed change to a policy or vessel was scrutinized. My task was to see that Green Haven, Maine, did not become what Gloucester, Massachusetts, was in the 1980s. An astonishing number of Gloucester men had decided to not go down with their ships or without a fight. They had tried to take the marine insurance industry with them.

In all honesty, the real job was not a lot of fun. Even after only a few days on the job, I had figured out that marine insurance surveying and investigating was rarely exciting or stimulating, which, I was easily able to convince myself, was all the more reason to dabble in things

I was not paid to do—like solving the murder of Nick Dow. Not that boredom alone was enough to make me do the things I was doing. But I did believe in our system of justice and was willing to work to see that Dow's murderer didn't skate. Handy, I thought, that in this case my extracurricular activity did have strings attached to my real employment. The *Sea Hunter* was a major connection, and I vowed to get aboard the boat to snoop before nightfall.

As mundane as the surveying gig could be, it was my only source of income. So, off I went in search of the sister ships *Desperado* and *Witchy Woman,* while trying to recall what other song titles fleshed out the Eagles' greatest-hits album that I had listened to over and over as a teenager. An image of Manny Gomez (the first of a string of Cuban boyfriends) playing the air guitar and lip-synching "Lyin' Eyes" sprang to mind. I put the past back in the depths of my personal archive when I spotted the two vessels rafted together along the end of a very rickety pier.

Picking my way along the dock, being careful to step over the many broken planks and spaces where planks were missing, I realized that I had found the low-rent district for half a dozen unfortunate fishing boats. The first two had weathered remains of Marshal stickers plastered to their windows. "Stickered" boats were legally tied up for unpaid bills or neglected mortgages, and these particular vessels appeared to have been abandoned some time ago. Sea grasses and kelps stretched in the current from just below waterlines that were no longer visible under scales of rust. Net drums and cable spools had been stripped bare. Even the hydraulic hoses and fittings had been scavenged. Anything of any value to anyone was long gone, similar to what happened to cars that broke down in the neighborhood where I had grown up. I was strangely at home among the derelicts.

The skeleton of a fish that had been on the deck of one of the abandoned boats so long it no longer drew flies was further testimony to the number of moons that had waxed and waned since the host vessel had weighed anchor. Dock lines were mostly odds and ends of different sizes tied together with awkward knots. Chaffed and frayed, spring lines appeared to have outlived their ability to stand up to their names. A rat the size of my toaster lumbered the length of a rusted deck and disappeared into a jagged black hole in a thoroughly disintegrating bulkhead. The only other sign of life on this sad pier stirred aboard my destination—*Desperado*.

Four young men—Webster's definition of a motley crew—stood with their hands in the pockets of jeans, the waistbands of which rested below their pelvic bones. With their boxer shorts exposed and baseball caps askew, they made me think I had happened upon Green Haven's gangsta rappers. Three green contractor bags, fishermen's suitcases, rested on the deck along with a lone canvas duffel that I assumed held the belongings of the boat's captain. "Hello," I called as I reached a stretch of dock that looked as though it might support all 135 pounds of me. The men looked up with what appeared to be disappointment. They were waiting for someone, but not me. Getting no response to my greeting, I thought I would try again. "Who's the Eagles fan?"

The men looked at one another and exchanged shrugs. One man finally emerged as their brave leader when he flicked a cigarette butt into the water over the stern. "We like the Patriots. Are you lost, ma'am?"

Patriots? Ma'am? These men were younger than I had originally perceived. No need explaining the Eagles connection, I realized. That would only result in my feeling quite ancient. "No. I'm not lost. I'm here to survey these two boats for appraisals. I'm looking for the owner, Mr. Marten."

"Hey, join the crowd. He was supposed to be here to settle up with us three hours ago."

I interpreted this opening statement as an invitation to climb aboard, and I did. Noting the fully packed garbage bags, I said, "Looks like someone's jumping ship."

"Yes, ma'am. We're all going home as soon as we get paid. This boat is a death trap." The other three guys nodded in agreement. "I hope we made enough to cover bus tickets. I tried to convince Mr. Marten to invest in a new net for us, but no way. We spent three days trying to repair that rag with nothing to work with." He pointed to the net haphazardly wrapped on the drum and draping over the stern. I found it interesting that he was offering an apology for quitting. "If we had some rockhoppers, we could have fished the hard bottom and caught something more valuable than these damn starfish." The man I now presumed was *Desperado*'s hired captain nudged a dried brittle star with the toe of his sneaker. Brittle stars appeared in some abundance in the nets and corners of decks of boats engaged in the cod fishery. I recalled their presence aboard *Fearless*.

Through continued conversation with the group's spokesman, whom I was told was indeed the captain, I learned that the young men were from a small fishing village down east. They had responded to an ad in last month's *National Fisherman* and had been hired with one short phone call. They had spent the last three weeks working like dogs, with dreams of record catches and promises of paychecks. They had hoped to return home at the season's end with bulging bank accounts and bigger reputations. So far they had struggled not only to get the boat and themselves safely offshore and back in, but also to sell enough fish to cover the running expense—primarily fuel and groceries.

"My father warned me about accepting the boat sight unseen, but I just couldn't bear the thought of working on the deck of his boat the rest of my life," the captain confessed. "Now I've dragged my friends away from paying jobs for this disaster." His sincerity was touching. And the mention of his father's warning confirmed this group's age for me. Late teens and early twenties, I thought.

"Hey, man, we came of our own free will. We're all in this together," said one of the crew members. "Let's just hitchhike home. Marten isn't coming. He knows we'll take the money and run. Where else will he find four fools who'll work for nothing?"

Following some quiet discussion during which all four weighed in, they decided to wait a while longer. After all, they reasoned, Mr. Marten was bound to arrive eventually, since he was expecting the insurance lady. I thought it was hopeless, but I did not want to say anything that might add to their downtrodden spirits. I had witnessed similar scenes on many occasions. In Florida towns where commercial fishing was on the skids—Fort Pierce, St. Augustine, Mayport—boats owned by investors who were not fishermen themselves were the first to circle the drain. Mr. Marten, I had learned from the paperwork, was an attorney who had invested in the fishing industry in the early 1970s, when there appeared to be no end to the resource. He had extracted every possible penny from his investment and had no history or intention of putting anything back in—until now, of course. He claimed to be applying for a loan for "improvements," using the boats as collateral.

The bank required a survey and full insurance. Liquidation? Maybe. Red flag? Certainly.

"What about *Witchy Woman?*" I asked. "Is anyone aboard her?"

"No. They quit last week. The captain's wife came and drove them all back home to Port Clyde. They said we were stupid to stay, and I guess they were right. How can he not pay us *anything?*"

He was not expecting an answer, I knew. So I excused myself to begin my job while they waited for money I knew they would never receive.

"You're going inside?"

"Yes. I'll start in the engine room bilge and work my way up to the top of the rigging. Good luck," I said as I started toward the fo'c'sle door.

"You're the one who needs the luck, from the engine room bilge right up the rigging," the captain said tentatively. "We're not responsible for the mess aboard here. We did our best, but she's a wreck. Maybe you should wait for Mr. Marten." The men shuffled their feet uneasily.

"I'll leave the waiting to you. Don't worry about me. I've seen it all."

As I groped for a light switch on a tacky bulkhead, I wished I had thought to bring a pair of rubber gloves. When I found and flipped the switch, I knew I had not quite seen it all but was about to further my education. Even the lightbulbs were greasy. I made my way down a slippery set of steel stairs to a dimly lit engine compartment. A thick, mealy coat of soot from an old exhaust leak frosted every surface like black powdered sugar. The diamond-plate steel decking was as slick as wet ice from what appeared to be years of grease, oil, and diesel fuel. Apparent total neglect of what I knew to be the heart of the boat said a lot about the vessel's overall health. My first impression was that *Desperado* would be put on the critical list—not yet terminal but in a bad way.

Something stank. Perhaps the holding tank for the head had been leaking, I thought. I wished for boots and coveralls along with the rubber gloves I did not have. I crept slowly to the forwardmost space ahead of the engine, shone my flashlight down, and found a steel plate small enough to remove in order to inspect the bilge. The plate had an oval hole just big enough to use as a handle. Lifting and sliding the plate aside, I discovered the source of the stench. I had smelled some bad bilges in my day, but this one reeked.

Casting the beam from the flashlight down sent the remains of my breakfast in the opposite direction. I swallowed hard against the bile that rose in my throat as I bolted back up the stairs and out onto the deck the men had since vacated. Leaning over the port rail, I hurled long, hard, and loud until dry heaves racked my weakening frame. Wiping tears from my eyes with a sleeve black from soot, I wondered what kind of human beings would defecate in the bilge with the entire North Atlantic Ocean surrounding them. I quickly recalled my intention to attend diesel mechanic school at the age of nineteen, and the advice of my mentor to try something else unless I wanted to spend my life in shitty bilges. Until now I hadn't thought he meant it literally.

No, I thought, I had not seen it all. I had investigated through grime and squalor, but nothing like the filth, human waste, decay, and maggots here. My ribs ached and my throat burned by the time I had checked off the last item on the survey list for the *Witchy Woman*. The day had me questioning my new career. What had I done? Never prone to depression, I had always fought the urge to wallow in self-pity. I reminded myself that I had important work to do. Sadly, I wasn't bothered by the possibility of Mr. Marten scamming the insurance company. Nor was I overly concerned about him ripping off his own employees. Sure, these were social injustices of the kind that would normally make me crazy. But I had more important things on my mind. There was a killer at large in Green Haven, and if I didn't hustle back to Turners' Fish Plant, I might miss an opportunity to gain another lead.

My sweatshirt and sneakers indicated (falsely) that I might be inclined to exercise, and I forced myself to run from Quarry Landing along the length of the waterfront to the gate outside the plant. The plant's parking area would be a natural place to stretch after a jog, and the dock where the *Sea Hunter* was berthed was the perfect spot to cool down. My smooth and athletic gait soon dissolved into what could be best described as a hurried limp. My unconditioned body refused the ruse midway up Main Street. Still, I pushed on, gasping for oxygen, while my messenger bag slapped my hindquarters like a jockey spurring on a crippled horse with every jarring footfall.

Feeling as if I had managed to pound my hips clear up to my shoulder blades, I finally saw the gate. Using it as the finish line, I slowed my pace and checked my wristwatch as I broke the invisible tape. Five minutes before seven o'clock—perfect. I could be stretching in the parking area in time to see Blaine Hamilton's arrival for his meeting with Ginny Turner. Then I might need to prowl around in search of a restroom, perhaps in the neighborhood of Ginny Turner's office, where I might accidentally overhear something of interest.

The only wrench in my plan was around the corner in the parking lot. There in midlot was Lincoln's pickup truck, along with Lincoln's brother, George, who sat on the open tailgate. George was darker-complexioned than his brother, not nearly as attractive, and perhaps a few years older, if the slight pot-belly and depth of crow's feet were true indications. Strange, I thought, that the only other time I had seen George was in this identical spot—hanging around the back of the truck in the plant parking lot. A second vehicle was parked against the building in a spot designated for Ginny Turner. George's presence would hinder my surveillance somewhat, as well as postpone my casing of his brother's boat. The best I could hope for was that George intended to leave in the next five minutes.

Stretching and pacing as if I were a real jogger, I caught my breath enough to consider approaching the truck to speak casually to George. But before I could open my mouth, George sprang from the tailgate to his feet, pumped a fist up and down, and bellowed, "Ortiz!" Startled, I took two steps back and watched this relatively large man complete a very immature victory dance around the tailgate of the truck. He was actually strutting, bobbing, and weaving in sheer delight as he chanted, "You the man. You the man. You the man . . ." Although he was ruining my game plan, his antics were brightening up an otherwise dank day. When he settled back on the tailgate, he acknowledged my presence. He removed the earpiece that was attached to a transistor radio dwarfed by his hand. He smiled warmly. The personal twinkle I found irresistible in his brother must be genetic, I thought, and I returned his smile. "Getting a little exercise, Miss Bunker?"

"Yes," I said. "I didn't realize how out of shape I've become. What are you doing here this time of night?" I hoped I didn't sound accusatory.

"Listening to a Red Sox game."

"Why here in the parking lot?"

"It's the best reception in town."

"Why don't you watch the game on TV?" I hoped he didn't feel like he was being interrogated.

"We don't get TV reception offshore, so I always listen to games on AM radio. I enjoy it more this way. Are you a fan?"

"No."

"We'll have to do something about that!"

"Is Lincoln aboard the *Sea Hunter?*" I couldn't believe I'd asked. I needed to practice some self-restraint.

"No. He's probably at home."

"Oh, well, of course. Well, I was just wondering because of his truck being here. And I was just here stretching and cooling off and happened to see his truck and thought he might be around. I'm not looking for him or anything." Now I was nervous and sounding like a cross between a teenager with a crush and a cop looking for a suspect. I needed to shut up.

"I can see how you might assume he'd be here, even if you didn't really care." George had a nice way of teasing, I thought. "But this isn't actually his truck. Not his alone, anyway. He and Quin bought it together to use for boat business. We call it 'the boat truck,' and it's driven by all of us, even Eddie and Alex."

That was good to know. The object of my lust needn't necessarily head up the suspect list. With multiple drivers, the odds were against Lincoln having been behind the wheel at Dow's.

A black Mercedes I recognized as Blaine Hamilton's pulled into the lot and parked close to the building. Placing the miniature speaker back in his ear, George said, "I'll tell Lincoln you were asking for him."

I wasn't asking for him, was I? Blaine Hamilton was heading up the stairs and through the door. I had to do something. Bouncing slightly on the balls of my feet, I asked, "Is there a ladies' room up there?" I pointed toward the top floor of the plant.

"No, that goes to Mrs. Turner's office." As he twisted the volume knob on the radio, I could tell I was beginning to annoy George; he wanted to follow the ball game. "The only restrooms are down by the processing area, and that's all locked up for the night. I guess you'll have to run home," George said, dismissing me.

"I don't think I can make it home," I said with some urgency. I crossed my feet, pressed my thighs together, and squirmed a bit. Forcing a look of anguish, I said, "It's an emergency! I'll go up and ask for a key."

"If it's that urgent, go aboard the *Sea Hunter*. That would be quicker."

"Great! Thanks, George," I said, and sprinted down the pier toward Lincoln's boat. Too easy, I thought. Like taking candy from a baby. When I turned to back down the ladder onto the deck, I noticed George coming along behind me. Damn. Wouldn't you know George would be a gentleman.

"Through the main door. It's the next door on your left," George called from the dock above.

Standing in the closet-size room into which were squeezed a marine toilet, shower stall, and tiny sink with vanity, I realized I had no time to search, with Mr. Manners waiting outside. Pulling the cell phone from my bag, I placed it in the corner of the floor, where it could not easily be seen by someone sitting on the head. The old "retrieving the forgotten item when nobody's home" trick was so basic, it was ridiculous. But as much as I hated to part with the phone, it was my best ploy to get back aboard and search for evidence like Dow's black book. Besides, this was Green Haven, Maine. It might work.

I remained standing in the *Sea Hunter*'s tiny bathroom

until enough time had elapsed to allow me to have emptied my bladder and washed my hands, had I actually needed to do so. Although the head was far from spotless, in comparison to where I had spent my entire workday, it was immaculate. Catching a glimpse of my reflection in the small round mirror mounted on the inside of the door, I jumped in fright. My face had a number of dark smudges, including what looked like running mascara but was a product of tears through soot. On top of my head, clinging to where my hair parted, was what looked like a wad of chewing gum that I knew to be a blob of hard grease. The closeness of this confined space reminded me of the *Desperado*'s bilge. I smelled like Homeless Joe, the shopping-cart-pushing hobo who wandered all of Dade County. I hoped that George would forgo the description of my present appearance when remembering me to his brother.

I thanked George and left him on the dock holding his transistor up at different angles to the sky and adjusting both earpiece and tuning knob. He was so preoccupied with the Red Sox that he probably would not have noticed if I had scooted up and pressed an ear to Ginny's office door. But rather than push my luck, I hurried home, anxious to get out of the foul-smelling clothes and into a hot shower.

I'd never anticipated that my new life would be glamorous in any way. I'd known that by accepting my present job, I would be starting below the bottom rung of a ladder I had not yet developed a desire to climb. But today's job-related activities had been a catalyst for major disillusionment. I trudged up the hill toward my tiny apartment. The lingering smell of scorched popcorn was actually welcoming after the stink of the bilge. At least that hadn't changed—I still couldn't cook. No sooner had I latched the door behind me than there was a single firm knock. Before I could say "Come in," the door opened, and in came Henry Vickerson, toting a lovely paisley satchel. "Hi, Mr. V.," I said, amazingly cheerfully, given my tolerance level at this point.

"Oh my Gawd! You look like you've been hauled through a knothole! And you stink! Where have you been?" he asked as he opened a window for some air.

"Work. Tough day." I was more discouraged than I let on. I was virtually at the brink of tears.

"Oh, you poor dear. The missus sent me up to invite you for dinner—mussels au gratin—sure looks good. Oh, and to deliver this." He held out the pretty satchel for me to take. "We found it hung outside the door. Thought it was for us. We read the card. Sorry." He pulled an envelope from his breast pocket and handed that over, too.

"That's all right. Thanks." I wondered how they'd thought it might have been for them when my name was clearly written on the envelope.

"Get cleaned up and come on over. We'll have a drinky-poo while we wait." He left without waiting for an answer. I suspected he and Alice had already had a drinky-poo or two.

A fitting end to a totally miserable day, I thought: cheesy mussels and the company of two very kind but toasted old folks who couldn't mind their own business.

Roses? Roses! I reached deep into the satchel and carefully pulled out the flowers. What on earth? God, I prayed they were from Lincoln. Laying the dozen plump red roses on my table, I reached back into the bag and retrieved a bottle of chardonnay. I could barely breathe. Had I ever received roses before? Not that I could recall, and knowing now how it felt, I was certain it had never happened before. And wine, too! This was too much. Please let them be from Lincoln, I thought. I couldn't stand the anticipation any longer. My hands were shaking as I slipped the card from its envelope. The outside of the card was the most gorgeous watercolor of Green Haven's waterfront. The inside was nearly filled with neat printing in black ink. I read and shivered with excitement.

> *"They are not long, the days of wine and roses;*
> *Out of a misty dream*
> *Our path emerges for a while, then closes*
> *Within a dream."*

> *Jane,*
> *I am looking forward to getting to know you. Thanks for accepting my invitation to the star show. Should we meet in the Clearing on top of Spruce Hill? Seven? As promised, I'll bring dinner and hope to hold you responsible for dessert.*
> *Fondly, Lincoln*

Dessert? I read the card over and over and hoped I was not misinterpreting. Oh my God! How long had it been since a man had asked me for "dessert"?

ELEVEN

Hurrying in and out of the steamy shower, being sure not to pass by the partially drawn shade in my various stages of stripping and dressing, I suddenly suffered a minor anxiety attack with the realization that my date was under twenty-four hours away. Before joining the landlords for their latest epicurean experiment, I thought it prudent to write a short to-do list for tomorrow. I had always adhered to a strict policy of not letting my personal life interfere with work. Come to think of it, this had been less than challenging as of late. I vowed that I wouldn't let the anticipation of getting together with Lincoln distract me from my job.

A bit ambitious, I thought as I put down the pen, grabbed the chardonnay, and headed to dinner. The paperwork required before submitting today's surveys would eat up the best part of tomorrow, and I had a lot of other things to accomplish. I hoped to get aboard the *Sea Hunter,* if I could find the boat unoccupied before she headed offshore for another cod trip; I assumed this would occur shortly after my date. The Duster needed gas, and I needed directions to Spruce Hill and a new outfit. Considering the last two items on my list "work-related" was a stretch, but the roses and poetry had soft-ened me from my usual rigidity to something somewhat more malleable.

Alice's timing was perfect. She and I entered her liv-ing area from opposite ends, as if on cue. Now that I was armed with the chardonnay and a mood made absolutely buoyant by fond anticipation for tomorrow's romantic in-terlude, I was sure to find my landlords' quirks, obses-sions, and strange habits far less bothersome this evening. Alice was fresh from the dispensary with her nightly battery of pills and seemed delighted to have my rapt attention as she tucked medications one at a time into the center of her bowled tongue. After washing each pill down with a swig of an iced tawny-colored liquid I suspected was Scotch, she was careful to show me her empty tongue. I resisted the temptation to praise her.

While Alice rattled on in graphic detail about her past twenty-four hours of health issues, Henry rearranged the boats competing in the fireplace mantel's regatta, making room at the rear for a new trinket. Alice paused before taking her last pill to proclaim the genius of her current doctor. The accolades were more than glow-ing, and I wondered, after witnessing the breadth of chemicals he had prescribed, what had become of Hip-pocrates' theory of natural healing. Nice, though, that Alice Vickerson revered doctors so. Such a contrast to my mother, who had a general distrust of the entire medical profession. I had warned her that her rejection of doctors would someday come back to haunt her. In my opinion, I had been correct. Perhaps doctors could not have saved her—then she could have gone to her grave saying, "I told you so." As the Vickersons bickered about something in the margins of my consciousness, I recalled the only time my mother had taken me to a doctor. As she'd stormed out of his office, dragging me along by a wrist, she'd shouted something about a hypocritic oath. Humiliated, I'd vowed at the age of seven to remain healthy. So far I had.

As Henry handed me a glass of wine, I realized that he and Alice were waiting for my reply to something I had tuned out. "I am sorry. I guess I am tired. What were we talking about?" I asked.

"That hideous ball of rust he's placed on my mantel!" Alice snapped down the cover of her pill separator. "I say he should throw it onto the beach where he found it and hope the tide is charitable enough to take it back. What do you think?"

"What is it?" I asked.

"It is a relic," Henry said in a tone that implied I should have known.

"A relic of what?" I asked at the risk of exposing my ignorance.

"See!" Alice shouted.

"It is a relic. That's all that matters," Henry defended the ball of rust. "Possibly Native American."

"But it's rusty! Where was the Indians' foundry?"

"A relic is an object of religious veneration." Henry pushed his glasses up snug against the bridge of his nose. "A trace of an earlier culture—it is a keepsake to be held dear."

"Have you been reading the dictionary again?" Alice asked.

I began to laugh. Alice quickly joined me, and Henry came along reluctantly after summarizing with "Women." A closer inspection of Henry's relic led to more hilarity when I commented on the threaded hole in its center. Although the piece was an interesting item, and somewhat mysterious in that I couldn't decipher from what type of equipment it had fallen, it really wasn't that old; in fact, it was hardly rusty at all.

Before I knew it, we were eating dinner and successfully avoiding the topic of my date, which they should not have known about but did in some detail. I held a mussel the color of a Cheez Doodle on my fork and admired it. Not caring much for the taste, I complimented the eye appeal of the dish. "This is really pretty, Mrs. V. Thanks for feeding me again."

"Yes," agreed Henry. "This certainly is a bright meal, sweetheart. The cheese, carrots, and squash are all the same color. Very nice indeed. And so . . . orange."

I started to laugh once more. This time Henry roared, and Alice clucked a couple of times after pledging to serve the dish again on Halloween. We all struggled to clean our plates. Henry was the first to put down his fork in concession. "Ahhh . . ." He rubbed his belly until he had our attention. "What's for . . . *dessert?*" He winked at his wife, and they both laughed harder than ever as I sat and blushed.

When they pulled themselves together, Alice wiped a tear from her cheek, cocked her head to one side, and shrugged in what I considered a slight apology. "Well, Jane," she said softly, "love makes the world go 'round."

"*Money* makes the world go 'round!" Henry corrected.

"Money isn't everything," Alice quipped.

"Money is the root of all evil," Henry countered.

"Love conquers all."

"'Did you ever hear of Captain Wattle? He was all for love and a little for the bottle,'" Henry sang, and shook the ice cubes in the bottom of his glass, signaling Alice to mix him another drink.

Amazing, I thought. Even their foolish, intoxicated

Ping-Pong proverbs could not irritate me tonight. I had a date to prepare for. I declined another glass of wine, opting instead for a wee dram of single malt alone in my apartment. I thanked them and excused myself.

"Shall we wait up for you tomorrow night, dear?" Alice asked before I closed the door.

"No, thank you, Mrs. V. I'll tell you all about it over coffee the next morning."

"You'd better!" they shouted in unison.

That had been a surprisingly fun evening, I thought as I propped my feet up on a box marked MISCELLANEOUS that I had yet to unpack since my move north. My new arrangement must be sort of like having parents—but better. How many moms and dads would keep their daughter in single malt and tease her about the possibility of "dessert" on a first date? And I wouldn't have the responsibility of caring for them when they grew senile or were no longer ambulatory. I'd be long gone by then, I was sure. In the meantime, I found their weirdness growing on me and hoped I was endearing myself to them. One of my lesser reasons for relocating here from a city had been the stories I'd heard about the generosity and welcoming spirit of the people. The Vickersons were holding up their end by treating me like what I imagined was family.

The last drop of the small glass of single malt I served myself was sweet and slightly nutty. I smelled a hint of toffee. How that conservative pouring had transformed from the brazen, smoky, burning first sip to a shy malt sweetness that clung to the inside of the glass fascinated me. Like people, I thought, all single malts are distinctly different. Like single malts, I thought, people are ultimately a product of their environment. Scotch was the

liquid existence of the only thing I remembered from
high school French class—*gout de terroir*—taste im-
parted by environment. People embody that concept,
too, I thought as I yawned and closed my eyes. Water,
air, soil, shape and age of the still, temperature . . . Maine
must be a great environment. I liked the people a lot. I
wondered if this was as close as I would ever get to Scotland. The home of single malt and golf—paradise.

Catching myself drifting off, I forced my feet to the
floor and my butt out of the chair. I was backlit by the
soft yellow bulb in my bedside reading lamp and figured
whoever was manning the telescope would see I was in
my nightshirt and tucking into bed. The knee-length
oversize cotton gown that I had slipped on behind the
closed door of my bathroom could hardly be considered
part of a burlesque show. But I knew the importance of
maintaining certain habits and routines when surveillance was suspected. I couldn't let on that I knew I was
being watched.

I clicked off the lamp and settled into comfortable
total darkness. Closing my eyes felt good. I took an extra-
deep breath and exhaled slowly into complete relaxation.
Then I counted lethargically down from ten, loitering
between digits lazily. At four, I was nearly unconscious.
Tempted to rush the countdown, I exercised patience and
self-control. "Three, two, one . . ." I flung off the covers
with a backhand, then rolled out of bed and onto the
floor. On my hands and knees, I was in the bathroom in
a flash and feeling around in the dark for my clothes.
Jerking a shirt over my head and plunging into a pair of
slacks, I dropped back to my knees and crept out and
under the partially drawn shade toward the apartment's
exit. I tiptoed downstairs in my socks and gently opened
and closed the door, letting myself out of the Lobster
Trappe. The twin dachshunds in the rear window of the

Vickersons' Caddy watched me put on my shoes, their shiny red eyes reflecting light from a nearby streetlamp.

I saw from their blackened windows that my landlords had passed out. Now that the town had gone nighty-night, I would turn the *Sea Hunter* upside down, I thought excitedly as I moved quickly down the hill. Darting around spots of light from the few streetlamps and dodging beams from a single passing car, I shot through the plant's gate undetected. Scampering around the corner of the building, I was deeply disappointed to find half a dozen or so cars in the parking area, including the boat truck.

I eased toward the truck as stealthily as I could for a better view of the boats at the end of the pier. The *Sea Hunter* and *Fearless* were lit up with deck lights that reminded me of night games at Dolphin Stadium. Keeping the trucks between the boats and me, I watched the activity on the decks. Someone, I assumed Quin, was welding around the base of his net drum while Eddie scrubbed and stacked penboards that were used to section off the fish hold. Aboard the *Sea Hunter,* George pumped grease from a gun into various fittings on each cable spool, while Lincoln mended a hole in the fishing net. Alex sat on the fish-hold hatch and filled a plastic needle with orange twine, loading it for his father to empty into the next hole or tear.

I leaned against the side of the truck, rested my forearms on the top edge of the bed, and admired Lincoln in a way that was possible only when no one knows you are looking. His countenance, even from this distance, spoke the perfect combination of strength and gentleness. He clearly enjoyed this work and appeared to be entertaining his crew with a story. I observed him pause, look up from the repair, and gesture with his arms in an animated fashion. His broad shoulders bumped up and down against the base of his neck as he laughed and returned to mending. The scene took on a dreamlike quality, and I felt quite adolescent, gazing unnoticed from afar.

"Kind of late for you to be out, isn't it, Miss Bunker?"

Although I was startled, I recognized Cal's voice and answered without turning around. "I could ask the same of you, Cal. It's a beautiful night, and I am out for a walk. So what brings you here at this time?"

Cal joined me on the side of the truck and said, "A load of bait from Canada. I came down to open up the plant and supervise a small crew to salt and store it. What's so interesting about the back of this truck?"

Embarrassed that I had been caught ogling Lincoln, I looked into the bed of the truck and remarked on its only contents. "I'm curious about that sprayer. It looks like something used by the Orkin Man to flush out cockroaches. There aren't any cockroaches this far north, are there?" I had always been quick on my feet—unless I was in the presence of a man with whom I was infatuated.

"I've not seen or heard of one in seventy-two years. That spray bottle is used to clean stuff with a bleach solution. They're great for killing and removing growth from the bottom of a skiff. The conscientious guys also use them to disinfect their fish holds."

"So these guys must be conscientious," I said, never shifting my focus from the *Sea Hunter*'s deck.

"Among the best. The Aldridges are good men." The low bass rumble of a diesel engine and the hissing of air brakes turned both of our heads as a tractor trailer pulled through the gate and backed into a loading dock. "I've got to get to work. Good night, Miss Bunker."

"Wait, Cal. Do you know of a place called Spruce Hill?"

"Oh, sure. It's a nice spot—used to be private land but was given to the town for a park. I haven't been there in years. It was the first proposed site for the wind farm."

"I'd like to go. Can you give me directions?"

"Tonight?"

"No, tomorrow."

"Stop by. I'll draw you a map." Cal hobbled off toward the truck.

"I guess I'll head home. Good night, Cal," I called after him. My disappointment in postponing the shakedown was lightened by what I considered Cal's positive endorsement of Lincoln. I had good judgment, and my first impressions were usually spot on. But still, I was happy for a second opinion of someone whom I hoped to grow closer to.

As I sneaked back into my dark apartment, I felt my way to the bathroom, probing with a foot to avoid stubbing a toe or banging a shin. Donning my nightshirt once again, I found my bed with some assistance from the illuminated numbers on my alarm clock. The red lights, which I appropriately kept on my starboard side, also indicated that I had two minutes before my coach turned into a pumpkin.

I woke at six A.M., alert and eager to start the day. Transposing the surveys of *Desperado* and *Witchy Woman* from paper to computer was tedious. The checklists retained a bit of an odor, which turned my stomach and served as a reminder of the boats' condition. Nowhere on the list was there a box to check for raw sewage in the bilge, so I was thorough in my "additional remarks."

I interrupted my work twice to travel down to the dock, hoping for the proper opportunity to get aboard the *Sea Hunter* under the guise of looking for the cell phone that I had "lost." But it was no use. The area was a beehive of activity. I did, on my second trip, run into an extremely tired-looking Cal. It must have been a very late night for him, I realized, and the lack of sleep exaggerated his disfigurement to quite a degree. Still, he was pleasant and uncomplaining and had taken time to draw a map with written directions to Spruce Hill. He didn't mention my get-together with Lincoln. Cal heard everything, so this meant word hadn't gotten out. From this I inferred that Lincoln hadn't confided in anyone, and I further deduced that he would not be one to kiss and tell. That would be my prerogative.

After another hour of paperwork that included paying monthly bills and balancing my checkbook, I gobbled down a peanut butter sandwich and headed back into town, this time driving the Duster. I said a few prayers and, by some miracle, managed to coast to a stop in position to fuel up at the Old Maids'. I hadn't seen the ladies since sitting with them at the coffee shop the morning Dow showed up in the seaweed.

The pump was somewhat antiquated. There was no slot for a credit card, and a sign read PUMP FIRST—PAY INSIDE. There was a piece of duct tape on the glass face that covered the wheels indicating the dollar amount of a purchase, on which was printed TELL CASHIER # OF GALLONS. This was not promising, I thought. The gas pump's mechanical wheels could not keep up with the price per gallon. The two matronly-looking gals watched through the store's plate-glass window as I added two gallons to the Duster's bone-dry tank.

Entering the store under a sign that read ISLAND HARDWARE AND VARIETY, I was greeted first by a friendly and overweight cat. The cat followed me to the cash register, where it rubbed against my lower calf. "Oh, look, she likes you!" exclaimed Marlena, who with Marilyn was squeezed behind the register. The cat's immediate fondness for me seemed to be key with the women. They were quite talkative, and although they invited me to look around their store three times, they were not as pushy as

I had been led to believe. They introduced themselves as Marlena and Marilyn, as if they did not recall our time together at the coffee shop. Oh well, I thought, Audrey had never introduced us, so now the formalities were complete. The cat was introduced as Sir Bunny of Wheat Island—quite a masculine ID for a female cat, I thought. As I waited for change for a ten-dollar bill, I learned more about Sir Bunny than I knew about most of my acquaintances in Green Haven.

Sir Bunny of Wheat Island, they said, was a Scottish Fold cat. Originally from Scotland, these cats were bred, among other places, right offshore of Green Haven on Acadia Island. Since I was a Bunker, they reasoned, my ancestors might have been responsible for the introduction of the breed to Maine. As it turned out, this remote possibility was reason enough for the women to be nice to me. Sir Bunny, I learned, was a type of Scottish Fold with folded ears, but Folds also came with straight ears. The women belonged to the Cat Fanciers' Federation and had won trophies in numerous shows. Folds, they said, made wonderful pets, cried with a silent meow, and stood on their hind feet like otters. Rather than question the silent cry and request an otter demonstration, I simply nodded and smiled, still waiting for my change. The smile came naturally with the thought that my family might have bred cats. My mother had had no use for cats, so I had never tried to adopt a stray.

"Did you know there is a Maine Scottish tartan?" asked Marilyn. "We've ordered some fabric for Sir Bunny. Spoiled rotten, she is!"

"I'll say." I was still smiling and waiting for four dollars and some cents that Marilyn was squeezing in a chubby fist.

"Would you like to donate a couple of bucks to Green

Haven High's basketball team? They're getting new uniforms this year."

"No, thanks," I replied. I needed every penny of my change to meet my very tight budget.

"Not a sports fan? How about the Animal Rescue Squad? They do wonderful work. Just last week they released a seagull that had been sick. They are also the dogcatchers here in town. We call them the Dog Squad."

The Fraud Squad was more like it, I thought. I shook my head and said, "No, thank you," while wondering how much of the money collected on their behalf actually made it to the animals.

"Not an animal lover? How about kids? You do like children, don't you? How about a small donation to benefit little Russell Trundy?" Marlena pointed to the clear plastic container identical to the ones I had seen beside every cash register since entering the state of Maine. On the front of this receptacle, in which anyone could see that the clientele of this establishment had been quite generous, was taped a picture of the cutest toddler. Beneath the photo was the tearjerking text defining Russell's disease and need for expensive treatment.

Unwilling to listen to another plea, I agreed to contribute the change that Marilyn held over what looked like a piano man's tip jar. She quickly released her grip and allowed the money to fall in and join the small fortune the Old Maids had managed to raise for little Russell Trundy. The two women thanked me profusely and wished me a good day as I left the store. Sir Bunny of Wheat Island stood on her hind feet looking otterly, as promised, with her mouth wide open but no sound emitting. I assumed she was meowing in silence—whatever that meant. Interesting ladies. Strange cat. I would be back many times, I thought. But in the future, I would have correct change.

With the Duster's gas gauge registering nearly an eighth of a tank, I moved across the street and up two blocks. I parked in front of Lucy Hamilton's boutique and then checked my face and hair in the rearview mirror. Sighing audibly, I braced myself for what would probably be an unpleasant experience. If I had more time, I would drive to Ellsworth for an outfit. But I did not have time, and Le Follie was the only game in town. So up the steps and through the front door I marched, ready for battle, if that was what would be required to emerge with a sexy little number fit for tonight's stargazing picnic dinner.

The boutique was overflowing with imported apparel and exquisite accessories. I doubted that I could afford even a simple belt. Still, it wouldn't cost me anything to look around. At the very least, I would leave with a sense of the latest fashion trends. I closed the door behind me, setting off an automated electronic tone that alerted whoever was in the back room—I assumed Lucy Hamilton—that a customer had entered. Muffled voices from the other room suddenly quieted; then I heard the opening and closing of a back door and the subsequent slamming of a car door in the distance. As I admired a display of handbags and satchels by the same designer as the one Lincoln had sent my roses and wine in, I nearly choked on the price: $115! No wonder he dared suggest dessert.

My contemplation of Lincoln's generosity was interrupted by the sound of a vehicle behind the building. The signature squealing of the boat truck faded as I gaped at rack after rack and shelf upon shelf of ladies' finery. Surrounded by fields of neutral-toned lush fabrics complemented tastefully by occasional splashes of color, I wondered if Lincoln might have driven the truck. I fantasized that he had come to purchase another gift, such as one of these gorgeous scarves. No, probably not, I rationalized. More than likely, Alex had simply come to visit his mother.

Running my fingertips over a teal-blue cashmere sweater, I saw Lucy in the blurry corner of my vision and wondered who would fire the first shot. As soon as she saw me, she plunked her hands onto her hips and began muttering unintelligibly. Picking up the cashmere sweater by its shoulders, I hugged it against my coffee-stained T-shirt and turned to admire it in a full-length mirror. She shuddered visibly as I attempted to refold the short-sleeved top. Rushing to my aid, she whisked her merchandise from my fumbling hands, the fingernails of which retained grease from yesterday's dirty work. "We don't carry Wrangler here," Lucy snarled. "Why don't you try Wal-Mart in Ellsworth?"

Before I could return her fire, the electronic tone ding-donged, forecasting the entrance of a legitimate customer and sending Lucy to her post as greeter. "Ariel Cogan! Do come in! I haven't seen you in weeks. You look marvelous. How has your summer been?" Lucy was more than cordial. The women exchanged small talk while I moved to a circular rack of sale items over which I could watch both Lucy and Ariel, whose back was to me, as choreographed by the proprietress. I had not met Ariel Cogan but was aware that she was Green Haven's most loved summer resident. From what I now saw and heard, I understood how she had gained her reputation as the consummate lady. Though her talk was pure polish and refinement, her messages were plain and direct. She was tall, with perfect posture, and her look was one of classic elegance. There was an aura about her. The human embodiment of pictorial harmony and enchantment, Ariel Cogan was indeed a person of distinction. The absolute antithesis of Lucy Hamilton in all of her flashy, flamboyant, dazzling gloss over white trash, Ariel Cogan was the genuine article.

Feigning interest in a black skirt, I listened intently to the conversation as it shifted to local politics. Ariel, it became clear, was on a fact-finding mission to help her make an educated decision about the proposed offshore site for the wind farm for which Lucy's husband was pushing. "I'm all for wind-generated power. But the fishermen are concerned about the loss of Penobscot Ridges. That area has been closed to them for so long! Shouldn't Green Haven's fishermen enjoy the bounty they have sacrificed to create?" Ariel argued passionately for the survival of the town's traditional lifestyle. She was saddened by the possibility that the approval of the offshore site would snuff out what remained of Green Haven's fishing heritage. It seemed to me that she wanted an advocate to convince her the fishing fleet could survive along with the wind farm.

But Lucy accomplished little with her insensitive, matter-of-fact statement: "Soon there won't be a single codfish left in the ocean—not even on Penobscot Ridges." That was harsh, I thought, and wondered how Lucy had come to that conclusion. It seemed painful news to Ariel, and I resisted butting in with some statistics to the contrary. I knew I would learn more from listening. Lucy skillfully changed the subject, probably sensing my urge to blurt out "Bullshit!" from behind the sale rack. "That suit is great on you, Ariel. I had you in mind when I ordered it. No one's styles are as clean as the Italians', are they? I'm expecting another small shipment by the end of the week."

"Oh, marvelous! Perhaps I'll find something to wear to your little fete. I haven't RSVP'd yet, but you know I adore your husband," Ariel said, ignoring Lucy's attempts to cut her off. "Saturday the twelfth, right?"

Now Lucy launched into a coughing fit. Ariel banged her on the back and kept talking. "Do you really think Blaine will be surprised, after thirty-seven years of birthdays, to be having a thirty-eighth?"

The twelfth? My heart and mood sank like a failed soufflé. I didn't hear another word of their conversation. The twelfth was my brother's birthday, too. How could I have forgotten my precious baby brother, Wally? Here I was, shopping extravagantly for myself, while I hadn't even purchased a card for Wally. I needed to exit the boutique before Lucy called my bluff and humiliated me into buying what I could not afford. As I left Le Follie without so much as an acknowledgment from Lucy, I received a warm smile and nod from Ariel Cogan.

On the drive home, I consoled my selfish, egotistical being by reminding myself that Wally wouldn't really care if his thirty-eighth birthday had temporarily slipped my mind. Of course, he would rather I was there with him, and I missed him fiercely. But he'd always hated phone calls and never much cared about his birthday. As long as I continued to send him goofy cards every week, he'd be pleased.

Self-centered me was back at the top of my game when I cheered out loud at the sight of the empty parking area at the Lobster Trappe. The Vickersons had actually taken the bobbing-headed plastic dachshunds for a ride in the Caddy. With any luck, they would remain away until after I left for my date. I had just enough time to complete today's tasks on the laptop, and send the surveys into cyberspace for someone else to deal with, before showering and finding something decent to wear.

Letting myself into the apartment, I was not surprised to find a note on the table from Alice. They had gone to a flea market in Belfast, hoping to find "a few goodies" to resell here at the Trappe, and would not be home until after dinner. They wished me a fun time tonight and left a red-and-white-checkered tablecloth to spread and enjoy the picnic upon, as "men never think of these things." They also mentioned something in the refrigerator for "dessert emergencies." I couldn't imagine what might constitute an emergency in this case or what would need refrigeration that could possibly help. I flung open the door to find a large basket filled to the top with strawberries.

The berries were ripened to perfection and were as heavy as a basket of berries could be. My mouth watered with one whiff of their sweetness. I sighed and realized the berries were actually a necessary addition to the evening. After all, what if I *had* misinterpreted his note and all Lincoln had in mind was a piece of pie? "Good thinking, Mrs. V.," I said aloud, placing the basket on the counter. Perhaps the best strategy would be to take just a few strawberries, leaving room for something more if anyone was interested. Hadn't I read somewhere that strawberries were an aphrodisiac, like oysters? Was I being too forward? Maybe I'd forget about the berries and pick up some cookies at the coffee shop, I thought. "Oh, for God's sake!" I berated myself. "Put a few berries in a bowl and be done with it!"

After plunking several of the biggest berries into a small glass bowl, I spent the next five minutes struggling with the Saran Wrap. First the end of the wrap was hiding on the roll. Then I couldn't get it to tear against the serrated metal teeth. Next the sheet I did manage to tear off wanted to cling to everything but the bowl. With wadded-up balls of plastic all over the kitchenette, I abandoned the wrap in favor of a plastic bowl with its own snap-on lid. Tucking the berries into the paisley satchel along with the tablecloth, I realized I had no time to waste. I booted up the laptop, proofread survey reports for *Desperado* and *Witchy Woman,* and sent them along through the painfully slow dial-up connection.

After jumping in and out of the shower, I upended my bureau drawers and tore through a few things hanging in the apartment's lone closet for something appropriate to wear. Too revealing, too frumpy, too stained, too tight, bad color . . . I settled on a crisp white pair of knee-length shorts and a canary-yellow cotton sweater. I threaded a multicolored necktie through my belt loops and tied a neat square knot at my left hip. Then I slipped into my strappy white sandals, grabbed the satchel and map that Cal had drawn for me, and headed out, feeling vibrant and put together.

Leaving Green Haven proper by the western route took me the length of Main Street, where the shops were already deserted. This town really closed up at five P.M., I thought. Even the Old Maids had left their plate-glass window. The only activity I saw was through the well-lit storefront of the coffee shop. It was Friday night, and an all-you-can-eat fish fry would keep the coffee shop hopping until the *ungodly* hour of nine. Soon I passed the turnoff to Granite Bluff and couldn't help recalling my most recent encounter with Lucy Hamilton. She remained with me, surrounded in hazy suspicion, until I passed the end of Nick Dow's driveway. What was their connection? I would, in time, get to the bottom of it. I knew I would. Perhaps Lincoln could shed some light.

Just as Cal had described in his written directions, I found the well-marked entrance to Spruce Hill exactly seven miles out of town. The road sign indicated this area was a public park open year-round. Smaller signs in the picnic area asked visitors to carry out all their trash and not to light fires. At six-forty-five P.M. I left the Duster under the only light pole in the parking lot and went on foot up a path marked THE CLEARING.

The sun was still well above the horizon. I resisted the thought to go back to the Duster for the flashlight I kept in my messenger bag, knowing that its batteries hadn't much life and certain that Lincoln would bring a light, because men always thought of these things. The grassy path led to a forest thick with tall spruce trees. The path was more like a trail here, winding up and around the hill at a lazy incline. A red squirrel chattered a welcome. Exposed roots crossed the trail, dissecting the well-traveled ground into many possible landings for feet. The woods gave way to a hillside dense with a tangle of wild raspberry bushes. A swath cut in the bushes for a walkway was wide enough for two people to travel abreast through plants so thick that I imagined only the berries along the edges were harvested by human pickers. It was beautiful. I was lucky to have been invited to share this special place.

I kept moving uphill and through what seemed like acres of raspberries not ripe enough to sample. The path flattened out into a plateau where the end of the thorny stalks of raspberry plants nestled against a low, lush mossy carpet. A wet field in front of another patch of spruce forest was bridged with slabs of trees cut lengthwise and laid hewn side up for sure footing. Breaking out of the woods into what had to be the Clearing, I was exhilarated by the sounds, smells, and sights of what some might experience as the absolute nothingness of nature. This simple area in the spruce held so much life that I was inspired, and wondered how I had endured city life so long. I reached the center of the Clearing and laid the tablecloth on a soft bed of ferns that appeared to have been matted down by deer. I thought of Thoreau and vowed to start reading more.

I paced around the square cloth until seven o'clock. Lincoln would be here any second, I thought. Not wanting to appear as nervous as I was, I decided to sit down and wait. Should I face the path? No, that would only make me look anxious. I spun around, putting my back to where Lincoln would soon appear. No, maybe side to was best. After all, I was expecting him, so shouldn't it look like I was eager for him to arrive? Cross-legged Indian-style wasn't much of a suggestive pose. Perhaps crossed at the ankles, legs stretched straight. No, too stiff. Not comfortable. Not relaxed. How about lying partway down, propping my top half up on an elbow behind me? That was comfortable. My tummy appeared nice and flat this way, too. What a perfect spot to see the stars, I thought as I looked straight up at the sky. The tops of the circle of giant spruce trees formed a crown through which I watched a blue sky dim in the fading light.

At seven-fifteen I reassured myself that all was well and that my watch was actually a few minutes fast. The sun was well below the tree line, and the air was cooling quickly. Seven-thirty had me wondering if I'd read Lincoln's card correctly. But this had to be the only clearing, and I was certain the invitation had read seven. Maybe I had the wrong night. No, he was probably running a little late and would burst through the opening in the spruce any minute now, full of apologies and armed with a picnic he'd put together himself. My anticipation had surged from a pleasant tingle to a nauseating burn. At eight, I faced the sad reality that I had been stood up. I hadn't thought it would matter this much. Feeling thoroughly defeated, I was angry not with Lincoln but with myself.

Well, no sense hanging around any longer. The mosquitoes had found me. I was cold and hungry. Standing up, I grabbed an edge of the tablecloth and gave it a good shake to rid it of any spruce needles or bugs. Just as the far end of the cloth fluttered to the ground, something tugged it, and a loud blast pierced the otherwise silent dusk. After two decades in law enforcement, I knew a gunshot when I heard one. Dropping to my belly and covering my head with both arms, I felt and heard another near-miss. This time I gasped. I had been set up to be killed—led like a lamb to the perfect spot. My life would end wrapped in a plastic checkered tablecloth.

Remaining motionless for what seemed an eternity, I waited for another gunshot while the mosquitoes did a number on my legs and neck. Waiting a while longer, I reasoned that whoever held the gun had assumed himself a better shot than he was, and had left me for dead. Then again, maybe the marksman hadn't left. When I decided it was dark enough to make a move, I crawled commando-style through the ferns to the edge of the woods, where I unfortunately missed the trailhead. Daring to stand only after I had slithered into the thicket, I felt my way in the general direction of the path, bumping into and being poked by prickly branches.

Out of the woods I emerged in a boggy area I hadn't seen earlier, and trudged through ankle-deep muck toward the raspberries. Once I found the berry patch, all I had to do was travel downhill. I would eventually come out to the main road, hopefully not too far from my car. Though I had the eerie sense that I was being followed, I knew it might just be my paranoid imagination running wild. Still, I had to move faster. As I thrashed my way through the raspberries, thorns scratched my bare calves until they felt red-hot. I ran, nearly tumbling, through the last of the spruce forest, red squirrels screeching all around me. Tripping over root after gnarled root, I stumbled miraculously close to the Duster, which sat alone in the yellowish spotlight.

Standing in the shadows, I fished the key out of my shorts pocket and made a mad scramble for the driver's-side door. The window had been smashed out, and the door had been unlocked. Checking the backseat for unwanted company, I hopped in, cranked the engine, and sped off. I didn't use the headlights until I turned left onto the main road leading back to town. I drove as fast as I dared. Among the pieces of broken safety glass on the seat beside me were strewn the contents of my messenger bag, including the crab I had collected at Dow's. The only thing I could determine missing was my camera. Even my wallet had been left behind, not that there was much money in it: eleven dollars, to be exact.

On the outskirts of town, I slowed to the speed limit to give myself time to think. I realized I had gotten too close to something. It had to be Dow's murderer. I had believed that poking around to solve the mystery of Dow's death had been my duty as a curious and bored bystander. Now it was personal. I would never be safe in Green Haven until the murderer was exposed. All I knew was that Lincoln had either forgotten about me or had set me up to be killed. Either option was bad. To be forgotten was sad. To be set up was terrifying. Or what if Lincoln was in danger? Maybe someone had interfered in some way, keeping him from our rendezvous. What if my poking around in Dow's death had injured Lincoln? What if he were in peril? Fear for my own life melted with growing concern for Lincoln's.

Although I had no appetite, the last place I wanted to be was alone in my apartment. So I stopped at the coffee shop. It was nine o'clock, but a few customers remained at tables, finishing meals. Clyde Leeman held down his usual spot at the counter, where he was reading the sports page. As I approached, he looked up from the paper and exclaimed, "Oh, geez! Miss Bunker! What's happened to you? You're a wreck!"

Examining what I could see of myself, I agreed. Partially dried mud was clotted between my toes, exposed in my filthy sandals. My legs appeared to have been clawed by wildcats—mostly superficial but deep enough to draw blood in a few of the gouges. The white shorts were stained with green streaks, and ferns stuck out from the top of my waistband. "I joined the women's rugby league up in Bangor," I lied.

"Geez. Rough bunch." Clyde made room for me at the counter beside him.

Before he could ask any questions that would force me to elaborate, I was saved by Audrey, who came crashing through the swinging doors laden with plates mounded with crispy battered fish and french fries. She stopped in mid–food delivery and mouthed something I read as "What? You have to be kidding me." Her eyes were as big as saucers as she shook her head in disgust. She moved on to a table of four and set plates down hard enough to make the customers jump. She said, "'All you can eat' is not supposed to be a challenge." Turning on a heel, she stomped back around the end of the counter, stopping in front of me. "Janie, Janie, Janie . . . What is wrong with your head, girlfriend? You stood up the most eligible bachelor in Hancock County! He waited in the plant's lot half the night for you. He just left here with a broken heart and a basket of fried chicken. Where have you been?"

Before I could answer in my own defense, Clydie jumped in with "She's been playing rugby."

"Yeah, right. And I've been singing with the Andrews Sisters." *Ding! Ding! Ding!* An impatient customer wanting to pay his bill slammed the bell at the register.

"I didn't know you singed," Clydie said, impressed. As Audrey moved to the register, she promised over her tattooed shoulder to return and continue our discussion.

Knowing that meaningful conversation with Clyde was not possible, I went for the safest topic. "So, Clyde, how did the Red Sox make out last night?"

"Oh, the Red Sox didn't play last night, Miss Bunker."

TWELVE

As promised, Audrey returned with a vengeance. Her eyes flashed with impatience as she ran a wet sponge the length of the counter. What little I knew of Clyde Leeman told me that I couldn't put much stock in his word that the Red Sox had not played last night, when I had seen George Aldridge—Boston's self-proclaimed biggest fan—vigorously enjoying the game. For all I knew, Clyde used the sports page only as an accessory to his lingering at the counter while nursing a malted milk. Frankly, I would have been surprised if Clydie could read at all. Before I could confirm or confute his statement by requesting that he share the newspaper, Audrey was scrubbing the finish off the Formica adjacent to where my forearms rested. She looked at me with what I assumed was a fiery need for an explanation. I tilted my head toward Clyde and raised my eyebrows in a not-so-subtle silent reply.

"Okay, cowboy." Audrey was firm yet cheerful, considering this late stage of what must have been a double or even triple shift. "It's time for you to saddle up and head for the barn."

"You fixin' to close the saloon, Miss Audrey?" Clyde played along in character. He ceremoniously donned his Stetson, stood sort of bowlegged, and hitched his pants up a notch with his wrists, his hands extended as if ready to draw six-shooters.

"This ol' gal has done rustled up enough grub for one night. I need some shut-eye. Now, get along, little doggie!"

Slapping a hand on the counter and removing it slowly, Clyde revealed a fifty-cent tip. "That's for your trouble, little lady," he said, and backed the entire width of the dining area toward the door.

As the cowbells clanged, Audrey called, "Watch your top-knot, partner." Then, under her breath, "Which, in your case, is a slipknot." A table of four exited with Clyde, leaving Audrey's parting shot on the safe side of the door. "Your ten-gallon hat's running on empty." The sponge of perpetual motion came to an abrupt halt. Rocking her head from side to side, then around in circles orbiting her shoulders, Audrey danced slowly to some inner music. "'I think we're alone now,'" she sang. I would have thought she was too young to know it.

"What is: Tommy James and the Shondells?" I asked in true Alex Trebek fashion.

"I'm not sure who performed it originally. But Uncle William, who has since become my stepfather, did a great rendition back in 1991. It was his stage entrance number every time he came to visit. He'd always bring me a bag of Oreo cookies, and I'd be allowed to watch cartoons in the living room while Mommy and Uncle Willy watched grown-up television in the bedroom."

"Ninety-one? You must have been all of five. And yet you were aware of what was going on in the bedroom?"

"I was quite precocious. Even cleaned up my own Oreo puke." I didn't know how to respond to that, so I didn't. After a short pause and a clatter of dishes behind the swinging doors, Audrey was back on topic—me. "So what gives, girlfriend? Why were you a no-show tonight?"

Although I liked Audrey a great deal and had the desire to confide, I couldn't burden this young girl, even if she was as precocious as she claimed, with the fact that someone had just tried to kill me. And I realized that, given her addiction to gossip, it would be unfair to expect her to keep a secret. "Well, it was a simple misunderstanding," I said. "I waited for him at Spruce Hill Clearing until after dark. *I* thought he stood *me* up. I guess we got our wires crossed, and now I'll never be asked out again." I looked sadly upon my hands as I picked at a cracked cuticle.

"Oh, Jane! You poor thing." My explanation had elicited some much needed sympathy. "This is like Romeo and Juliet! You have to go find Lincoln and explain!"

"There's no sense. His fragile male ego has been destroyed." Audrey, who loved the drama and romance of it all, was riveted as I told her of the mysterious delivery of roses and wine and quoted the poetry from the card. Against my better judgment, I even told her about dessert. Lincoln had gone so far out on his sentimental limb; I explained to the less experienced Audrey that this meant he would almost certainly avoid me to save face. "And," I continued, "it might be some time before he finds the courage to pursue another woman." I knew this last was too hopeful and for my own benefit.

I continued to pick my cuticle in a most forlorn state of mind. How pathetic, I thought, to be lamenting outwardly and so confused inwardly about what had actually transpired tonight. Was Lincoln a villain? Had he set me up? Was he the victim of an honest misunderstanding or a bad memory? None of that would explain the gunshots. Or perhaps the gifts had been sent by an imposter in attempt to frame Lincoln for my murder. The thought raised my spirits considerably, because I felt in the core of my soul that Lincoln must be innocent.

"Some people recover from total devastation more quickly than others," Audrey said as she stared absently out the windows behind me. Or maybe not so absently, I realized as her eyes followed some motion outside. Spinning the stool 180 degrees, I looked out in time to see Lincoln and Ariel Cogan passing arm in arm on the opposite sidewalk. "There goes your chicken dinner, girlfriend." Lincoln didn't appear to be as broken up as Audrey had described. In fact, he looked quite content.

I thought briefly about running onto the street and screaming, "Bastard!" Instead, I laughed and said, "I'll be damned. Poor crushed Lincoln couldn't bear to be alone. He's getting some much needed consoling from that older woman. Men's psyches are so fragile! There's a sort of mothering thing going on there, don't you agree?"

"Yes. Absolutely. Right on. Look at his fake smile. He's hiding his pain *really* well. If I didn't know that his heart had been ripped out, I'd swear he was rather happy. He's very convincing. Look! They're almost skipping!"

Pivoting my stool back around to face the counter, I said, "I've seen enough. I feel bad enough about ruining his evening without watching him suffer so."

"So much for dessert," Audrey said with an expression I interpreted as genuine concern for me.

I nodded and said, "Don't waste any time worrying about me. I'm a tough lady. And I have a bag of Oreos at home." I left my young friend stacking chairs onto tables in preparation for sweeping.

The short walk to the Duster was dark and cool. I caught myself looking nervously over my shoulder and preparing to dart behind or dive under a parked car at any unexpected sound. My heart was racing when I reached the car door with the missing window. I took a deep breath and looked up and down Main Street. All was quiet. When my pulse had resumed a normal rate, I opened the car door and moved quickly behind the wheel. The dome light flickered on and off in its usual half-functioning way. Before I pulled the door closed, I sensed something moving in the passenger seat. I gasped in fear and sprang from the car. Crouching behind the open door, I prepared to sprint back to the coffee shop. But then the dome light came wholeheartedly to life, illuminating big, fat Sir Bunny of Wheat Island up on her hind legs and enjoying the crab she had managed to fish from the plastic bag. I wiped cold sweat from my forehead and again consciously managed my heart rate down from a near-boil. I'm a nervous wreck, I thought as I shooed the evidence-eating Sir Bunny from the Duster and vowed to put Mr. Vickerson on window repair first thing tomorrow. Henry would surely have a sheet of plastic and some duct tape that would suffice until I could get to Ellsworth for a permanent replacement.

Green Haveners certainly go to bed early, I thought as I drove the narrow stretch of Main Street that separated private properties into waterfront and not. I noted that an amazingly large percentage of residents fully utilized their right to bear arms as I counted trucks with gun racks and NRA stickers. A far cry from Miami, where firearms were primarily concealed handguns; the only body without a hunting rifle in this town was me. Stopping at the intersection where I would normally turn left up the hill toward home, I turned right instead, into Turners' Fish Plant.

No cars, no boat truck, no lights: Here, finally, I thought, was my opportunity to sneak aboard the *Sea Hunter* and conduct a thorough search. As I completed the turn through the gate, the Duster's engine began surging. Great, I'm out of gas, I thought as I coasted to a stop between two loading ramps. I could deal with the gas problem later. I grabbed my messenger bag and hustled down the pier. The moon, partially obscured by cumulus clouds, cast just enough light to allow visual perception of shapes at a distance. When I was abreast of the *Sea Hunter,* the moon moved out from under the clouds enough for me to see that the pier was not totally vacant. Four young children slept wrapped in blankets lined side by side like sacks of potatoes. Eddie Quinby was perched behind his telescope at the far end of the dock. The distinct smell of pot smoke lingered. He had his back to me and seemed engrossed in some astrological event. I knew he wouldn't see me climb aboard the *Sea Hunter.* I assumed the babysitting charges were his much younger siblings; they had apparently fallen asleep during the meteor show. No witnesses.

Aboard the boat, the first order of business was to retrieve my cell phone. I opened the door to the head and was surprised not to find the phone. I knew I had hidden it from view of the casual glance, but perhaps Alex or George had swept it out of hiding in a cleaning spree. Down a phone and a camera. This hobby was getting a bit expensive. I should give up the gumshoe for ceramics or knitting, I thought. Well, I could report the phone lost and cancel the service. Fortunately, I had downloaded the photos into my laptop for the real job. So all was not lost.

I moved quickly through a short gangway and entered the galley. Dow had been the *Sea Hunter*'s cook, so this seemed the logical place to begin my search. Not quite daring to turn on the overhead lights, I used my penlight. Climbing onto the galley table and across a counter, I pushed ceiling tiles up and aside and back into place one at a time until I had disturbed years of accumulated dust and spiderwebs over the galley area. Next I opened, emptied, and refilled every cupboard. I disassembled and reassembled the stovetop and thoroughly scoured the oven, freezer, and refrigerator. The bench seats fore and aft of the galley table functioned as storage lockers where canned goods were stowed. Just as I removed the cushioned cover from the aft bench, I heard voices. Listening closely, I determined that they were adult and getting closer. In any other compartment of a boat, there would have been a number of places to hide. But in the galley, my choices were few.

Suddenly, the deck lights came on, sending a beam through the fo'c'sle doorway and directly at me. Someone was aboard! Diving in with Dinty Moore and Campbell's, I pulled the seat cushion over the top, leaving a small crack to peek through. Two sets of legs entered the galley, walking along the ribbon of light streaming from outside. The overhead lights came on, fully illuminating George and Alex. George tossed a duffel bag into the bottom bunk. "Besides," George said, "it'll only be two or three days. Stay home. I can handle the deck alone." He sat on the bench opposite my cramped quarters.

"I need the cash for basketball camp next week," Alex replied as he stuffed a canvas bag into a forepeak locker and kicked the door closed with what looked like a size-twelve Nike Air. George brushed some crumbs off the galley table and watched his disgruntled nephew stomp and slam in disgust from under his faded Red Sox cap. "Two or three days of gutting fish, eating out of a can, and sleeping in a dead man's bunk." With an attitude as black as his pin-straight hair, Alex unzipped a duffel bag with strength enough to have torn it open. He yanked a handle on a drawer beneath a bunk; it opened partway and caught. The drawer resisted a healthy shove and a sharp nudge with Alex's knee. It refused to budge either in or out—it appeared the drawer was off its track. After struggling unsuccessfully, Alex finally gave up with a heartfelt "Fuck" and began stowing socks and underwear in another drawer.

George inhaled deeply and audibly. His bushy reddish eyebrows peaked into arches above large blue eyes. "Well, la-tee-da! Is that spring-fresh Tide with bleach alternative I smell?" he asked, playfully teasing Alex.

His nephew shot George a look of impatience and quickly covered a filthy mattress with a crisp white sheet. "Fuck you."

"Hey! Watch your language. We don't talk like that aboard the *Sea Hunter*." George scowled. I was barely breathing with anticipation of a chance to be alone with the jammed drawer.

"Oh, yeah. I can see that. Only gentlemen aboard this fine craft," Alex remarked snidely as he drew a bony index finger across a cupboard door over the stove, leaving a furrow in the grease. "This piece of shit ought to be burned."

"Hey! Come on. Lighten up." George removed his cap, exposing a totally bald head above his thick fringe of hair, which now looked like a blond wreath. "Where's the happy-go-lucky kid I used to know?"

Alex smirked. "I'm seventeen. I'm *supposed* to be miserable." Brushing by his uncle toward the fo'c'sle door, he stopped to slap the top of George's head with two sharp smacks. "No wonder I'm depressed! I hope this isn't what's meant by a bright future." Alex gave the shiny skull another tap. "Put your fuckin' hat on. The glare is killing me!" He disappeared with another warning from George about his language.

The canned beef stew began to feel quite uncomfortable under the weight of my upper body. If I shifted at all, I stood the risk of being detected. So I waited patiently, curled on my right side and looking directly at George through the slit of light between the bench and the seat top. When he finally stood and put on his hat, I held my breath. He opened the top of the bench where he had been sitting and shuffled through the contents, which sounded to me like more cans. As he replaced the cushion and turned toward my hiding spot, I imagined my predicament couldn't get any worse. My stomach turned, and I broke into a sweat as he reached for the seat cushion above me. "Hey, George," Alex called from the deck. "Dad wants you to start the generator."

"Coming right up!" George replied and pulled his hand from the edge of the cushion. As soon as he was gone, I pushed the cover off the bench and climbed out. Ignoring the cramp in my calf, I hustled to work on the stubborn drawer. This had to be it, I thought as I wiggled and jiggled the drawer back and forth, up and down, a fraction of an inch. This was the logical place for Dow's stash. Men, as a rule, don't touch other men's underwear.

The generator engine started, and the lights went out and then back on. I knew I was running out of time, but I couldn't leave the boat without whatever was keeping this drawer from cooperating. Kneeling down, I forced my right hand into the narrow opening beneath the drawer. Yes! There was a bulge secured to the underside of the wooden panel. I picked at the edge of what felt like duct tape until I pulled a ten-inch strip from the opening. Reaching in again and feeling my way to another edge, I pulled and released a second strip. The bulge dropped, allowing me to remove the drawer completely. There on the deck, within the cavity, was a package wrapped in plastic and sealed with clear tape. I thrust the package into my messenger bag and quickly replaced the drawer, making sure to jam it off its metal track. Now all I needed to do was escape before the lines were cast off the dock.

Poking my head around the corner, I saw Alex and George on deck. With all the engine noise, I couldn't hear what they were talking about. As I contemplated my options, black boots appeared at the top of the wheelhouse ladder. Lincoln! Without a second's deliberation, I slid down the ladder to the engine room fireman-style. I needed time to think. As I ducked out of sight behind the massive diesel engine, a black boot stepped down onto the top rung of the ladder and was followed by another on the rung below it. Shit! I flipped an extremely heavy deck plate on edge, which gave me access to a bilge compartment. I stepped down into it, trying to disappear. I slipped on the greasy steel hull and fell into the hole, and the deck plate came crashing down onto my head. Out cold.

When I came to, it didn't take me long to collect myself. I knew exactly where I was and how I had gotten there. The only thing I didn't know was how long I had been unconscious. There was not a single ray of light to be seen through the gaps in the deck plates above me, so I assumed Lincoln had turned off the lights and returned to the wheelhouse. A slow, rolling motion confirmed that my situation had indeed gotten worse. I was now an unintentional stowaway aboard a vessel heading offshore that was captained by a man who might well be a murderer.

I fumbled through my bag for a light and realized that I must have left it in the galley. Of course, I owned the cheapest possible wristwatch on the market, so it did not have an illumination feature. I did recall from the galley conversation that the voyage would last only two or three days. Hell, that was nothing, I thought. I'd spent longer durations in worse places. I had completed a two-month tour of duty in the Everglades, sleeping in a tent. Bugs, alligators . . . now, that was torture. Then there was the failed drug bust when I barricaded myself inside a dog kennel to keep from being eaten by angry pit bulls. I was so hungry by the time my partner showed up, I was ready to eat the Purina.

But this wasn't exactly what I'd had in mind for my first all-nighter with Lincoln. I would have to be more careful about what I wished for. I had what I came for, so I could afford to be patient. The pounding in my head indicated a sure concussion. Stretching out along the turn of the bilge above the keel, I lay uncomfortably against the cold, damp steel hull and didn't have to worry about falling asleep.

My resolve to remain entombed in this greasy steel box for what could be forty-eight hours was being steadily sapped by hunger, headache, and shivering muscle spasms. I measured the first six hours in two-hour intervals between routine checks by captain and crew. Like clockwork, the lights came on every two hours for approximately one minute, just time enough for me to stare at my wrist and for whoever was on watch to ensure that all was well in the engine compartment. The next twelve hours crept along in three-hour epochs marked by a slowing of the main engine and growling of hydraulic power. I must have dozed a bit between tows.

I knew the drill. Although we'd never come far enough north to fish for cod, my mentor, father figure, and fishing captain had dragged me along on every boat he'd

captained during my summer vacations for eight years.
I had worked aboard a number of stern trawlers similar
to the *Sea Hunter*. So although I was in the bilge, I was
acutely aware of all activity above. I imagined the routine, timed the engine room checks, and knew within
minutes when the hydraulics would again engage. My
desire to climb out of the bilge grew with my hunger and
the onset of hypothermia. My best bet was to emerge at
night, just prior to the hydraulics signaling time for the
fishing net to be hauled aboard. It was risky, but I had to
make my move while I still had some wits about me.

The thought of food bolstered my diminished strength
and allowed me to push aside the deck plate. Stiff and
sore, I struggled out and slid the steel plate back into
position. As if I'd gone from refrigerator to oven, the
temperature gradient between under and over the deck
plate was extreme. The heat from the engines, even
with the fumes of diesel and exhaust, was like a delight-
ful injection.

Desperate for food and a new hiding spot, I hurried
up the ladder and into the galley. I counted on my past
experience to know the crew was sound asleep. The deck
light through the fo'c'sle door was adequate for me to find
half a sleeve of Ritz crackers on the table and a partially
eaten breast of fried chicken in the trash can. I couldn't
open the refrigerator for a drink, for fear of the interior
light waking George or Alex. So I drank from the kitchen
faucet. Rusty and stagnant-tasting, it was all I had to
hydrate. I forced several gulps.

Out through the fo'c'sle door with my stash, I scurried
like a rat to find a dark hole. The engine slowed suddenly.
Opening a door ahead of the port winch, I stepped into
a booth-shaped space and latched the door behind me
just as the hydraulics engaged. Perfectly cozy, I thought,
as I realized I had stumbled upon a storage locker through

which ran the exhaust stack from the engine room. There was no room to lie down in my clandestine closet, but I could stand or sit, and ventilation grates in the door allowed a full view of the work deck. After my time in solitary confinement, this would be downright sociable. I was sure I could endure a day or two here until we were back ashore.

"Haul back! Let's go, boys," Lincoln called through the open fo'c'sle door as I gnawed cartilage from the chicken breast. The captain engaged the main winches, released their brakes—port, then starboard—and hurried back topside, where I knew he manned engine and hydraulic controls at an outdoor station aft of the wheelhouse.

The winches turned, winding two steel cables out of the ocean and onto their drums. As the wires rubbed against flanges, surface rust flaked and fell to the deck, forming small piles of brown scales and dust that lay under each winch, undisturbed in the absence of even the slightest sea breeze. The groaning of the winches as they strained to pull the wire and accompanying trawl, consisting of net and doors off the ocean's bottom, was like spurs prompting the crew of two to hustle into oilskins. Both men squinted in the bright deck lights following the nap they had just been awakened from. George was ready first. He grabbed the five-foot steel steering bar from its resting place against the port rail and took a position facing the port winch. The steering bar was to be used crowbar-fashion to help guide, or fairlead, the wire onto the winch evenly, keeping it from building up on one side or the other. Alex was seconds behind, taking his position with an identical piece of steel to guide the starboard wire.

The lack of wind and apparent slack tide made the job of fairleading the cables nearly effortless. I watched as I ate crackers. The two men stood steadily on the deck, which moved predictably in the gentle swell. The men's rapt attention moved back and forth from winches to the large single-sheaved bollards that hung high above each stern quarter and through which the cables traveled as they were slowly hauled from either side of the boat's churning wake. Salt water trickled from the bollards back into the ocean in a steady stream. Bright orange spray-painted marks were loudly noted at twenty-five-fathom intervals by each man as the marks reached bollards. Subtracting twenty-five from the total set overboard three hours ago, the men kept a running tally of the length of wire remaining to be hauled before the doors and net would break the surface.

The minute or so between sets of marks was filled with George's words of caution to his nephew as the cables snapped with increasing tension on each rotation of the drums. They needed to watch themselves and each other, he warned. He told a gory tale of a crewman who had somehow been pulled into the winch while his shipmate was fetching coffee or using the head. By the time the horror was discovered, the body had been around the winch several times, each wrap of wire severing another piece of the man. Alex appeared to have heard the warnings and stories before, but he still winced when his uncle described removing the body from the winch.

"One-fifty!" called George loudly as an orange mark entered the port bollard.

"One-fifty!" echoed Alex as the mark on the starboard side ran through the massive block. They counted down in segments of twenty-five until a white mark appeared, indicating the final sections of wire were on their way to the winches.

"Last mark!" both men barked simultaneously. They stowed the steering bars on the deck between winches and gunwales and hurried to the stern, each man in his own far corner with the net drum between them. George leaned heavily on the port rail and peered down into the water, looking for the six-hundred-kilogram steel oval trawl door, as the last few fathoms of wire strained through the bollard over his head. Alex scanned the water where the wake flattened out behind the boat, I imagined looking for the cod end to pop up and float on the surface. If the catch was good, the end of the funnel-shaped trawl where the fish were eventually trapped would float with fish bellies bloated with air, a result of being pulled from the depths.

Bang! The port door was up and resting against the steel hull. *Bang!* Up came the starboard door. The back straps, or chain bridles connecting doors to the net, made steep angles with the surface of the water. The links worked hard against one another, with the weight of the gear remaining overboard. A smaller-diameter chain, the idler, dangled freely from each door. The slack in the idlers allowed the crew to detach them from the respective doors and connect them to large links hanging from either side of the net drum. When both idlers were hooked up, Alex and George stepped back into the far corners of the stern and gave the captain okay signs to engage the net drum. A few rotations of the huge drum between them took the tension off the back straps, allowing the men to disconnect the trawl doors from the net. The doors hung loosely from the bollards, the full weight of the net supported by the drum. Not a damn thing had changed in the years since I had worked the deck of a dragger.

Although I couldn't see him, I knew Lincoln was carefully working the valve controlling the net drum. Soon the mouth of the net broke the surface. The lower lip of the mouth was constructed of a series of ten-inch black plastic disks connected by chain through their centers. This rig, or roller frame, allowed the leading edge of the trawl to roll along the ocean floor, up and over ledges and other obstructions on the bottom. The upper lip of the funnel-shaped net's mouth was rigged with brightly colored plastic floats, or cans, that kept the mouth open vertically as the trawl doors stretched it horizontally while being towed through the water.

The net drum, controlled by the captain above, slowly and methodically wound out of the wake the orange and green webbing of panels and sections of twine formed by tens of thousands of stitches and knots sewn into diamond-shaped mesh. George examined the port side of the trawl for damage as it passed by him on its way to the drum, noting any holes or tears that may have needed mending. Alex absentmindedly gazed out over the stern and into the ocean under a flock of herring gulls diving after small creatures that had escaped the net. The cod end still hadn't popped to the surface. In fact, the twine stretched tight onto the net drum, which I knew was not a good sign. "Long tear in the port wing," George informed the captain. The net continued to come aboard. "Three or four holes in the belly," George called out as the narrowest section of the funnel was pulled up and onto the drum. "Looks like a bag of rocks. It's wicked heavy," George said in reference to the cod end, which now hung straight down under the surface at the *Sea Hunter*'s stern. The six-inch diamond mesh collapsed into vertical bars with the weight of whatever had been caught in the cod end.

Lincoln gently stopped the drum as the thicker-diameter twine of the net's chaffing gear reached the spool. "Alex, honey, grab the sewing basket from up in the gear locker," Lincoln called down, referring to a container of tools and twine needed to repair the net. If I had been in the gear locker, the jig would have been up. Alex obediently traveled the length of the deck in long, graceful strides and disappeared into the black hole contained within the steel frame of the fo'c'sle door. I let out a quiet sigh of relief.

George retrieved the spliced loop of braided line used to strap, choker-style, the net just above the cod end. He pulled his hood on over his cap and moved quickly under the drum to a position where he could place the strap. As George hugged the section of twine that hung between the drum and the water, Alex emerged with the milk crate overflowing with tools, placing it on the deck against the starboard gunwale. George tucked one end of the strap through the opposite end, cinching the rope loop around the twine with a sharp jerk. Lincoln slacked the wire of a cargo winch mounted at the base of the boom and hinged to the mast. The wire ran through a block at the end of the boom and down to a cleat welded to the base of the net drum. The slack in the wire allowed Alex to remove the blunt hook shackled to its bitter end from the cleat and hand it to his uncle, who crouched under the drum raining salt water. George placed the hook in the free loop of the strap and moved out from under the drum and back to the port rail, removing his hood. "Just like Christmas morning, isn't it?" George said cheerily.

"Bah humbug," Alex replied while staring down at the toe of his boot. He and George leaned on opposite rails while Lincoln worked hydraulics to pull the cod end out of the water, up the stern ramp, and onto the deck. Lincoln skillfully pulled up on the cargo winch while backing off the net drum. As the bulged end of the net was dragged through the U-shaped ramp in the *Sea Hunter*'s stern, the grinding of rock on rock was heard over the crying of the gulls still diving into the distant wake. The cod end slid forward and came to rest with a crunch in the middle of the workspace. George grabbed the tail-like line leading from the bottom of the cod end, wrapped it around the cleat at the base of the drum, and signaled Lincoln with a thumbs-up. Lincoln once again cracked open the valve operating the cargo winch, putting enough tension on the tail rope to pop open the clip that secured the purse line sealing the cod end. The distinct *pop* of the release of the brass clip cued George to free the end of the tail rope from the cleat. The purse line cinching the cod end relaxed, immediately dumping the net's contents noisily onto the steel deck.

Two dozen rocks—boulders ranging from substantial girth to grapefruit-sized—spilled onto the deck with a smattering of scalers, fish whose usually shiny scales were chafed up or missing as a result of their ride in the cod end with objects other than fish. "A handful of scrod and market, Linc," George said to his brother as he and Alex worked to clear the deck of rocks. The larger boulders were rolled aft and pushed out the stern ramp, while smaller, more manageable rocks were picked up and tossed over the sides. Alex flipped the codfish into two orange baskets.

Lincoln joined his crew on deck to help mend the net as the *Sea Hunter* drifted west with the remains of a moon. Alex gutted, gilled, and washed the meager catch and disappeared into the fish hold, where I knew he would bury the cleaned fish in ice. Once the fish were put to bed, Alex reappeared and assisted with the net repairs. He refilled plastic needles with mending twine as his uncle and father emptied them into holes and tears, snapping knots tight with needles in their right hand and twine knives held in their clenched jaws. The sun had risen before the net was declared back together, and Alex yawned loudly as he examined a small cut on his index finger.

George and Alex sat and waited quietly under bright lights flooding the deck as Lincoln steamed the *Sea Hunter;* I assumed he was getting the boat back to towable bottom. The rumbling of the diesel engine hushed to an idle. "Here we go again." Alex exhaled with mixed fatigue and discouragement.

"Cheer up. It ain't over till the fat lady sings. We have plenty of time yet," George said as he patted his nephew's back fondly.

"Yeah. That's what worries me," Alex said out of the side of his mouth, avoiding eye contact with his uncle as they took their respective places in the far corners of the stern.

The trawl was backed off the drum and into the wake of the *Sea Hunter* as she jogged into the growing daylight. The net, streaming at its full eighty-foot length behind them, was connected to the doors and disconnected from the drum. The heavy oblong steel trawl doors were lowered into the water as Lincoln backed the tow wire off the winches. The doors submerged, dragging the net down with them. The throttle increased to a good steam as Lincoln released the winches, allowing the wire to free-spool over the stern while the trawl dove to bottom.

"Twenty-five," sang George as the first mark ran through the port bollard.

"Yep," mumbled his shipmate as the starboard wire reached the same mark.

And so it went for the next nine hours. The crew napped at three-hour intervals while their captain tried in vain to put them on the fish. I worried constantly about someone opening the door to my closet, but it seemed I had chosen a little-used space. I sneaked out once more for water from the tap and whatever scraps of food were lying around, and I prayed for the end of this trip. The Vickersons would be worried to death. I would have a hard time explaining my absence. I was so exhausted that I no longer had the urge to open the package I hoped held the evidence to convict Dow's murderer. It could wait.

"Haul back!" Lincoln's voice jolted me from near-sleep. I stood and watched the routine through the ventilation grate. Alex's mood appeared to have brightened as he and George took steering bars in their hands for what I supposed would be the final haul back. According to my count, we had been fishing a full twenty-four hours, and unless this tow produced a miracle, the *Sea Hunter* would return to Green Haven with fewer fish than what I imagined would be needed to cover the expenses of fuel, mending twine, and groceries. But Alex would be cut loose from what he apparently considered torture, and so would I. I caught myself humming Carly Simon's "Anticipation." The end was in sight.

"Seventy-five!" Alex called out loudly and was echoed by George. "Hey, Unc! What time do you think we'll hit the dock?"

"I don't know. Alex, honey, pay attention to the wire now," George said. "Watch out for that splice. It'll—"

"I know, I know," Alex interrupted. "It'll catch my sleeve and pull me into the winch, and if it doesn't kill me, I'll wish it had." He mimicked his uncle's deliberate speech. "At the very least, I'd lose an arm. Wouldn't do much for my basketball game, would it?" He smiled for the first time I had noticed. "Fifty fathoms!"

"Roger, fifty!"

Alex dropped his steering bar in the middle of the deck as soon as the white mark broke the surface, then he hustled back to the stern in anticipation of the final bang of doors against hull. George methodically stowed his steering bar in its usual spot and walked purposefully toward the stern, arriving well ahead of the doors.

Starboard then port doors climbed from the water, up the sides of the hull, and came to rest hanging comfortably from the bollards. Alex quickly ran the end of a short rope through a shackle on his door, pulled tight, and wrapped a few figure eights around a cleat on the gallows frame, securing the starboard door for the steam home. George was in the process of securing the port door when Lincoln stopped him. "Hey, boys. Not so fast. We've got fuel enough for a couple more tows." My heart gained ten pounds.

"Aye-aye, Captain," George answered as he removed the tie-down line from the port door.

Alex, clearly as unhappy as I was with this news, whipped the line from his door and slatted it against the rail. He complained through his clenched teeth, loudly enough for me to hear. "What the fuck." Idlers were hooked up. "Has he lost his mind?" Back straps were disconnected. "We've caught every rock on Schoodic Shoals." Thumbs-ups were sent to the captain. "Two more tows. Give me a break." The men stepped away from the drum as it turned, retrieving the trawl. Alex continued to mutter obscenities to no one in particular as the usual entourage of swooping and soaring gulls went into a frenzy. Stoic birds left their flank positions from the *Sea Hunter*'s beams and joined the tight cluster diving and screeching above the bloated white bellies within the cod end that popped to the surface, silencing Alex's rant.

As the inflated bag neared the boat with every revolution of the drum, my excitement mounted with the closing of the gap between it and the stern. My anticipation of a successful Hail Mary effort grew with the volume

of the feeding gulls. Maybe we'd be going home after all.
Within the ball of white bellies flashed something large
and dark. "Did you see that?" shouted George as he
peered more intently from under his Red Sox cap. Something huge and very much alive was thrashing among
the small and swollen codfish all belly up, with tails
barely wagging. God, how I wanted to come out of hiding and join them in the stern!

"What is it?" Alex asked as he leaned over the stern,
stretching to get a closer look.

"You'll be among the first to know!" said George excitedly as he grabbed the strap, donned his hood, and
moved under the net drum just as it came to a stop.

The bag was strapped and pulled up the ramp. George
wound the tail line around the cleat. *Pop!* Out onto the
deck fell the usual handful of cod and one giant bluefin
tuna. The tuna, seven feet long and as big around as a
barrel, flopped around the deck frantically. Alex let out
an excited whoop and mounted the magnificent fish, riding it like a bucking bronco. "Yee-ha!" Alex yelled, circling an imaginary lasso above his right shoulder. "This
fucker's got to go eight hundred pounds! What a beast!
Twenty bucks a pound—yee-ha! Pay dirt! Head her to
the barn, old man. Alex honey is in the money!" He dis-
mounted and bowed low, like a triumphant matador. His
uncle laughed hysterically at the antics, and I fought the
urge to let out a whoop myself.

"Okay, boys. Get that fish overboard before someone
gets hurt," Lincoln called from above.

"Right, boss," responded George as he attempted to
herd the silver and blue monster toward the stern.

Alex stood, dumbfounded. "What do you mean? What
are you doing? This is a godsend! Let's go home." His
voice cracked nearly to a whine.

"I'm sorry, Alex, but we don't have a permit for tuna.

We'll have to release it. Give your uncle a hand before someone gets hurt. Come on, boys. Two more tows." Lincoln sounded less than enthusiastic.

In what appeared to be beyond mere immature frustration, Alex picked the steering bar from the deck at his feet, raised it high in the air, and brought it down at full strength directly into the tuna's skull. "Fuck!" he screamed. The fish quivered and then laid motionless, its head badly smashed.

THIRTEEN

Stunned, I remained as still as the dead tuna. A sickening take on catch and release, I thought. My appetite for Ritz crackers disappeared with the fish as George slid it easily out the stern ramp. Alex's violence went beyond the throes of youthful impetuosity. It hadn't taken much to detonate this savage display. Lincoln and George appeared to be unmoved by the violence. Were they used to this sort of behavior? They didn't scold Alex. Did homicidal rages run in the family? And if an eight-hundred-pound lifeless mass could be so easily disposed of, why not an average man? The unbridled tantrum scared me back to the bilge, where I would patiently wait out the *Sea Hunter*'s fuel supply, out of the Aldridge boy's range with the deadly steering bar.

The icy condensation trickled down the side of the hull and wicked into my shorts and T-shirt. The cold kept me alert, while my inner furnace was fueled by a desire to expose Dow's murderer, whom I believed, now more than ever, was a deck above me.

I toyed with the hopeful possibility that Lincoln had

changed his mind about making any more tows. The engine's steady speed indicated that we were steaming back toward Green Haven. Just as I considered climbing out of the bilge for a peek around, the main engine slowed to an idle, and the hydraulics jolted me back to the reality that the captain was indeed leaving no stone unturned in his attempt to put a profitable trip aboard. The weather had deteriorated to some degree. Even from the short end of the pendulum here in the lowest part of the bilge, I felt a steeper angle in the roll and an occasional jarring slat of sea increasing with wind velocity. I sensed a course change after what I guessed was approximately an hour after the seas had picked up. The *Sea Hunter* was being driven directly into the wind and ramrodding into seas that seemed to be growing taller and farther apart. The main engine growled louder with more throttle; I imagined Lincoln had increased the RPMs in order to maintain the net's optimum speed over ground in the worsening conditions.

Three hours into the tow, I was again resisting the urge to climb aboveboard, since the motion of the boat was becoming unbearable. It was difficult to brace myself from sliding fore and aft on the slick steel as the hull pitched up and over waves that were hitting directly on the *Sea Hunter*'s nose. The only consolation I could take from the beating was my assumption that the nasty weather would necessitate that this be the last tow. The hull dropped into a trough, leaving me hanging for a fraction of a second before it surfed back up the next crest and hit me hard enough to punch the breath from my lungs. God, I thought, this would be a slow, painful death. One more shot like that, and I would have to risk detection.

The final blow, delivered seconds later by the unforgiving steel tomb, may have broken ribs. As I gathered my strength to push aside the plate above me, the engine sang out in what I thought must be full speed ahead, and I felt the boat fall off to starboard—the waves were now pushing on the port bow. Far from comfortable but no longer in a life-threatening position, I nestled back against a frigid longitudinal I-beam and prayed for the hydraulics to signal the final haul back.

I imagined that the weather had become too severe for Lincoln to continue towing the net into, or even quartering, the seas. I sensed the boat's motion running fully in the trough and then before the wind. The main engine's throttle had been pulled back a bit, and I enjoyed the slow, deep roll, knowing that the end of the trip was near. The gentle push was followed by the glide of seas on stern and accompanied by a gradual slowing of the engine. It picked up my spirits as I realized that I would endure the bilge for only a few more hours. I waited with acute anticipation for the welcome sound of hydraulics engaging. I squeezed my messenger bag to support my burning rib cage. I hoped its contents held the evidence to unravel the twisted snarl of all I had encountered since moving north. But I knew that no matter what, I would have some explaining to do to Alice and Henry regarding my absence. I hoped we would reach shore after dark so that I might immediately sneak home, and no one would be the wiser. I wouldn't have been missed by anyone other than the Vickersons. Audrey might have wondered where I'd been, but not to the point of hysterical concern or suspicion. Cal would need an explanation of my long-term parking and the Duster's broken window. I appreciated the advantage I had gained by not allowing close relations to form. I had learned and relearned this: Questions and answers must be vague among mere acquaintances. I had learned that Mainers were, above all, polite. I didn't feel the need to be totally honest with anyone. Not yet, anyway.

An abrupt stern-down lurch of the *Sea Hunter,* followed by the wallop of a wave slamming her aft port quarter, was disconcerting. This was not the usual dip-and-launch move of a boat towing before the wind. The sharp strike with no reaction of caroming down sea was an unnatural halt of the perpetual motion one takes for granted after days offshore. Another shove on the stern with no equal and opposite thrust forward confirmed what I'd suspected: We were hung down, or anchored by the stern as the net and/or accompanying ground gear had fetched up solid on some protrusion from the ocean floor. The main engine slowed to an idle, and the hydraulics clunked on.

The next slap on the stern was more severe and made me quite nervous. A stream of cold water blasted me in the face, awakening my worst nightmare. The ocean was surging over the stern and had forced its way into the engine room, flowing down through the spaces between the steel plates above me. The water must be rising quickly in the bilge below me, I thought. Although it was pitch dark, my sensation of partial submersion illuminated the horror. Pushing on the plate above me was useless. The weight of the water coming down was too great for me to overcome. Remain calm, remain calm, I thought as my steel casket continued to fill.

The *Sea Hunter* rolled to starboard. The volume of water yet to seep into the bilge sloshed and held the boat in an extreme starboard list, not allowing her to right herself. Bracing against the port side of the steel plate with the back of my neck and shoulders, I pushed hard with my legs from a deep squat to a low crouch and managed to move the plate aside, leaving an access just wide enough to squeeze through. A murky halo of light daw-dling at the top of the ladder on the opposite end of the engine room was my catalyst for action. I needed to reach the doorway through which the rogue waves had flooded the engine compartment before the crew was able to latch it closed in a somewhat belated attempt to keep what re-mained of the airspace below them watertight.

Creeping along the low side of the engine room, I leaned against the port fuel tank, knowing that if the *Sea Hunter* suddenly listed the other way, I could be cata-pulted into one of the moving parts of the engine, which was, miraculously, still running. I waded through knee-deep water to the bottom of the ladder and held on tight as another wave broke over the stern and rushed the length of the deck. A mass of green water darkened the doorway above me. Gripping the sides of the steel lad-der, I ducked my head and held my breath. A deluge of salt water sluiced down through the open door and onto my back, buckling my legs. When the water stopped, I raised my head to a shower of sparks on my immediate right. I scrambled up the ladder and onto the deck, where the water that hadn't found the engine room door was rushing in retreat out the stern ramp. The noise from the engine room fell silent to the peal of raging wind and sea as both engines were snuffed out.

Three men in full foul-weather gear held on to winches, wire, and gunwales to keep from washing overboard with the escaping water. When the deck had cleared, all three men seemed to notice me at once. I had a real vi-sual of someone looking like he had seen a ghost. We all understood that this was no time for questions. "Close the doors!" Lincoln yelled into the howling wind and creaking rigging.

I secured the engine room door while George did the same with the fo'c'sle. Since the wind seemed to be increasing exponentially, I assumed we were in the middle of a squall that would subside quickly as it blew by and off to the east. Until then we had nothing better to do but hold on and hope not to roll over. I had experienced storms at sea while fishing with my mentor, but nothing as perilous as our present situation—full of water, no engine, and hung down by the stern. We shipped another mountainous sea. This one ripped Alex from the winch he had been hugging, sending him hard into the forward bulkhead and then adrift in the rushing tide until he was able to grab the base of the net drum as he sailed toward the open ramp. As soon as the water cleared again, Lincoln bolted to help his son back to a safer spot ahead of the port winch.

Wedged between the winch and the bulkhead, Alex cowered limply as his father and uncle discussed a game plan. A short debate over the merits of turning off the twelve-volt bilge pump in order to save the battery power for restarting the main engine, versus leaving the pump running to dewater the engine room, ended when Lincoln gave the order to save the batteries. Commanding his son to get up to the wheelhouse, where he might be safer from the next onslaught of salt water, and to shut off the pump was met with no response. Alex, whose face was the color of baby aspirin, was clearly in shock and would be of no help to us.

"Where's the switch?" I asked, ready to climb the ladder to the bridge.

"Starboard console panel."

"Mayday call?" I asked.

"No radio."

With no time to question Lincoln's reply, I flew up the ladder and turned off the bilge pump circuit breaker. I agreed with the captain, not that anyone had asked my opinion, that we seemed to have survived the amount of water already aboard and that the batteries would be imperative for our eventual return to the safety of Green Haven. A quick glance around the bridge on my way back to the deck blew my mind. "No radio" was meant quite literally. There was no VHF radio—not even a bracket for one—anywhere. In fact, there was a complete absence of electronics altogether. Filing this to contemplate after we'd dodged sure death at sea, I charged back below to assist the men in maximizing our chances.

The wind was lashing at about fifty knots and sending every fourth or fifth sea barreling up the deck to sweep us off our feet and out the ramp to a salty grave. The port list was enough to bury the stabilizing outrigger, which looked as though it might be snapped like a pencil or torn from the hull at any moment. A stay wire strung from the end of the boom to the top of the mast slackened slightly with every downward mushing into each trough, and it hummed with tension like a muted guitar string at the top of each crest. I wondered how many times this would happen before the turnbuckles exploded, leaving us in even greater danger.

"We need to get rid of the gear. Man the port winch, George," Lincoln hollered over the whistling and creaking as he positioned himself at the manual brake of the starboard winch.

"Wait!" I yelled. "If we let the net go, we'll end up drifting with the wind on our beam. There's a lot of water in the engine room. We could roll over!"

"It's possible. But if she rolls over, she'll stay afloat for a while. If we keep taking shots on the stern, she may begin to break up. She'll go down like a rock," Lincoln said emotionlessly.

"Why not let one winch off, take the slack wire to the bow, and secure it there?" I asked. "Then let the other side go, and at least we'd be anchored by the bow. Wouldn't that be safer?"

Lincoln thought about my suggestion as another sea crashed and flooded the deck. When the port outrigger came out of the water, the top stay parted with a stomach-wrenching *bang!* Lincoln said, "Okay, let's try it. I'll ease this side off. George, as soon as there's enough slack on deck, you pull it up to the bow and take a wrap around the bit." George nodded, seemingly eager to take action. Lincoln carefully timed the relaxing of the brake between slams and managed to run a large coil of wire onto the deck. Just as George summoned the courage to dash to the open deck, the port wire parted in the bollard with a *twang,* sending him skittering back to safety. The loop of slack wire sprang from the deck before Lincoln could tighten the brake. The result was a bird-nested mess of backlashed steel cable jamming the starboard winch.

"Now we're fucked!" Alex yelled. "What's the insurance chick's next plan?" He put his head between his knees and began to vomit.

"Back to plan A," said Lincoln calmly and loudly. "We'll get rid of the gear. That'll buy us some time. Get the hacksaw, George."

"Roger." George opened the closet door behind the winch. A gust of wind blew half a sleeve of Ritz crackers out and overboard, where they immediately disappeared in the white shock of a breaking wave. The wind was relentless and showed no sign of flunking out. The seas were building, and daylight was diminishing. At this point, our chances were better adrift, even if upside down. We were running out of time.

"What about cutting torches?" I asked. "That would be a lot faster than a hacksaw."

"I lent them to a friend," Lincoln replied.

"Some friend," George added as he stumbled out of the locker, hacksaw in hand. The blade was rusty and apparently not very sharp; he spent several painful minutes giving short strokes back and forth across the cable, which refused even the slight scar for the effort exerted. Lincoln took a turn with the saw as George rested, Alex vomited, and I wondered how much longer it would be before a plate dropped from the hull as waves continued to hammer the *Sea Hunter*.

"Where's my cell phone?" I asked George, who was now standing beside me.

"In the cubby above my bunk. The battery is dead."

I began to tremble with cold and offered to take a turn with the hacksaw, thinking the work would warm me up. The men refused my help but each insisted I take their foul-weather clothes. I reluctantly took a jacket from George and pants from Lincoln and struggled into them between blasts. George then directed me to his sock drawer and a dry pair of boots in the fo'c'sle. Lincoln instructed me to grab the life vests above the galley table. Their concern for me seemed to disgust Alex, who mumbled something derogatory about "the insurance chick" between bouts of dry heaves and rants about our plight.

I timed the opening of the fo'c'sle door carefully and managed to secure it behind me without allowing any water to enter. I hurried into dry socks and boots twice the size of my feet, the fear of being trapped inside pushing me to hustle back to the cold, wet deck. I took a few seconds to retrieve my cell phone, on the outside chance that the battery had one more call in it. Dropping the phone into my soggy messenger bag, I grabbed the only two life preservers above the table and scrambled back to the deck, where Lincoln was working intensely with the saw. "Put one of those on and give the other to Alex," he commanded.

As I handed the orange flotation vest to Alex, he ripped it from my grasp and threatened, "If my father drowns because you're wearing his life vest, you're dead meat." I knew he meant it, but I also knew not to argue with the captain. If we spent any time in the frigid water, the vests would only ensure that the buoyed bodies were found first. Snapping closed the two plastic buckles and tightening the vest's straps around my torso until my ribs screamed in pain, I gazed over the stern, wondering what else I could do to help with the battle.

Something caught my eye. The weather conditions limited visibility, and the seventy-knot salt spray felt like torture and made focusing nearly impossible. Squinting and blinking, I searched the horizon and thought I saw a boat, but before I could be sure, it dropped out of sight in a deep valley among the mountain range of waves marching toward us. When it rode up on the next cresting peak, it was close enough for me to read the name on the bow. "Look! It's the *Fearless*!" I shouted, and pointed to where the boat quickly settled back out of view.

"It's about time," George said.

"Wait up here until they get close enough to throw a life ring over," Lincoln ordered. "Alex will go first, then Jane, then George, then me. No one jumps without the ring." He was calm and seemingly relieved. At that moment I knew his plan had been premeditated. Of course, I thought, they had planned to scuttle the *Sea Hunter*. That explained the absence of so many essentials, such as a life raft, acetylene torches, or electronics. The boat had been stripped of most anything of value. That also explained why George had tried to talk his nephew out of making this trip, and why there were only two life preservers. Lucky for me, I thought, Quin had finally come to our rescue, living up to what I suspected was his part in an insurance scam.

It would not be an easy transfer. Getting and maintaining a position close enough to reach us with a hand-thrown life ring in this violent wind would require exceptional boat-handling skills. In all of the scheming they had done to pull off an intentional sinking, they surely hadn't planned for the weather to be this bad. But the convenient storm would leave less room for suspicion and accusations.

As the *Fearless* approached our stern, she veered right and passed close to our starboard side. "What's he doing?" asked Alex.

"He has to turn around and come alongside with his bow into the wind to keep control," Lincoln answered confidently. As *Fearless* surfed by on top of a wave that nearly capsized us, I saw Quin's son, Eddie, looking at us through binoculars from the open wheelhouse door. When the waist-deep water drained to below my knees, I dared to release one hand from the security of the winch and waved. Eddie returned a tentative raising of an arm. Then a hand—I assumed his father's—reached out, grabbed his shoulder, and yanked him into the wheelhouse. The door closed. We watched *Fearless* shrink in the distance.

FOURTEEN

He doesn't see us," cried Alex. "Dad! Do something!" We watched the stern of our savior fade into the distance and gathering dusk until a cable supporting the main boom parted, sending the end to crash down onto the net drum. With it plummeted my optimism that the *Sea Hunter* would withstand whatever remained of the beating Mother Nature was dishing out. In complete desperation, I tried my cell phone, but no go. George held his transistor radio at arm's length and twisted it at different angles to the sky to catch a weather report. When a voice promised more of the same, George quickly stifled it. Three heads hung in moods of sheer doom and helplessness. The fourth, belonging to the captain, was busy working with the few teeth that remained of the hacksaw.

"Don't worry, Alex, dear. The wind is coming around. It won't blow much longer," Lincoln vowed. He shared a look with his brother that I was sure was meant to keep George quiet; then Lincoln added, "We'll be fine." Back and forth he swept the saw blade tirelessly. Just as I'd dragged my psyche out of the doldrums to think again about what I could possibly do to help, Lincoln said, "Alex, you and Jane go find some buckets. We'll need to bail the engine room as soon as we're free of this gear."

"Buckets? You're fucking kidding!" Alex replied. He wedged himself back behind the winch and began to sob uncontrollably. "We're going to die aboard this fuckin' wreck!"

Lincoln's resolve spurred me to action. "This chick ain't going down!" I defied the sullen brat. "Come on, pull yourself together! Let's find something to bail with." Fully aware of the volume of water in the engine room, I was skeptical about bailing by hand, but I kept that to myself as I entered the fo'c'sle in search of anything that might be useful in dewatering. Ahead of the bunk area was a door that led to a small storage room in the boat's forepeak. I shuffled through boxes and shelves of years of accumulated boat junk and didn't find anything I considered handy for ridding the engine room of water—no hand pumps, no lengths of hose. Stacked on the deck were three clean white five-gallon buckets rigged with tiny aeration pumps and tubes. I figured this must be how Nick Dow had transported the crabs to his aquarium. Leaving the aeration equipment in the forepeak, I grabbed the buckets and hurried back to the main deck to await Lincoln's next order.

The men's determination with the saw finally paid off: The wire was parted with help from a wall of green water that exploded on the stern. We all waited, silent with our own prayers, to see how the *Sea Hunter* would react to being set free from her shackles to the bottom. She wallowed up and down a couple of times, then was spun around ninety degrees so that the wind and sea were now on her port beam. The night was pitch dark but for a bit of hazy moonlight sifting down through the wind-driven spray, so it was difficult to decipher whether our new predicament was more or less dire.

A wave waltzed effortlessly aboard over the port rail, totally swamping the deck. When the water receded over the rail, I thought we might roll bottom up. But we didn't. I felt the port side lifted on the back of the next wave, tipping the contents of the bilge and pouring it to the leeward side. "Hold on!" yelled George and Lincoln in unison as the *Sea Hunter* lurched to an even keel, then landed heavily on her starboard rail, sending the end of the boom skittering to the other side of the net drum with a gut-pulling slat. Again I thought we might roll completely over. Again we did not.

What remained of the broken port outrigger dangled in the water off the *Sea Hunter*'s bow by one skinny guy wire that had yet to give up. Fascinating, I thought briefly, that the cable of the smallest diameter had outlasted those of greater girth and breaking strength. With that tenacious wire in mind, I became the top link in the chain of three that comprised a bucket brigade working doggedly through the night to reduce the water in the engine room to a level that would enable us to attempt to restart the main engine.

Lincoln stood in seawater up to his midthigh and scooped with five-gallon buckets, handing them full over his head to George, who was positioned halfway up the ladder. George then passed the buckets up to me on deck, where I dumped closer to four gallons after all the sloshing and spilling along the way. After I'd emptied the buckets, I had to get them back down the chain to be filled again. Lincoln and George changed positions every fifty buckets or so, as being the middle man necessitated working with one hand while holding on to the ladder with the other. The engine room door was secured open in a way that did not allow enough reaction time when a deck swamping was imminent. I couldn't close it fast enough to prohibit part of what washed aboard in our deepest rolls from seeping down and refilling what we were determined to empty. In true "two steps forward, one step back" mode, we were an obstinate team. Alex emerged from the fo'c'sle once to take a leak and quickly slunk back to where I imagined he sat and waited to die.

By the time daylight trickled over the eastern horizon, George and Lincoln were exhausted and switching bailing stations at ten-bucket intervals. A somewhat triumphant report from the bottom of the chain described the depth of water there as ankle-deep. The stubborn stay wire holding the port outrigger at last gave way as the relentless sea succeeded in pulling the cable's grip from the bow one finger at a time. The loss of weight with the release of the wire pinned the *Sea Hunter* in her starboard list even with the reduction of what the bilge once held in water. There had been little conversation among the three links during the all-night bucket brigade. I supposed talk was unnecessary and kept dumping buckets as they appeared at my feet. My mind wandered briefly to my favorite daydream as I dumped buckets. If, by some miracle, I survived this, I swore I'd play golf in Scotland someday.

Numbed to the biting wind and seas that threatened our tenuous stability, I had stopped warning Lincoln and George to hold on with every rogue wave hours ago, as even shouting was getting difficult. The wind continued from the same direction, and the seas grew to new heights. Occasional waves crested and broke so high in the *Sea Hunter*'s rigging that no antenna had been spared by midmorning. When the radar dome was ripped from the top of an A-frame bracket, it swung in the wind by its thick cord, smashing against the steel bracket until its entire housing had been shattered to bits that flew downwind like potato chips.

Though I was on the verge of physical collapse, unwavering determination kept me in pace with the men until they ascended from the dark and joined me on deck. George and I stared at the captain, waiting for orders. Lincoln scanned the horizon thoughtfully. "Still southeast," he said with a hint of discouragement. He took a deep breath that appeared to bolster his courage and continued, "Well, the weather hasn't improved, but I'd say our situation has. George, see if you can get an update on the storm while I gather flashlights and tools." George did as he was told, this time being careful to keep the radio close to his ear, I supposed for my own protection if the truth was that we had not seen the worst of this system. Lincoln soon returned with a canvas bag that held an assortment of rusty tools and a single functioning flashlight. "Any good news?" he asked his brother.

Speaking directly to Lincoln and over me, as if I were a small child who couldn't possibly understand, George replied, "An intensifying low is moving *slowly* to the east." He looked as though he'd like to cover my ears before finishing. "They're calling for storm-force winds out of the northwest on the backside until midnight."

Refusing to be left out of the conversation that could determine the length of the rest of my life, I asked hopefully, "Shouldn't the Coast Guard be searching for us by now?"

"Not without a mayday call or a signal from an EPIRB," Lincoln answered. So I knew that among other things, we also had no emergency radio beacon that could send a signal to the Coast Guard.

"What about Quin? Wouldn't he have radioed for help on our behalf?" I asked.

"I'm not counting on it. We're on our own. Do you know anything about waterlogged diesel engines?"

Dismayed to learn the unlikelihood of being saved by the Coast Guard, I was glad to at least be welcomed to try to save myself. "I can turn a wrench," I said, completely understating my knowledge and ability.

"Good. Let's go." Down the ladder we went, the three of us, to work in ankle-deep ice water, on a platform in perpetual motion, on an endeavor that was of highly improbable success, by the light of one narrow beam and without proper tools. The good news was that we were sheltered from the wind, which made verbal communication less taxing. Not that any energy was wasted on small talk. In fact, all conversation was to the purpose of reviving the main engine, which had expired as a result of immersion. What we did not know was the exact cause of death. Best-case scenario—the twelve-volt electrical system needed for fuel injection had been shorted out. If the loss of battery power had caused the engine to stop prior to salt water being sucked into the air intake or washed into the crankcase breather, then there was a chance that we could, with a lot of work, restart it. Worst-case scenario—permanent damage. Perhaps the engine had seized due to sea water, with its absence of lubricating properties, entering moving parts that required oil. If the latter were true, the only hope we had was to survive the thrashing promised by the weather forecast and be rescued by the chance passing ship. Unwilling to leave our survival to chance, we got busy in the engine room.

That we had only one performing flashlight aboard mandated that we all work together, which we did amazingly well, considering the series of events that had led us to this juncture. When strength was needed, I held the light and passed tools. When tight workspace necessitated small hands and dexterity, I was chief mechanic. Both labor and thought processes were so intense, I forgot about the raging storm. The immediate goal was to get the engine running. Without propulsion, we were completely defenseless. No one spoke of the what-ifs we would face in failure. We had no backup plan.

The battery terminals were fried beyond recognition. The lack of new ends required us to cut the leads back a few inches and hose-clamp them securely to their respective posts. Leads were chopped with a fire ax, a hammer, and a block of wood. The dipstick exposed a milky sludge that clung to the strip of metal like frothy maple syrup, confirming that water had indeed penetrated the engine's lube oil. There was barely enough clean oil aboard to do a complete change, but we were able to replace the polluted filter with an old one, the discarding of which, luckily, had been neglected. Next we worked to disassemble the top of the engine, exposing the fuel injectors. Each of the twelve injectors was removed, cleaned, and replaced while a manual fuel pump was pushed in and pulled out endlessly to bleed fuel lines. Primary and secondary fuel filters were spun off, dumped, and refilled with diesel free of water. The saturated air filter was removed, squeezed dry like a sponge, and replaced with a prayer.

An auxiliary belt-driven bilge pump that hadn't been used in years was next on the fix-it list. Working its shaft with channel-lock pliers, back and forth and back and forth, then around and around and around until it turned relatively freely, we searched for an appropriate-sized belt. Finding none, I removed the necktie from my belt loops, stretched it around the pulleys on the pump and main engine, drew a slipknot as tight as I could, and cinched it with an overhand. Even if it worked for only a few minutes before the necktie shredded, I reasoned, that would save hundreds of buckets.

The bit of light from the door above the ladder was fading fast. We had been working in the engine room all day. We had been as thorough as we could be and were anxious to hit the starter button. Lincoln checked and re-checked all we had done to ensure that nothing had been missed. By the time he was satisfied that there was nothing more to do, we had all suffered bloody knuckles and jolts of stray twelve-volt current. We understood that the batteries would sustain only a certain amount of cranking and that the fuel supply was critically low. There would be no second chance. I dreaded this moment as much as I yearned for it.

Warning George and me to stand back, Lincoln put a thumb on the rubber plunger that protected the starter button. Lincoln took a deep breath before pressing, and I actually crossed my fingers—something I couldn't remember ever doing, even as a kid. Lincoln's thumb went hard into the rubber. The engine turned over three or four times but failed to catch. Releasing the button, Lincoln expelled a great sigh of relief. I was glad he couldn't see the utter grief in my face. "She's not seized up," he said triumphantly. I knew this was good news but had wanted so badly to hear the engine start and run that anything less was tragic in my mind.

Before I could contemplate what would become of the *Sea Hunter* and Mother Nature's four hostages, the backside of the storm began to trample us. Lincoln ordered George and me into action again. "Get on that priming pump! Hold the light so that I can see what I'm doing! Hand me the seven-eighths open end!" We did as we were told: I pumped until my arms burned with pain, and Lincoln and George bled air from fuel lines that led to the injectors. As bubbles disappeared and clear fuel ran, each line was closed snugly until all twelve injectors were bled. Lincoln again placed a thumb on the button and said, "Stand back. And pray this time."

"I prayed last time," George said sadly.

The engine let out a sickening groan before turning over hesitantly. This was it, I thought, the batteries were nearly drained. If the engine did not catch now, we were goners. Lincoln kept the button depressed and yelled, "Come on!" The beat of the cranking quickened slightly and caught. The engine was running—roughly—but running. Lincoln dove on the manual prime pump and began thrusting it in and out vigorously. The engine broke into a coughing jag, hacking and spitting and threatening to die. Lincoln pumped as if administering CPR to his most beloved, and the engine responded positively. Though it was not the steady rumbling I had prayed to hear—more of a ragged hiccup and hiss—even the poorly running diesel was nothing short of a miraculous accomplishment. I suddenly understood the name on the stern of a pretty red lobster boat I'd seen back in Green Haven: *Joyful Noise*.

Lincoln grasped my wrist firmly and pointed the flashlight I held to a panel of gauges. I focused the beam on the ammeter, and we watched the needle climb slowly into the green zone, indicating that the alternator was indeed functioning and charging the tired batteries. Lincoln gave my wrist a couple of victory squeezes before letting go. The water in which we had been standing was now below the deck plates. The necktie was working! I had nothing to squeeze, so I pumped a fist in the air. Lincoln pulled a string that hung above the engine, illuminating a single bare bulb. It was the first time we had seen one another's faces, although we'd been working side by side, for what I guessed was better than ten hours. Overwhelming stress and physical exhaustion had deepened the lines around Lincoln's eyes, and his usual ruddy complexion had paled to geriatric tallow. I couldn't begin to imagine my own appearance and didn't much care.

"I'll check things topside and head her for the barn," Lincoln said loudly. "Open that valve, and drain water from the hold as long as the necktie hangs in. Don't let the water get above the deck plates." He pointed out the gate valve low on the bulkhead between the engine and fish hold. "If the engine sounds worse than it does now, pump that primer until she clears." Up the ladder he went, leaving George and me to monitor the bilge and nurse the engine along if need be.

Whether thanks to my state of mental exhaustion, my enfeebled mental capacity and emotional fatigue, or just the human tendency to bury painful experience, things blurred. I didn't know how many times I opened the valve, allowing water to gush in and up to the deck plates, before the makeshift belt disintegrated. I didn't count the number of times George brought the engine out of epileptic seizure by jamming the pump in and out like a piston. But the occasions of knowing that the end was near were numerous. Every time the *Sea Hunter* climbed willfully up the face of a charging sea and raced down its back, I believed we were close to the safety of Green Haven. Each time the *Sea Hunter* failed to reach the summit before being pummeled by a crest that must have caused structural damage above, I thought we were losing ground. But it was the shuddering that I found most disheartening. The quaking of solid steel, like a profound shiver running the length of the boat, shook my core in a way that was unequalled by either entrapment in a bilge filling with water, or being shot at in an open field. The shuddering jolted me out of dazed lassitude to an outright cold sweat. With each deepening tremor, enduring became the remotest of all possibilities.

Eventually the roaring shudders dissipated to a swaying clacking that I associated with the railroad. The pounding and crashing and thrashing and wallowing gradually came to an end, too. We were either in the lee of land, or the wind had blown itself into extinction. Eager to learn the truth of our situation, and not daring to hope for too much, I followed George up the ladder when he beckoned me to do so. Walking out onto the main deck just as Alex came out of hiding, I realized the weather system had fought to the bitter end. We were indeed entering the channel leading to Green Haven Harbor. The air, as languid as a stalking predator before attack, held a fresh quality that opposed the staleness of the engine room's fumes. Wisps of cloud obscured and dulled the edges of the moon setting on the western horizon, the orblike fuzziness reminding me of an old black-and-white close-up of a Hollywood starlet looming on the big screen. "We made it," I said softly and to no one in particular.

As we approached the dock, I was surprised to see a crowd of people ready to catch our lines. Although it was rather late for Green Haveners, I reminded myself of the speed at which news travels in a small town. Cal caught and secured the aft spring line over a piling when Alex enthusiastically threw it at him hard enough to nearly knock the old man over. Clydie was there and was the first to yell an excited greeting: "I knowed you was fine! I been watching for you out my window for hours. When I seen you coming, I rung the church bell. Quin said you was sunk, but his boy said you was still afloat." Someone stepped out of the shadows and hushed Clyde. It was Lucy Aldridge, looking and acting like her usual highbrow-socialite self. She calmly dispersed the crowd, thanking them for their concern and sending them home to bed.

When the *Sea Hunter* was fully secured at her berth, Cal caught my eye with an expression that silently asked if I was okay. I smiled. He shook his head and said, "Good night," then headed up the pier behind the small group, leaving only Lucy on the dock above us. I assumed that the condition of the boat and the appearance of her crew spoke volumes. Words were not needed. There would be plenty of talk tomorrow at the coffee shop, I was sure. Alex was up the ladder and into a hug from his mother as soon as Lincoln joined us on deck from the wheelhouse.

I handed George his jacket and boots and promised to launder the socks he had lent me. He left quickly, anxious, I was sure, to walk on solid ground, promising his brother to reappear first thing in the morning and begin what looked like endless repairs. As I dragged my legs out of the oilskins I'd borrowed from Lincoln, I was amused by Alex's account of his own bravery to his mother, who was quite impressed. Mother and son had an uncanny resemblance—not just their physical but also their emotional makeup. Lucy called down to Lincoln that she would take Alex home with her and get him to basketball camp the next day. Lincoln agreed and bade them good night. I folded the orange rubber overalls and returned them to Lincoln with a "thanks."

Lucy laughed above. "Some women will do anything to get into a man's pants!" She left before my tired brain could fully register the insult.

Ready to get some sleep before facing my landlords' interrogation, I said, "See you around," and pulled my aching body up the ladder.

"Wait!" Lincoln said as he hurried up behind me. "I don't know how or why you ended up aboard my boat this trip, but I'm glad you did."

Was this a come-on? "I wish I could say the same."

"I guess you've decided that you made the right decision about standing me up on our first date."

Was he fishing? "Well, long story, as it turns out."

"Will I get another chance?"

Another chance for what? To kill me? I walked away, clutching my messenger bag to my broken ribs, and said over my shoulder, "Not tonight, Captain."

FIFTEEN

My eyes and brain were clouded in exhaustion and darkness. The neighboring boats appeared thick and motionless against pilings and distant buildings, as though some artist had spread them with a palette knife from a tube of black oil to gray canvas. After the riot of sound and motion I had experienced in the past forty-eight hours, I found the stillness nearly as overwhelming. The clapping of the sole of my sandal with its torn strap against the bottom of my left heel was the only break in the silence. Parked between the loading ramps precisely where I had abandoned it (was it only two nights ago?), the Duster was a most welcome sight in my otherwise greetingless homecoming. Although it would have been nice to have worried somebody—anybody—to the point of sleeplessness and wringing of nervous hands, the fact that I owed no explanations for my short sabbatical was oddly comforting. The Duster, like a loyal Labrador retriever, sat and waited and would ask no questions.

The thought that perhaps my only unconditional emotional attachment was directed toward an automobile was disturbing and mildly depressing. As I dug in my bag for the keys, I absentmindedly began humming Simon & Garfunkel's "I Am a Rock." Positioning myself behind the steering wheel, I was surprised to find a note taped over the horn: "Miss Bunker, I took it upon myself to have your window replaced before the storm struck. Hope that's OK. Lee (my nephew) at Sunrise Glass has a bill for you to sign and send to your insurance company. Cal." With all that had happened since, I had forgotten about the broken window. How thoughtful of Cal! Maybe my feelings of friendlessness and disconnection in Green Haven were false or the product of fatigue and the aftermath of trauma. I wiped a single tear from my eyelashes before it escaped down my cheek. Some island I am, I thought. Glad to have no witnesses to my emotional weakness, I stomped the accelerator to the floor three times and turned the ignition switch. The engine refused to start. The recollection of running out of gas sent a fresh flood of tears. God, I was so tired. I wondered when was the last time I'd cried. Before I could figure that out, I was hiking up the hill toward home.

Feeling my way through the gift shop and up the stairs, I didn't turn on a light until I was safely inside the apartment. Another note, this one from Alice and Henry, was mostly lighthearted teasing about the schedule I had been keeping and an invitation to dinner on Thursday. Unless I had missed an entire day along the line, Thursday was the following night, so I vowed to accept the invitation and found myself actually looking forward to seeing the landlords. As for the rest of this evening, I needed food, a hot shower, and sleep. Strawberries did the trick for my hunger, and fifteen minutes under a steaming showerhead washed away salt, grease, and the chill. Somewhat revived, I was now considering things other than my bed.

As much as I squirmed to dance around the spending side of one of my Scottish dilemmas, I caved in and plugged my cell phone charger into a socket behind the table. Wondering how many messages I had missed from my employer, I turned on my laptop and ran the phone line over to the bottom of the wall-mounted unit that Henry had so expertly repaired after the popcorn disaster. As long as I was splurging on high-end electricity, I might as well go for a little long-distance dial-up, too. While waiting for my somewhat antiquated computer to come to life, I casually drew the window shade. Then I locked my apartment door with the deadbolt, took a deep breath, and willed myself to relax. I'm alone, I told myself. I'm safe.

Lunging for my soggy messenger bag, I opened its Velcro closure with such exuberance that my ribs sang a painful reminder. My patience had been stretched to a tautness that had until now been unknown. Fear of either discovery or disappointment fed a palpitation in my chest that surged the length of my arms and dead-ended in my trembling hands. The package was meticulously wrapped in plastic and taped to a fare-thee-well. As I began picking tape from a corner, I suspected I held in my hands evidence to convict. This was the sought-after item that had sent Green Haven residents combing the shoreline, and also the catalyst for someone to visit Dow's house. Anything worth hiding must be worth finding, I hoped as I ripped a length of tape, exposing the package's contents.

Dow's black book was, in actuality, dark green and just the right size to tuck into a back pocket. The vinyl cover was worn and shaped in a way that indicated the book had spent a great deal of time being sat upon. Inside the front cover was an envelope containing cash, mostly tens and twenties, that added up to just three hundred dollars. Not exactly high stakes, I thought. I pulled a loose sheet of paper, folded letter-style, from between pages in the middle of the notebook. It was a rather formal letter addressed to Lincoln Aldridge from the dean of the admissions office at Boston University, politely denying Alex Aldridge any financial aid in the way of athletic scholarship and encouraging Mr. Aldridge to apply for need-based aid, which would make Alex eligible for a campus job. A surreal image of Little Lord Fauntleroy serving up scoops of pasty mashed potatoes vanished with the growing mystery. Why, I wondered, would this letter be in Nick Dow's possession?

Dow's book was pretty much what I'd imagined it would be, given all that I had heard about his activity as the local low-level bookie. Entries were dated and clearly printed. No names were used; numbers represented gamblers and buyers into various pools. As far as I could tell, there was no methodology in the numbering system. Some players were represented by single digits, others up to five digits, as if they had chosen their own codes to be easily remembered. Nowhere in the book did I find a key that matched names with the secret gambling codes. I was not surprised. This could be Dow's assurance to his flock of gamers that if the authorities ever leaned on him, nobody but Dow would be in any legal trouble. Speeding through the entries page after page, I couldn't imagine what all the fuss had been, with so many folks discussing the book and the wad of cash they'd surmised would accompany it. Most bets were in the ten-to-twenty-dollar range.

Then, two-thirds of my way through the book, I noticed a large increase in the individual bets placed by gambler 34. The first sizable bet was listed on a page

headed with "MLB American League East": 34 had bet
$2,000 on the New York Yankees and had lost. Following
that loss, 34 had wagered increasingly large amounts,
apparently drowning in the typical gaming spiral: circling
the drain and hoping that a huge win against all odds
would pull him or her out. But luck was not on his or her
side. IOUs were taped to many of the pages and signed
with 34. By the time I reached the page where the last
bets had been placed, a rough calculation showed that
34 was in debt to Nick Dow for over $50,000. This was
not petty cash. People have killed for less.

Several unused pages led to the back of the book. The
very last page had some notes scribbled on it, including
what looked like a toll-free telephone number and a series of digits and letters that I associated with an order
or shipping confirmation. Curiosity got the best of me.
My cell phone now had enough charge to place a call
while remaining plugged in. I let my fingers do the walking. "Thank you for calling Saltwater Exotics. All as-
sociates are busy with other customers. Please stay on
the line for the next available associate. Your call is
important to us." Interesting, I thought. But not incrimi-
nating. Dow had a hobby and had placed an order for
his aquarium. This I already knew. Before I could hang
up, a pleasant man thanked me for holding and asked
how he could assist me.

"Oh, hi. I'd like to check on an order, please."

"Do you have your order number?"

"Yes. GN337DC."

"Okay, let's see." A short pause was followed by: "*Hemigrapsus sanguineus,* ten male and ten female, right?"

"I'm sorry, but I didn't place the order with the Latin
name. What was ordered?" I asked.

"*Hemigrapsus sanguineus* is the Asian shore crab, or

Japanese crab. And I show them delivered. Mrs. Hamilton, right?"

"Yes, Lucy Hamilton," I lied. "I purchased them as a gift and never received a thank-you, so I wanted to see that they had actually been delivered. Some people have no manners! Thanks for your trouble."

"No trouble at all. Anything else I can do for you, Mrs. Hamilton?"

"I would like to know more about these crabs. I know it's strange that I purchased them without knowing exactly what I was buying, but like I said, they were a gift. How do you spell the Latin name? Maybe I can research them on the Internet."

"You should have received a fact sheet with your invoice. We always send a fact sheet."

"I'm not sure I remember seeing the invoice, but I suppose it could be here somewhere," I stalled, hoping for something more that might help.

"The envelopes we use stand out. They have a red border along the left edge."

"Oh, yes. That sounds familiar. Where did I see that envelope?" My mind immediately flashed to the envelope Lucy Hamilton had grabbed from the urn wreckage. "My memory isn't what it used to be. Have I placed any other orders with you?"

A long sigh indicated that the salesman was getting annoyed with me. "Let's have a look here. No. My computer indicates this was your first and only order."

I thanked him again and hung up. If Dow hadn't been bringing home crabs from sea, then how could the travel buckets and aeration pumps be explained? To what extent was Lucy Hamilton involved? And for what purpose? Lucy had gone to such lengths to conceal the evidence of her crab purchase that I knew she and Dow must have had evil intentions. But what? So far Dow's book had done nothing but add to my confusion.

Launching my Internet browser, I waited impatiently through the clicks and electronic sounds that accompanied the dial-up service. When I finally connected, I Googled "Asian crab." Pages listing websites and articles on or including *Hemigrapsus sanguineus* appeared on the screen. Selecting the site topping the list, I scrolled down through the information, then skipped around and through a number of articles, mostly excerpts from science publications, and learned more than the average person would care to know about Asian shore crabs. The physical description of the Asian crab was identical to what I remembered seeing in Dow's overflowing aquarium. I cursed the Old Maids' cat for eating what could have confirmed the match.

Asian crabs, I read, were highly reproductive, with a breeding season twice the length of native crabs. Females were capable of producing fifty thousand eggs per clutch, and they produced three or four clutches per breeding season. This would account for a shipment of twenty crabs growing quickly to tens of thousands, I reasoned. More interesting to me was the fact that Asian crabs were touted to be versatile and able to thrive in a range of habitats. They were "opportunistic omnivores," feeding on larvae and juvenile fish. Prolific reproduction, broad diet, and hardiness gave these crabs the potential to disrupt food chains and devastate indigenous populations of crabs and fish.

Nearly every article I read listed Asian crabs as highly invasive, bringing to my mind a Miami media blitz following a lawsuit that eventually convicted a man for the illegal importation of the highly invasive koi fish. The man had been selling koi to owners of Chinese restaurants for display in tanks. I clearly remembered the man's reaction to mandatory jail time and the outrageous fine; he stressed that he had absolutely no intention of releasing the koi to the wild, which would have been a serious threat to native species. I couldn't imagine it was legal to sell these crabs except for scientific research. Who knew what kind of story Lucy Hamilton had manufactured to have her order filled?

Dow never had to worry about being chased down by the dogs of journalism in Green Haven for the illegal release of Asian crabs. But had he had intentions other than the entertainment and wonderment of watching them multiply? What if his intentions had been to release the invasive crabs to hasten the total devastation of the cod stocks, as predicted in his letter to *National Fisherman*? I saw how this would also benefit Lucy Hamilton. Wind farmers could better justify their desire for a piece of ocean floor if there were no cod there. Things were falling into place. But who had killed Dow? And why?

Exiting Google, I clicked on my e-mail icon. Deleting the myriad of electronic sales pitches ranging from low-interest loans (which overestimated my interest in them) to wrinkle creams, I opened the single e-mail sent from my boss. After reprimanding me for not being attentive to incoming calls, the note quickly outlined serious business. "First," he wrote, "I must make my priority the completion of the survey of Blaine Hamilton's sailboat, *Fairways*." It seemed Hamilton was in the process of "mortgaging his eyeteeth" to purchase shore property for his proposed wind-generated power plant. Hamilton's willingness to have everything riding on a wind farm that had yet to win Green Haven's public approval was surprising to me. The implication that the Hamiltons didn't have enough cash to purchase the entire state of Maine, as I had been led to believe, indicated desperation more than willingness.

My employer's other immediate concern was what had been reported as the "total loss of the *Sea Hunter*" by Alan Quinby. Quin was apparently entitled to the entire insurance settlement, as his partners, Lincoln and George Aldridge, had been lost at sea with the vessel. The insurance company was anxious to know whether I had surveyed the *Sea Hunter,* as they had requested, so they could begin the process of minimizing cash outlay. My, it hadn't taken Quin long to start the wheels of financial benefit after leaving four of us, including his best friend, for dead. But as anything other than a condemnation of Quin's character, all of this was irrelevant, since the vessel had not gone down. I would straighten this out with my boss in the morning. I wondered what the ramifications of attempted insurance fraud were.

Next I checked my cell phone's voice mail and found that my boss had not left any messages. The phone's call log indicated three missed calls, all from the agency and all prior to the boss's resorting to e-mail six hours ago. The call log also listed outgoing activity, and I wondered who had placed calls before the battery had died. There were five calls, all to the same number—367-5009, a Green Haven exchange. None of the calls appeared to have connected, as the longest was twelve seconds. I guessed that Alex had used my phone to call a girlfriend. I knew that teenagers were apt to dial anyone's phone at any time, without regard to permission from its owner. I wondered whose number had been dialed so persistently and so late at night. Well, it was my phone, I reasoned. I felt justified in attempting the number myself, even at this late hour.

After four rings, a machine picked up. "You have

reached the office of Ginny Turner at Turners' Fish Plant. Please leave a brief message after the beep." Ginny Turner! My instincts had told me that she was up to something. But what? What had I missed? Alex wouldn't have called Ginny. It must have been Lincoln. As much as I had wanted to deny Lincoln's involvement in anything scandalous, there were just too many signs pointing in his direction. I was absolutely positive that Lincoln had planned and aborted the scuttling of *Sea Hunter*. Perhaps it had been planned prior to Dow's murder, but because Alex had filled in on deck, Lincoln couldn't go through with it. There was a good chance that he had indeed been driving the boat truck the night I was caught at Dow's. Lincoln could be 34. That could have been his age when he placed his first bet. Although I would have liked to blame anyone else, the odds were that Lincoln had set me up to be killed under the pretense of a date. He'd probably even fired the shots himself. But how did Ginny Turner fit in? Were the two of them joined in some conspiracy? Had one or both of them murdered Dow?

Oh, what I wouldn't give for fifteen minutes alone in Ginny's office. She was hiding something. I felt it in my gut. She seemed like the type to be sloppy about deleting messages. If I could listen to her phone messages, perhaps I would learn something about her connection to Lincoln. Well, I thought, she's not in her office now. And I can pick a lock with the best of them.

SIXTEEN

Sleep is overrated, I thought as I hurried into jeans and a navy blue sweatshirt. I have the rest of my life to sleep, I reasoned while double-knotting the laces of my tennis shoes. My second wind was kicking in as I added a few items to my bag that might be useful in breaking or picking whatever locks I might encounter between my apartment and Ginny Turner's inner sanctum. Henry's rechargeable flashlight would come in handy, so I took that, too. I wasn't even tired, I realized as I left on foot and jogged down the hill toward the fish plant.

The dogged persistence that had always been my strength had earned me the name of the Pit Bull among the detractors I had left behind in Florida's crime-fighting community. I'm back, I thought as I passed through the gate and into the deserted parking area. What I lacked in physical strength and intellect, I gained in pure and simple stubbornness. I was never a contender in the hundred-yard dash; my strength was endurance. Super-condensed, I was the absolute epitome of "chronic." I also happened to be very good at bolstering my own confidence and courage.

All that had been simmering in me since Nick Dow's body washed ashore was now approaching a boil. Every bit of advice I had received from my mentor through the years had come down to some analogy with hard-boiled eggs. He would never advise to strike while the iron was hot; he would say it was time to put the eggs in the water. That time had come. I simply could not wait until tomorrow.

Circling the perimeter of the plant, remaining close to the building to minimize my exposure in the light from the moon, which was nearly full, I was disappointed to find that all entrances were locked from the outside. I could pick any of the inexpensive, generic locks using a bobby pin, but I'd hoped to find a way in that was less illegal. Trespassing was preferable to breaking and entering. The plant's floor plan was fresh in my head from the survey I had done, so whatever entrance I used would lead to Ginny's office, as there were no interior locks. Because the ground floor of the plant consisted of a processing area and refrigerated spaces, there was only one window—a little natural light and fresh air for workers on break—located high in the external wall of the lunchroom. It was open.

If it hadn't been for my broken ribs and (I hated to admit) my age, I probably could have reached the lower sill and pulled myself up and through the window in a flash. But I had recently begun to realize that people really do get smarter with age—something of a necessity as other things ebbed. Just around the corner of the building was a stockpile of empty wooden lobster crates. Pulling two crates from the pile and dragging them under the window, I stacked them and climbed on top, putting myself in a position to ease my rear end onto the ledge rather gracefully. A table conveniently located under the window allowed me to drop into the lunchroom without any show of athleticism. Vending machines hummed loudly, and I found the door by their multicolored lights.

Entering the fish processing area, I pulled the flashlight from my bag and wove my way around the sleeping stainless contraptions. With blades and belts at rest, the cold and sterile machinery reminded me of a scene from a horror movie. An imagined snapshot of my body being filleted, skinned, and frozen urged me to hustle through the field of hulking steel. Parting heavy strips of plastic, I entered the salt storage area, where I slowed my pace through pallets of nonthreatening seventy-pound bags until I reached the next plastic curtain, which led to a long corridor. I passed several rusty metal plates the size of barn doors—they sealed expansive refrigerated rooms and freezers—and finally reached the door that opened onto the stairwell to Ginny's office.

At the bottom of the stairs was another door, this one exiting to the parking area and locked on the outside. Up the stairs I went and entered the small waiting area outside Ginny's office. Remembering her office window, I turned off my flashlight before trying the doorknob. A bit of light from a streetlamp streamed into the otherwise black office. After drawing the blinds and pulling the cloth curtains together, making sure the edges met in the center of the window, I was satisfied that I could safely use the flashlight to prowl around.

As I'd suspected, Ginny had not cleaned up the messages on her telephone's answering system. Illuminated red numbers indicated seventeen old messages. I hit the playback button and listened. The first recording was a short pause and a hang-up. That must have been me, I thought. A number of calls from delivery truck drivers sounded like routine check-ins before and after Ginny's usual office hours. There were calls from fish buyers and sellers, all of which shared a common theme: Sellers complained of low prices, and buyers lamented what they considered too high. This is leading nowhere, I thought as I continued to listen to benign messages.

Finally, message fourteen was of interest. I replayed it several times, trying to decide whether it was Lincoln's voice, but the connection and recording were not good enough for me to determine. "We're headed offshore. I hope your price goes up by the time we get back in." Strange, I thought, that a fisherman would assume Ginny would recognize his voice. Stranger still was "*your* price," as opposed to "*the* price," which had been used in every other message. It was a fairly poor recording, very static-filled, as from a cell phone. I listened again, this time focusing on the syntax. Yes, I was certain that he had said "your."

So what? I thought. Had I come here for this? The message was strange, but strange was not nearly enough. Strange did not lead to conviction. Strange was nothing. Discouraged that I had wasted time and taken an unnecessary risk, I listened to the answering machine wind through the last three calls. And there it was, the final message, from a female: "Hi. Where are you? Thirty-four has agreed but wants more money. Call me." Most unfortunately, I had no way to determine the date or time of any of the messages. I was certain this last one had been left by Lucy Hamilton. So she knew the gambling code. She and Dow had been involved in something beyond the crabs. Ginny, too, was aware of the code Dow had used in his book. Although this was far from what I needed to ignite the lightbulb over my head, it was

enough to form a possible scenario. I sat in Ginny's chair
and closed my eyes in concentration.

Of course, I thought, 34 had to be Lincoln. He was in
deep debt to Dow and might have killed him to avoid
paying up. The letter denying his son scholarship money
might have driven Lincoln to consider scuttling the *Sea
Hunter*. Before dumping Dow's body overboard, Lincoln
probably had removed the book of evidence from his
back pocket and stashed it, along with the letter from BU.
Or Dow had hidden the book himself, and Lincoln was
still searching for it. As I was the only person in town
poking around the circumstances leading to Dow's death,
I had become a target. Lincoln couldn't kill me aboard
the boat—two witnesses, one of whom was his beloved
Alex. But what had he agreed to do for Ginny and/or
Lucy that he needed more money to complete? Maybe
they had paid him to murder Dow? No, I was certain that
the fourteenth message had been a call made from my
cell phone, and that had been in my sole possession until
well after the murder. That didn't make much sense at
this point.

Maybe I could find something helpful in Ginny's
books or her desk drawers, I thought. I was now so tired,
I could barely hold my head up, but when would I get
another opportunity to sneak a peek at Ginny's business?
Timing is everything—the eggs again, thanks to my
mentor. If I could find the company checkbook, maybe
that would shed some light.

God, I needed sleep. Shuffling through the contents
of desk drawers, I had difficulty focusing. The top page
of a stack appeared to be a pending sales agreement
between Ginny Turner and Blaine Hamilton. The document's description of the property and location made it
clear that it was the plant and surrounding area. Jesus,

where does she keep the checkbook? I thought. My eyes were stinging. The beginnings of a headache were encroaching. A dry throat sent my thoughts to the Coke machine in the lunchroom. Keep searching, I urged myself, and I fought the nauseated feeling mounting in my gut.

The hint of an acrid odor caught my attention. Jesus! Headache, fatigue, nausea, dry throat, and confusion: the classic symptoms of carbon monoxide poisoning. Something was horribly wrong. Dropping papers on the floor, I scrambled out of the office, through the waiting area, and down the stairs. I needed to reach the lunchroom window while I had my wits about me. At the stair door, my flashlight outlined a tunnel of thick smoke moving rapidly toward me. Crouching low, I was able to get beneath the billowing mass and breathe a bit easier as I duckwalked the length of the corridor. Even in my oxygen-deprived state, I was aware that the plant was on fire and that my only exit was the window. All exit doors were locked from the outside, right? I questioned whether I had checked every door before entering through the window. But I knew there was no time to waste. I had to make it to the window.

As I hustled through the storage room, I wondered what happened to salt when it caught on fire. I wasn't about to stick around to find out. Although the processing area was filling with smoke, the high ceilings allowed me to transit under the poisonous mass nearly upright. When I reached the lunchroom door, a loud roaring on the other side squelched my exit strategy. I placed the back of my hand against the steel door to confirm my living nightmare. Yanking it away before I burned myself, I knew the room on the other side must be fully ablaze. Now what? I wondered. I couldn't possibly go back to the office and jump from the second-story window, as all of the smoke was going that way. I wouldn't survive long enough to open the blinds. I couldn't depend on being resaved by the Green Haven Cellar Savers. No one even knew I was in here. Or did they?

I had always refused to depend on luck for my own survival. If you rely on luck, it will eventually run out. Or, in my mentor's terms, it's time and temperature that ensure proper eggs—not a guessing game. But here I found myself facing sure death and deciding to scurry around the plant, hoping that I had missed an unlocked door. If I'm lucky, I thought, I'll find an open exit. If I'm unlucky, I'll die from smoke inhalation. Around and around I went, like a caged animal, frantically pushing on doors that refused to budge. On my second lap, I pounded on the doors and called for help. The smoke now hung lower from the ceiling, crowding me closer to the floor. The walls were getting hot, and puddles along the edges of the concrete floor sizzled. On my third lap, I banged my knee on a large PVC duct. The gurry chute!

The plant's gurry chute, or sluiceway, for the waste products from every fish-processing machine, was my way out. There was a large stainless steel bin, or hopper, into which ran plastic pipes that carried blood and guts, or gurry, from the automated stations as well as the troughs that lined the tables supporting manual cutters of fish. One end of the bin was fitted with the large PVC duct that I assumed ran in a downhill straight shot through the external wall and into the harbor. Flames had found a path along the crease joining the wall and ceiling, casting an eerie orange glow through plumes of smoke. At this rate, it would not take long for the roof to collapse. I took a deep breath and climbed into the gurry hopper.

Feet first, I decided, and hoped the duct was of a large

enough diameter to allow me passage. Having no other option, I slithered in. Like entrails, I slid quickly down the greasy pipe and splashed into the ocean. In no immediate danger, I treaded water and gulped in full lungs of fresh salt air. Clearing my smoky brain, I swam the short distance to the closest ladder. The tide was at just the right height for me to reach the bottom rung. As I pulled myself up, the pain in my ribs was a most welcome sensation. Oxygen, cold water, or both had revived me to the point where I believed I could evaluate my situation and make sound decisions. Feeling naked without the bag that almost never left my side, I realized that it and its contents were gone forever.

Standing firmly on the pier, I had a front-row seat to the plant, which was fully engulfed in flames. The blaze roared and crackled as bright sparks climbed in the cloud of heat, then fell, drifting and extinguishing themselves before making contact with the ground. The fire had spread to the head of the pier, barricading me from the small crowd that had gathered in the parking lot to watch what would be the demise of life as they knew it. My friend Cal's silhouette stood out among the others. I worried about his livelihood. A loud creak was followed by the deafening crash of the plant's roof folding into the inferno. The audience of stunned faces reflected the glow like scores of setting suns.

The steady drone of an outboard motor grew near. A skiff carrying three men, one of whom was Lincoln Aldridge, pulled alongside the *Sea Hunter*, which was tied where we had left her a few hours ago. Lincoln climbed aboard his boat, and the skiff continued on to the next boat. The engines of the boats soon started, and deck lights came on. Here was my ride to safety, I thought. I could easily dive back into the water and swim to the beach, but that could be considered another unnecessary risk. Turning my back to the fire, I walked the pier to the *Sea Hunter*'s berth and called hello to George, who was standing on deck, watching the plant burn. My voice startled him from what appeared to be a pensive mourning of what was sure to be the total loss of the cornerstone of this community.

"Ms. Bunker! You turn up in the strangest places! What are you doing? You're soaked!"

"I came down to see what was on fire and realized that I'd left my purse aboard the *Sea Hunter*. My whole life is in that bag. The only way to get around the fire was to swim to a ladder, so I did."

"You had your bag when you went home earlier, but come aboard. We're moving to another dock in case the fire travels the length of the pier. You need a ride, don't you? I noticed you left your car here. Is it broken down?"

"Just out of gas," I said. Happy to have been invited aboard, I felt safe. If Lincoln had been aboard alone, I probably would have chosen to swim ashore. Lincoln appeared at the controls behind the wheelhouse above us. Before he could question my presence, George called, "The lady from Atlantis thought she'd help us move the boat. I'll give her a ride home after." I suspected Lincoln was as confused and exhausted as I was. He shrugged and gave us the command to release the lines from the pilings. He didn't look pleased to see me, confirming now more than ever that he had indeed known I was in the plant when he set it on fire. Like a bad penny, I thought, I kept coming back.

George and I worked quickly to let the lines go and coiled them into readiness to resecure to the pier we were headed toward. As Lincoln turned the boat sharply around the end of the pier, she listed away from the turn, sending everything on deck in motion. Tools that I guessed had been used during the night to get the generator going cascaded off the hatch cover. The Orkin Man–type spray bottle that Cal had explained was used for bleaching and disinfecting rolled onto its side and stopped against the bulkhead. Before we could begin to pick things up, we were against the dock and tossing lines to a very stoned-looking Eddie, who had his telescope set up adjacent to where the *Sea Hunter* now rested.

Blue lights from a number of police cars raced down the hill and into the plant's parking lot. "I guess they didn't want to miss the fireworks," said Eddie as he lethargically looped eye splices over pilings. Moving quickly from wrapping the spring line around a cleat to the stern to do the same, I stepped over the spray bottle; the nozzle was in a puddle in a divot on the steel deck. Drippings from the nozzle sent rainbows across the top of the puddle. Bleach didn't do that. Tossing the stern line onto the dock, I waited for Eddie, who was at the bow catching a line from George.

Lincoln climbed down the ladder and sat on the starboard rail. He looked like a thoroughly defeated man. He hung his head in what appeared to be shame as George returned from the bow. Lincoln couldn't bring himself to look at either of us. If my developing theory were accurate, Lincoln had just failed in his second attempt on my life. In this case, he had been paid to commit arson, so my death would have been a great bonus in a "two birds with one stone" way. The closer I got to pounding the final nails into the coffin of his conviction, the more careless Lincoln would become in trying to stop me. I stayed close to George and was careful to keep an eye on Lincoln, who had gotten up to pace the deck nervously. He was distraught, I thought. There was no longer any doubt that I was on to him.

Lincoln drew a deep breath through flared nostrils,

held it in an extra-long time, then exhaled loudly through puckered lips. "I should move the truck out of the way. I'll be back in fifteen minutes," he said as he pulled on the spring line, drawing the *Sea Hunter*'s rail closer to the ladder on the dock. Oh, sure, I thought. He's probably going to get a ring-side seat to view his handiwork.

"I'll get it, bro. I wanted to drive Ms. Bunker home anyway," George replied quickly.

"I'd appreciate it if you would pick up the deck and secure the boat before you leave. I am happy to drive Ms. Bunker up the hill," Lincoln said. He held tension on the line and motioned toward the ladder, offering to let me go up first.

What? Is he out of his mind? Like I'm about to give him another shot at me? Third time's a charm . . . I said, "Oh, thanks. But I'll wait for George. I think I lost my penlight aboard and would like to look for it. You go ahead. I'll stay here."

"If we find your light, we'll gladly return it to you. Come on, now. Let's go," Lincoln insisted.

"I'm not ready to go yet. I can help George tidy things up. And I prefer to walk home. Thanks anyway." I began picking up tools from the deck and placing them on the hatch cover from which they had fallen. Lincoln hesitated, then climbed the ladder and disappeared. I knew he would come back, and I planned to be gone when he did. Now that the pieces were falling into place, I would once again place a call to the chief detective. Maybe he'd listen this time. I had done all the work for him. He could take the credit for solving both the murder and the arson. But until Lincoln was arrested, I was in danger.

"I'll walk you home as soon as I'm done here, Ms. Bunker," George said softly. He hustled around the deck, stowing tools and tying things in their proper places. When he broke out in a sweat, he pulled his hooded jacket off over his head, exposing the Boston Red Sox jersey he wore underneath. The consummate fan, I thought. Grabbing the spray bottle from the deck next to my feet, he turned toward the forward bulkhead to secure it with one of the many lines that appeared to have been cut and spliced for hanging up gear. When George wasn't looking, I stuck an index finger into the sheen on the puddle. Holding it to my nose, I confirmed the undeniable smell of gasoline. No wonder the fire had caught so quickly. When I called the detective, I'd insist that he hurry to get this bottle for evidence. I made sure to keep a sharp eye on George so I knew exactly where he was securing it.

I nearly fainted when I saw the back of George's Red Sox team jersey: ORTIZ 34. Shocked, I couldn't move. George was 34! I watched as he nervously tucked the bitter end of the line through the bottle's handle and tied a double-sheet bend. Through the loop he passed the bitter end and went around the standing part twice, clockwise. How awkward, I thought. He's left-handed. Right-handers would go counterclockwise. Where had I seen that before? I flashed back to Dow's body on the beach. His makeshift belt had been knotted in the same backward fashion—clockwise. Another flash took me back to Dow's house. I had swung his pitching wedge—righty. George must have killed Dow and tied the line around his waist to assist in moving the deadweight overboard. In his haste, he ignored belt loops. I am alone with a murderer, I thought. But does he know that I know? Forcing myself to remain calm, I went to the stern of the boat and looked up the pier for Eddie. The telescope stood unmanned. The six-hundred-dollar tripod, now missing, could have been the murder weapon. Henry Vickerson's "relic" was probably the part of the tripod that the telescope had screwed into. I knew I needed to get off this boat.

"I guess I'll walk home now," I said as nonchalantly as I could. I began leaning in to the spring line.

"Wait. I'll go with you," George said. He picked up the steering bar from the deck.

"I'm all set. See you later." I stretched for the ladder but couldn't quite reach it. I pulled as hard as I could on the line and hopped up on the rail, waiting for the *Sea Hunter* to move another inch or two closer to the pier. Deck lights cast the shadow of my figure, stretched from boat to ladder, onto the glassy black surface below me. Another shadow joined mine and outlined my death. I didn't even have the energy to scream. I could only watch as the shadow raised the weapon. I closed my eyes and waited.

SEVENTEEN

G eorge! stop!" Lincoln yelled urgently from the deck. I opened my eyes and watched the water below as George tentatively lowered the steering bar from over his head to rest it on his shoulder. Releasing my grip on the ladder, I stepped back aboard and slowly turned to face the murderer. George twisted his hands on the steel bar like a batter concentrating on the pitcher from the on-deck circle. A fine dusting of rust, like rosin, fell on the front of George's jersey. Our eyes met, his frozen in hostility and mine blazing in rage that slowly faded as the clues began to line up into a plausible scenario. Enlightenment eased what terror had produced, and my mind juggled puzzle pieces, some falling into place and others not quite snapping together.

Locked in a stare, neither of us flinched until Lincoln hurried down the ladder and positioned himself between us, interrupting cognitive warfare. George's blue eyes darted back and forth between the ladder and the opposite side of the boat, as if he was planning an escape.

Like cornered prey, he was now driven by fear, and desperate actions were often the result of fear unleashed.

Lincoln looked up to the top of the dock and motioned the police officers to holster guns that had been aimed at his brother. "Put the bar down, George." The sound of Lincoln's voice seemed to penetrate. "This trip is over, bro," Lincoln went on. The iron rod hit the deck with a thud that melted my fear and nerves. George took three steps back and sat on the hatch cover among the scattered tools. Holding his head in his enormous hands, he cried. Placing an arm across George's shoulders, Lincoln silently consoled his brother. After a long and sob-filled pause, George removed his ball cap and used it to mop tears from his cheeks. "Come on, bro. If we survived that storm yesterday, we can survive anything, right?" Lincoln said.

"That storm was nothing compared to what I have been living." With this vague admission, George seemed to pull himself together. The police officers shuffled their feet impatiently on the dock above us.

"This storm has passed. Come on, bro. Let's go."

"Passed? No, we're in the eye, Captain. Hold on. The worst is ahead." I took these words of George's as a warning to Lincoln to be prepared for what would soon be revealed. I wondered how much Lincoln already knew.

Finally, Lincoln urged George to join the state police officers on the dock. "They are going to place you under arrest and take you to the Hancock County jail," he explained, as if speaking to a child. "I'll hire the best attorney and meet you in court at your arraignment."

"Don't waste your money on an attorney. Ms. Bunker has the evidence to put me away for a long, long time." George took a minute to compose himself. Taking a deep breath, he smiled and said to me, "Weird. This feels nothing like what I imagined it would. You should have turned me in sooner." Although I was certain that George had not meant to humiliate his brother, Lincoln looked as though he had received a punch in the gut. I had witnessed reactions similar to George's on a number of occasions in the past. When basically good people get caught in the maelstrom of bad actions, incarceration actually liberates them from their inner moral conflicts. Stating publicly that they are getting what they know they deserve seems to cheer even the most distraught of criminals, somehow making them feel less guilty. The brothers embraced in a short and awkward hug, making me think they had never exchanged anything more physical than a handshake. George climbed the ladder and was met with handcuffs and an apology for having to use them. The men in blue surrounded the large, distraught man, and all five moved along the pier as a single unit.

Lincoln and I stood together on the *Sea Hunter*'s deck. But other than our relative proximity, I felt that we couldn't have been further apart. Naturally, he appeared to be regretting what had transpired, while I was relieved and silently rejoicing. Lincoln had saved my life and, at the same time, may have ended George's life as a free man.

A pale yellow crease on the eastern horizon trumpeted the arrival of a new day while noisy gasoline engines drove the pumps that jetted salt water from the shore to the now-smoldering plant. Two police cars climbed and crested the hill, leaving Green Haven to its usual lawless devices. The crowd of emotional townspeople began to disperse as Lincoln and I approached the parking area. Some muttered in disbelief and shock at what they had seen by the blue flashing lights. Their friend and neighbor George Aldridge, handcuffed and escorted by the state police, would be fuel for many rounds of coffee shop discussions.

"Ride home?" Lincoln asked as we passed through the gate and onto Main Street.

"No, thanks. I'd like to walk," I said.

"Mind if I join you? It would be good to stretch my legs a bit."

"Not at all. Come on," I replied, thinking that the leg stretching would be accompanied by a just-as-needed head clearing. We walked side by side slowly up the hill, until the hissing of water upon embers could no longer be heard and the smells from the fire had dissipated into the darkness. Standing with our backs to the Lobster Trappe, we had a bird's-eye view of all we had left below. This section of Green Haven's working waterfront that had for so long resisted new-wave development now lay in repose. I wondered if Blaine Hamilton's dream of wind-generated power would rise from the ashes of the plant, or if insurance fraud would negate the funding: tradition bowing to progress, to no avail. "What will happen to the fishing fleet now that the plant is gone?" I asked.

"We'll sell our fish in Rockland. We'll get more money for our catch and pay less for fuel. We all stayed with Turners' out of loyalty and nothing more. My father did business with Ginny's father, and our grandfathers and great-grandfathers . . . as far back as anyone can remember."

"But what about the plant employees? Don't many Green Haven families depend on those jobs?" I asked.

"Same thing. The cutters and packers can find better-paying jobs in Rockland. It's only a forty-minute commute. Everyone sacrificed for the good of the whole community. Ironic, isn't it?"

"Ginny doesn't appear to share your feelings of community and loyalty," I said.

"That's the ironic part. She was desperate and took

the only course she saw as the way out. I assume that her financial selfishness led to what will be best for Green Haven in the long run. Inexpensive, renewable, environmentally friendly power and the breaking of the shackles of time-honored family tradition that had outlived its usefulness. I deeply regret my brother's involvement, but I didn't know until it was too late."

"How much do you know?" I asked, hoping that Lincoln could clarify some of what remained fuzzy in my theories.

"I had no idea that George was in as deep as he was with Dow. I mean, I knew about his gambling debts because I was the first to see Dow's little record book, but I thought I had that all figured out. By sinking the *Sea Hunter,* I would have money for Alex's college tuition, George would be free of Dow's ghost, and Quin would put some money into *Fearless* and employ all of us until I could buy another boat. I even hid Dow's book aboard the *Sea Hunter* to be lost forever and protect George from future problems," Lincoln confessed, as if thinking out loud.

That explained the presence of the letter from Boston University among the things Lincoln wished to be lost. "Was the other day a failed scuttle attempt? Did you have to abort because Quin left the scene without us?" I asked.

"No. I backed out of the whole deal before we left the dock. Second thoughts and the changed situation—Dow's death and Alex's being aboard to replace him for the trip—I chickened out. We really were sinking, as you know. But it was accidental and purely coincidental. I'll never know if Quin left us for dead to collect all three shares for himself, or if he was trying to save himself, his boat, and his son."

I wondered if Lincoln was being honest, but I realized it was of no consequence now. "That is something we'll never know. Will Alex go to school?" I asked.

"He'll get there somehow. I was offered money to torch the plant, but I refused, knowing that would be the end of the bit of fishing heritage left here. That old, dilapidated building meant the world to a lot of families, including mine. Not in employment, as I explained, but in what it represented. I should have known that Lucy would approach my brother with the same offer. I'm pretty sure she sucked him into the invasive-crab ploy, too. Do you know about that?"

"I saw the crabs at Dow's place the night I thought you caught me there, but as it turns out, it must have been George. Anyway, I assumed Dow had a weird interest in crabs, since his aquarium was overflowing with them. Last night I was able to piece together what might be closer to reality. Dow and Lucy Hamilton and possibly George were conspiring to ensure that the proposed site for the wind farm would never be open to fishing again. Right?" I asked.

"Right. They planned to raise them at Dow's and release them by the bucketful when we steamed over the closed area on our way to the fishing grounds. I guess they believed they could inundate the area with enough crabs to destroy whatever might otherwise develop for commercial harvest. The whole thing seemed so ridiculous that I ignored it. Lucy has always been a conniver. She knows her future rests on that power source, and she'll do anything to get there. Now my brother is going to prison for arson."

"Arson and murder," I corrected.

"I don't believe George is capable of murder."

"Really? That bar would have crushed my skull exactly the way it did Nick Dow's. He knew I was on to him, and that's why he tried to do me in. If he hadn't killed Dow, why would he have wanted me dead?"

"Maybe he thought you figured he had tried to kill you

by burning the plant with you in it. I saw you slide out of the gurry chute from the skiff. George couldn't have known you were inside. He's not that bad a guy. He probably assumed you were on your way to rat him out and freaked." He sighed. "It doesn't look good, does it?"

I didn't bother sharing what I knew about the knot. I would wait to hear what George confessed to. I chose not to tell Lincoln about the first murder attempt on the night of our broken date. He'd probably excuse the gunshots, as Cal had. Just some guy out jacking deer saw the white side of the tablecloth flashing around like a deer's tail . . . good thing he was a poor shot. . . .

George had sent the roses and wine and written the note to lure me to the Clearing so he could either kill me or scare me badly enough that I'd drop my investigation. He had purchased the satchel at Lucy Hamilton's boutique. Perhaps she had helped with the note. She may also have penned the letter to the editor of *National Fisherman*. It must have been George who slipped out the back door of the boutique when I entered through the front entrance. George had broken into my car, hoping to find Dow's black book, and he'd taken my camera in order to destroy whatever evidence I had gathered. I recalled that George had been in the plant's parking lot, listening to a ball game, and the next morning Clyde had said the Red Sox hadn't played. Perhaps George had been waiting to see Ginny that evening, or perhaps he'd been eavesdropping to maximize his payment for the torch job. I had not even a shadow of a doubt now. But I would let Lincoln find out when the rest of the town did. And knowing how fast news traveled in Green Haven, I figured word would be out by lunch.

Now it was my turn to think aloud. "So Ginny Turner was double-dipping. She didn't have the interest or money for the improvements necessary to keep the insurance policy, so my bet is that she wanted to collect the insurance before it was canceled. Then she'd sell the property to the Hamiltons to be utilized as the shoreside facility for the wind operation, and everyone would be happy." Lincoln either didn't have an opinion on this, or he was still ruminating about the distinct possibility that George had indeed committed murder. I continued, "I'm confused about Dow. Why would Lucy need to involve him? I thought the Hamiltons were filthy rich."

"They *were*. Blaine has squandered his entire inheritance on different schemes. This wind farm is the latest. They don't even have enough money to pay half of Alex's tuition. That's why Lucy is so desperate to ensure that wind power comes to fruition. She and Nick Dow were friends since kindergarten. I've suspected there was more to it than friendship, but since our divorce, I haven't really cared. I'm sure that Lucy used Dow for whatever she needed, and that she was the only person in Green Haven who knew he didn't drink. His ruse as the town drunk fit perfectly. He was able to bring in a substantial amount of cash under the table. He even disappeared for a month every winter and came back all tanned. The honest working people of this town can't afford vacations." He must have spent that month on a golf course, I reasoned. "No matter what he did or where he was seen, everyone excused him as a drunk. People lose inhibitions around a drunk. He must have seen and heard a lot. He was always prowling around at weird hours."

"Pretty twisted," I said, wishing for more. When nothing more came, I figured it was time to say goodbye and wait for the real authorities to tie up any loose ends. Just as I was about to thank Lincoln for walking me home (not to mention saving my life, even if he was in denial about his brother's capabilities), I felt eyes on my back. Turning toward the house, I saw the Vickersons' faces pressed up tight against a window. I waved, eliciting the opening of the window. "Good morning, Janie," called Alice. When had I become Janie? I wondered. "Would you like to invite your friend in for a blueberry muffin?"

"Hi, Mrs. V. No, thank you. We were just saying goodbye, and I have to go to work," I lied, knowing that I was headed for the shower and bed.

With this, Lincoln nodded and said, "See you around." Then he turned and headed back down the hill.

"We're cooking up a new recipe. Mussel risotto! Will you join us tonight for dinner?" asked Henry.

"You bet." The window closed, and their faces disappeared. A trip to the Old Maids was in order for gas and a container in which to carry it to the Duster. Maybe a little nap would loosen my wallet. It would be good to support my community by buying locally. I would eventually need to use the Duster, after all. I found myself reflecting back to just one week ago, when I could only imagine what my new life in Green Haven, Maine, would be like. Tranquil, it was not. I hadn't yet sought out any of my Bunker roots, as I had tentatively planned to do. But I was beginning to feel stronger family-like ties with the Vickersons, Cal, and Audrey than I'd ever felt in Florida. Who says you can never go home? Happy with the knowledge that I hadn't been able to fully escape my love of solving crimes, I wondered whether the murder of Nick Dow would have been investigated if I had remained in Florida. I suspected Dow's death would have been regarded as accidental suicide for eternity. As capital crimes didn't often occur in these small towns, I was content to assume that my life would meld into what I had originally imagined. I would be the insurance lady and nothing more. Until the next time.

Acknowledgments

So often acknowledgments include apologies to those forgotten among the scads of people being thanked. This is no exception. I have been working on *Slipknot* for one year and am bound to forget to mention a few people whose help, encouragement, and support I am most grateful for. If you are among those slighted, please know that I am eternally grateful for whatever you did or said.

Thanks to the great folks at Hyperion for all you've done to get this book airborne. To name a few: Will Schwalbe, Brendan Duffy, Leslie Wells, Bob Miller, Ellen Archer, Jane Comins, and Christine Ragasa. Here's to book number five!

Thanks to my literary agent, Stuart Krichevsky, and all of the ladies at the Stuart Krichevsky Agency.

Thanks to my friend Drew Darling. Your beautifully written correspondence has inspired me to the point of near plagiarism.

One of the more difficult things about writing is finding just the right spot in which to sit down and do it. I am fortunate to have generous friends with perfect places.

Thanks to Marie Lane for the use of Uncle Walter's cabin in Rich's Cove. Thanks to Andrea Fassman for the time at her condo in Florida. And thank you, Pete Sheehen, for the week in your ski haus in Jackson, New Hampshire, when I was really under the gun to finish this book.

Thanks to the Smithwick brothers, who have provided marine insurance as well as contact information for others in the industry. I owe special thanks to Dave Dubois of Marine Safety Consultants for facts and a willingness to help in the future.

Thanks to photographer Todd Holmes and diesel mechanic John Pride.

Thanks to the talented and hardworking gals at Seabags for designing and producing the awesome Jane Bunker bag. I love mine!

Thanks, Mom and Dad, for proofreading. And thanks, Simon, for your help typing from time to time and for your companionship throughout.

There. Who did I forget?

Author's Note

Slipknot is, of course, a work of fiction, but included in the plot are some very real issues that confront today's coastal communities.

From California to Florida to Maine, species like the Japanese Crab are devastating our aquatic ecosystems. If you want to learn more, there's lots of interesting information at www.epa.gov/owow/invasive_species/.

As for wind farms, with ever increasing global energy demands and the growing movement toward developing renewable energy sources, wind farm projects are becoming more and more popular. But they're no magic bullet, and they have their own set of environmental consequences. You can learn more about the pros and cons of wind farms and other forms of alternative energy at http://environment.newscientist.com/channel/earth/energy-fuels.

Finally, there's the delicate issue of fishing regulations. The struggle between government agencies trying to safeguard our natural resources and fishermen simply trying to feed and clothe their families is ongoing.

Passions can run high on both sides of this debate, and it's difficult (and not always constructive) to choose sides. A site that has a lot of informative links on everything from fishery research to Department of Marine Resources websites is www.bdssr.com.

Oh, and one more thing—the slipknot itself. The knot that I had in mind when I titled this book was the slipped sheet bend. This is a basic knot that's particularly useful when it comes to connecting two ropes of different diameters. It's easy to tie and works best when under a lot of strain, like when you connect a line to the rigging or when you need extra leverage while dragging a dead body overboard.

Here's what it should look like:

Read on for an excerpt from

SHIVER HITCH
by Linda Greenlaw

Available from St. Martin's Paperbacks

ONE

Except for the time I was digging my own grave at gunpoint on the edge of Biscayne National Park, I hadn't much experience with a shovel. Now, my first winter in Maine was providing a cram course in the form of snow. Back in Miami, a sore back was the least of my concerns. And when I was able to crack the gun-toting drug lord's head with the back of the shovel and run for the mangroves, the real terror began. That night spent hiding, half submerged, I was unable to decide which was worse: leeches or mosquitoes. Neither of those was a threat here in deep, dark February in sleepy, frozen Green Haven, Maine.

I had been warned, and was fully expecting and prepared for a "wicked" winter, or so I thought. The locals whose holy books are *The Farmers' Almanac* and *Uncle Henry's,* who had advised me that there would be a record amount of snowfall—as forecast in "FA"—and that I could get whatever I needed to cope with it in "UH," must now be enjoying the fact that I had been skeptical. Of course it didn't help that my parking space seemed to be at the vortex of a snow funnel. Every time the wind blew out of the northeast, which accompanied most large storms, my 1987 Plymouth Duster had been buried. To be honest, my car is actually a Plymouth Tourismo. Plymouth did not make a Duster in 1987. I just think a Duster is more my style—less extravagant, more practical. Today, just the tip of the antenna marked the car entombed in flakes so big I could almost see their individual differences. I laughed to myself. My present situation was a far cry from chief detective of Miami-Dade County. If anyone from my past could see me now—Jane Bunker, bundled up like a goddamned Eskimo—living in an apartment over a trinket-selling tourist trap in this remote outpost—making ends meet financially (just barely) with a combination of insurance consulting/investigation and a job as the assistant deputy sheriff of Knox County—shoveling snow!

My landlords, Alice and Henry Vickerson—Mr. and Mrs. V to me—had been gracious in offering me the use of their snow blower. But that offer had come with the stipulation that it not be fired up until eight a.m., the time at which "anyone with an ounce of civility" should wake. I suspected the ounce of civility was in direct correlation to the ounces of Scotch whiskey consumed the night before, but might also have been age related. The eight a.m. mandate, in conjunction with the price of gasoline to power the blower, had me, at six sharp, digging a path with a red plastic shovel from the door of The Lobster Trappe (the V's gift shop over which I reside) to the antenna under which lived my wheels. Not that I am opposed to Scotch. I have been known to imbibe. But I am frugal; some would say "cheap."

When a crease of golden light warmed the eastern horizon, I figured I had been shoveling for nearly an hour. Not that I was counting, but I was aware that we were gaining over a full minute of daylight every twenty-four hours. I yearned for the four a.m. sunrise that would come again with the spring solstice. I thrive in daylight. And, I've come to find out, I am not crazy about the cold. Mr. V had secured a big, red, lobster thermometer ("Lobster Thermadore," as advertised in the shop) on the largest spruce tree on the lot. The black line whose height signified the temperature barely showed on the tail, displaying a frigid eight degrees this morning. Exercise within multiple layers of clothing resulted in full warmth by the time I had exposed the hood of the Duster, allowing me distractive thoughts while I found the car's doors.

Maine had become home, again, sort of. Although I still struggled when asked about my past, I had at least confided in the Vickersons and my new friends enough to stop their incessant questions that were born out of curiosity and rumor. People make more of what is unsaid than what is said. Not one to wear my heart on my sleeve, I am weirded out by strangers who bear their souls over a cup of coffee in public, or share intimate and minute details of their daily existence over social media. The surge in popularity of reality TV has everyone thinking their lives are ready for prime time. Just eight months ago, I was the new kid in town. What preceded my arrival was the knowledge that I had been born on Acadia Island, was basically kidnapped by my own mother (along with my baby brother, Wally), and was transplanted to Miami, where I grew up in a predominantly Latino section of the city and worked as a police detective until this past June. Rumors of a highly decorated career in drug enforcement cut short by some undefined, yet insurmountable scandal may have been exaggerated. But I have never been one to kiss and tell.

Although I hadn't yet visited Acadia Island since my move back to Maine, I could see it, as I stood to rest my back in the distance across the bay, looming mysteriously over smaller islands and ledges that dotted the way between it and Green Haven. Someday, I thought, I would initiate a family reunion. Someday, when I could stomach the possibility of having a door slammed in my face. Or worse yet, learning that the Bunkers were not the catalyst that sent my mother sneaking off in the middle of the night, settling at the farthest reach of the Eastern Seaboard, into the looney bin, and finally to suicide. The way my mother told it qualified her for sainthood. To my five-year-old mind, she had been heroic. At forty-three, I wasn't as convinced. What I "knew" was this: My mother had disappointed my father's family when she gave birth to a girl, as boys were needed to perpetuate both the Bunker name and the heritage of lobster fishing. The Bunkers had fought long and hard to acquire and protect their private sliver of the ocean floor that provided their livelihood and identity, and needed to seed the future with young Bunker men willing and able to carry on the territorial war. I always wondered how my life would have been different if the Bunkers had considered women capable of fishing and fighting. No matter, because when dear Wally was born and it was clear that he was a Down syndrome baby, that was the final blow to our "family." My mother, according to her, was treated like a pariah until she found the courage to escape. Nearly forty years later, here I was, a short boat ride to the truth, but unable to climb aboard; my fear of disillusionment crippling. Or perhaps it was confirmation I feared.

My move to Maine from Florida was indeed a knee-jerk reaction, and one that brought with it an inherent dichotomy that I straddled awkwardly. What remained constant in my life was my affinity for the law. This passion for fighting crime and solving cases ranging from petty theft to first-degree murder was what bolstered me through all lows. In the short time I had been in Maine, I had seen the crime rate change dramatically. Although the downeast coastal villages were quaint, sleepy havens where tourists enjoyed tranquillity and lobster rolls, there had been an explosion of drug use and overdoses among the young population of year-round residents. Meth labs were being discovered weekly, and synthetic opioids had become the new heroin. I had cut my law enforcement teeth in the era of the War on Drugs in Miami, the highest drug trafficking area in the Continental US. The older folks who live here are shocked by the seemingly rabid increase in drug-related topics in their local newscasts and print. But when you see young people harvesting a very abundant and lucrative resource like the Maine lobster, it was just a matter of time before the drug lords would tap into that cache. Timing may indeed be everything. Or is it location, location, location? Time and place. I was in the right place at the right time to make a difference, I thought.

When I was able to pry the driver's side door of the Duster open wide enough to squeeze in, I did. Three pumps on the gas pedal with a foot clad in the requisite, insulated L.L.Bean boot, a twist of the key in the ignition, and "Vroom," off she went—purring contentedly. I hated wasting gas, but thought it might be okay to let the engine idle while I dug out the back tires and dished out a couple of wheel wells behind them and out to the main road. The price of gasoline in Down East Maine was all the motivation I needed to throw snow with a real hustle. Just as I was finishing the job, the phone inside the house rang, piercing the stillness of the icy air. I leaned the shovel against the rear bumper and started toward the house. One ring later, the phone stopped. Two rings and a hang up was the code I had worked out with my boss at Marine Safety Consultants, Mr. Dubois, and was my signal to call him back pronto.

Cell phones are all but useless in this particular nook of coast, so my personal calls all come through a "party line" that I share with the Vickersons. The code was worked out in an attempt to gain a bit of privacy. At first, Mr. and Mrs. V had been discreet about listening in on my calls. But once the cat was out of the bag, rather than stop doing it, they became more blatantly nosy—even jumping into conversations to offer opinions. Most of my first-time callers end up saying "Who the hell is that?" before the end of the conversation. I then have to be polite and introduce whichever one of my octogenarian landlords happened to be near the phone when it rang. At the start it was disconcerting, then it really began to piss me off. Now, I laugh. And of course outsmart them.

Torn between allowing the Duster to remain running and thus climbing into a toasty warm car and shutting it off to feed my frugality, I opted for frugality. Besides saving gas, I needed to toughen up, I thought as I made my way back to the house. Carefully closing the door behind me so as not to wake my landlords, I brushed snow from the bottom of my pant legs that were frozen stiff, and pulled my feet from my insulated "Beanies" with the lobster claw boot jack. Yup, The Lobster Trappe sold anything and everything lobster related. There were lobster trap birdhouses, lobster beanbags, lobster coloring books, lobster cork screws . . . Well, you get the picture. The shop was now in its off-season, so the Vickersons were busy researching new items to add to their inventory, which led to many interesting conversations at their dinner table, where I had an open invitation to be any night at 7:30—five o'clock if I wanted cocktails. I tiptoed my wool socks across the shop and started up the stairs to my apartment. Halfway up, the door below that connected to the main house opened and I heard a very cheery, "Good morning, Janey!"

"Hi Mrs. V. I hope I didn't wake you."

"No dear, the phone did. Two rings and a hang up. Must be your boss. Better call him back right away." Oh no, I thought, they were on to me. I wondered how many conversations they had tapped into since I had schemed the code. The Vickersons were so good to me in every way that I had never been able to bring myself to scold them for eavesdropping. What the heck, I thought, at eighty-two and eighty-six, if they find pleasure injecting themselves into my fairly unexciting life, so be it. It's not as if the happenings in Down East Maine and outer islands (my territory in both my insurance and deputy gigs) required security clearance. The last two assignments I had been given by Mr. Dubois were surveying minor damage to lobster boats in a late January blizzard. One boat's mooring parted and it was blown into another boat before landing luckily on the only patch of sand beach in the county. And the only task I had been assigned as deputy sheriff since September was following up on leads that often led to busting meth labs, arresting addicts and hopefully beginning to snuff out what had reached epidemic proportions. Often, the entire community knows about a case or incident before I do, I realized. The Vickersons just like to be in the loop. I assured Alice that I had come in to call my boss, and hoped I could discreetly give Mr. Dubois a head's up that they were listening before they jumped in.

"Hello?"

"Hi, Mr. Dubois. Jane Bunker here, *we* are returning your call."

"Alice?" Mr. Dubois asked.

"Present," Mrs. V said promptly.

"Henry?"

"Standing by," answered Mr. V dutifully. Oh God, I thought, now there wasn't even any pretending. The only thing keeping me from being terminated from either of my jobs was the total lack of anyone else to do them. That, and the fact that I *am* good at what I do.

"Okay, team, here's the deal," the boss started. "Jane, I need you to go out to Acadia Island to survey damage suffered in a house fire. It's a summer home owned by a good customer for whom we insure several properties, three vehicles, a boat, and a business. The fire was just last night, and I want to move quickly to accommodate these people."

"Since when do we survey house fires? I thought you handled only marine-related insurance?" I asked to stall, and hoped to conceal an oncoming loss of composure about a trip to Acadia.

"It's called bundling, dear," interjected Mr. V. "Everyone is having to gain bandwidth in *any* business to stay afloat. Insurance is very competitive. Alice and I have all of our insurances under one roof as well—it's the only way we can afford it all."

"Besides," Mrs. V weighed in, "you really should go to Acadia and get that demon off your back."

"I think you mean monkey, dear," Mr. V corrected. "And maybe Jane needs to let sleeping dogs lie."

"Either way," Mr. Dubois interrupted what I had come to know as ping-pong proverbs before Alice could send one back over the net, "I assume the place is a total loss. Not much in the way of firefighting on these islands— all volunteer, and no real training or equipment. All I need from you is to go out and take lots of pictures to document what I already know," said Mr. Dubois.

"Yes sir, I'll get out there ASAP." Yet again, I am reduced to a photographer, I thought.

"Great. When you get off at the dock, take a right on the main road, in about half a mile you'll see a yellow Cape on the right. The Proctors are expecting someone from the Agency. They are caretakers for the Kohls, whose house you'll be surveying. They will get you where you need to be and back to the dock," the boss instructed. I breathed an audible sigh of relief when I registered "Proctor"—not any of the family names associated with my kin.

We all said our goodbyes and hung up, leaving me to contemplate the trip "home." Within seconds the phone rang again. I grabbed it and was not at all surprised to be speaking with the Vickersons. They advised me of the ferry schedule to and from Acadia, adding that I had already missed the first boat out to the island. The winter ferry schedule to Acadia did not give a passenger many options—the "early boat" departed from South Haven (a ten-minute ride from home) at seven a.m., and the "late boat" was a three p.m. departure from South Haven. Following the forty-minute cruise out, the Vickersons informed me, the boat would remain at the dock on Acadia just long enough to unload people and freight, before returning to the mainland. I thanked my landlords for the info, and told them I would find an alternate ride out, snap a load of pictures, and return on the last and only remaining ferry this evening. "Better get a wiggle on," advised Mrs. V. "Time is of the essence."

"What's the rush? Remember, haste makes waste," instructed Mr. V.

"He who hesitates is lost," admonished Mrs. V.

"Fools rush in where angels fear to tread!"

"The early bird gets the worm!"

"Good things come to those who wait."

"Tide and time wait for no man. And damn few women! There, top that, Henry," Alice challenged.

"I need to deice the Duster. I'll let you know my plans, thanks!" I wasn't quite sure what I was thanking them for, but slammed the phone down, bolted down the stairs, yanked on my boots, and hustled to my chilly and waiting Duster. For all I knew, the old folks were still volleying proverbs. Their game used to irritate me. Now I enjoyed it, I thought as I quietly quipped, "A stitch in time, saves nine."

My warm gloves melted the thin layer of frost on the car's steering wheel, leaving distinct handprints at ten and two. Nothing upsets me more than waste, I reminded myself as I waited for the Duster's defroster to clear a porthole in the windshield. I don't mean global, all-encompassing misuse and extravagance. That does not concern me. I only pay heed to the wastefulness of which I am responsible—me, myself, and I. Perhaps a gut reaction to my very unusual childhood; my personal frugality is just that—personal. I don't preach. I don't boast. I don't admire extreme economy in others. I find nothing more annoying than conversation regarding the "great deal" someone got on something following a compliment on that something, or the fuel economy of any particular hybrid automobile. Nor do I care about membership on the Fortune 500 list, or who the top-paid athlete is at any given time. My mother's routine of frittering away the monthly welfare check from the State of Florida in a single day, leaving us to "get creative" for the remaining thirty days to the next installment left its mark. Not that I didn't enjoy and look forward to the first of every month and whatever my mother had planned for us, but I knew at a very early age that my mother suffered with chronic immaturity with money. We ate and enjoyed government cheese, and the neighborhood ladies were forever dropping leftovers off for us, which sustained our family of three until I was old enough to work. I heard but didn't agree with the same ladies' whispered, negative opinions of how Wally and I were being raised. The ladies whose husbands worked long, hard hours, barely making ends meet, knew the value of a dollar. And I remember the look of envy in their children's eyes each and every month when we arrived home by taxi—not the bus, a taxi—armed with gifts, souvenirs, and stories of adventure. They said we couldn't afford such extravagance as a day at the circus. My mother said we couldn't afford not to. I'll never know which is true. But this morning, had I left the car running for fifteen minutes while I was on the phone, I would have been sick to my stomach.

Publicly, I am not big on sentimental journeys. My wanderlust is limited to the future. Privately, I spend a lot of time wondering about my roots, especially since moving to Green Haven. The only family I have left is Wally, I thought. Five years my junior, and an adult with Down syndrome, living in an assisted, yet independent situation, my baby brother has always been more well balanced and adjusted than I have been. He makes friends easier than I do. All of the reasons that I had for *not* uprooting him to come along to Maine when I bailed, were the exact same reasons why I should have done so. He's happy there, I justified as I backed out of the driveway. But Wally is always happy. The last shrink I saw before the big move north told me that I was over-protective of my brother. Maybe so. I just couldn't risk dragging him off into the unknown where, if my mother had been truthful, he would be mistreated by mean people blinded by ignorance—and those were blood relatives! Now I faced the probability of actually meeting what remains of the Bunkers, and hoped some of the hatefulness my mother spoke of had withered in the past thirty-eight years. I reminded myself that this trip to Acadia was not a quest for the truth or an opportunity for a family reunion. It was work, period.

Normally I would walk the mile to the Harbor Café, but there had been so much snow lately, it was banked high on either side of the street, leaving a gap so narrow that an oncoming vehicle presented a challenge. No sidewalks and not much time to find my buddy Cal were reasons enough to forgo the exercise today. As I nosed the Duster into a too-small parking space, I hoped this latest snow had not disrupted Cal's morning ritual of coffee and a newspaper at the café. Cal had quickly become my go-to guy for just about everything, including a boat ride, which was foremost on my request list this morning. Cowbells swinging on the inside of the café's door announced my entrance along with a good gust of cold, fresh air that formed a wispy vapor where it mixed with air permeated with donut grease. The place was crowded, and I stood in the doorway looking for Cal while I wiped snow from my boots onto a not-so-welcoming doormat that read "Many Have Eaten Here. Few Have Died."

"Close the door!" Yelled a chorus of apparently chilly breakfast guests. Pushing the door closed behind me, I spied at the counter the back of Cal's head with its thinning white hair. Luckily, the only empty seat was next to him. Unluckily, the seat was unoccupied because of the presence of Clyde Leeman, the unofficial town crier, on the other side of it. I tried to be discreet about putting my back to Clydie when I took the stool between him and Cal, like the people on the airplane who stick their face in a book to avoid having to speak to their seat mate. I liked Clydie well enough, just wasn't up to his nonstop complaining and nonsensical jabbering. It was clear to me how and why Clydie had developed a very thick skin.

It was virtually impossible to insult the man. And believe me, everyone tried.

"Hi, Cal," I said pleasantly, as he lowered the newspaper onto the counter, exposing his quick smile, and removed his glasses to reveal twinkling, blue eyes that defied his age. Cal had a natural ability to make everyone feel as though he was genuinely happy to see them, even when he wasn't. Before Cal could speak, Clydie broke in with his usual, too loud voice.

"Well, hellooooo, Ms. Bunker! You must be freezing. You ain't in Kansas anymore, are ya? Hey, I hope you don't have to pee. The pipes are froze in the bathroom." With that, the couple seated on the other side of him got up to leave.

"Clyde Leeman!" shouted Audrey, my favorite (and only) waitress in the café. "Will you stop with the announcements? Every time you open your pie hole, a customer leaves." The sassy, heavily tattooed and pierced Audrey was headed my way with a cup of coffee. Clearing a used paper place mat printed with local advertisements with her right hand, she plunked the full cup onto a clean one with her left, and slid it in front of me.

"Well, I just think it's good to let people know that your toilets are not working. What if someone has an emergency? This coffee is like mud! If anyone makes the mistake of a second cup, you're gonna have an awful mess," Clyde yelled.

"I thought the out-of-order sign on the door was sufficient," Audrey said. "But I guess that would require the ability to read." Audrey rolled her eyes, and sighed in exasperation. "Want the usual, Janey?" she asked, seemingly hopeful to exclude Clyde from any more conversation. I hesitated, not knowing what my usual was. I didn't recall being that predictable.

"I can read!" Clydie defended himself. "And you'd better avoid the prunes this morning, if you know what I mean, Ms. Bunker. Those pipes is froze solid. They won't get a flush down until April at this rate."

"Why don't you take some of that hot air into the bathroom and thaw the pipes?" Audrey asked sarcastically.

All the talk revolving around the status of the toilet was making me nauseous. I quickly agreed that I wanted my usual, whatever that was.

"English or day old?" asked Audrey. When I met this with a puzzled look, she elaborated. "Your usual is the least expensive item on the menu. Today that's a tie between a toasted English muffin and yesterday's special muffin."

"What was yesterday's special muffin?"

"Raspberry, a buck fifty."

"What's today's special muffin?"

"Apricot bran, two bucks."

"I'll have the toasted English, please," I said.

"Ha!" Clyde chimed in. "Good idea to avoid bran with the nonfunctioning facilities." Just as I thought Audrey would pour coffee into Clyde's lap, the cowbells announced another customer, causing Clyde's head to swivel toward the door. The incoming customer looked around in vain for a place to sit other than next to Clyde, and shrugging hopelessly, shuffled over and took the least coveted seat in the café. As Clyde began chewing an ear off the guy, I turned my attention to Cal.

"Cal, I need a favor," I said.

"You name it. I'm your guy," Cal replied immediately, never breaking eye contact. To my mind, only the best of friends will agree to a favor before knowing what it is. This was testament to the mutual trust we shared; trust that had been won quickly and tested frequently.

Not that I had been involved with many investigations since my arrival in Green Haven, but when I had, Cal had been at my service in any way needed.

"It's an easy one today. I need a ride to Acadia Island this morning. Seems that I missed the boat, so to speak." I went on to explain my mission to document damage caused by a house fire, and my plan to grab the late ferry back ashore later. Cal confirmed that I was in luck. He was happy to accommodate my request, especially at the expense of the insurance company who would reimburse all expenditures. I had learned that Cal was delighted to collect money from an insurance company with whom the vast majority of cash flow had always gone in the opposite direction. And since his retirement from a number of careers including commercial fishing, Cal had the time and appreciated a little extra money.

"Besides," Cal added, "the *Sea Pigeon* needs to stretch her legs a bit. And it's a great day for a boat ride. I haven't been to Acadia in years. No reason to go."